Jackie is happily retired living in Sussex with her husband, Bill. She worked in sales and in retail for a number of years and had always enjoyed writing but never 'had the time'. Lockdown changed all that. They have two children and five grandchildren, their son is in Sussex and their daughter is in Derby, and they enjoy spending time in both these wonderful counties.

Jackie McIntosh

THE PRICE OF LOVE

AUSTIN MACAULEY PUBLISHERS™

LONDON • CAMBRIDGE • NEW YORK • SHARJAH

A CIP catalogue record for this title is available from the British Library.

ISBN 9781035841349 (Paperback)
ISBN 9781035841356 (ePub e-book)

www.austinmacauley.co.uk

First Published 2024
Austin Macauley Publishers Ltd®
1 Canada Square
Canary Wharf
London
E14 5AA

The input I have had so far with Austin Macauley Publishing as they have offered me this opportunity to publish my work. Family and close friends who have encouraged me to do this and my daughter who read my work.

The early morning sun was shining through the bedroom curtains when Ma-donna began to stir—she stretched across the king-size bed and felt the empty space next to her. Still half asleep, she snuggled back down under the duvet, thinking that any minute now she would hear Derek's footsteps coming upstairs with their early morning tea.

Suddenly, Ma-donna became fully awake as she remembered that yesterday had been Derek's funeral. Today was the first day of the rest of her life. She stayed where she was for a while despite realising that if she really wanted this cup of tea she would need to get up and make it herself as she had done for the last few weeks.

Yesterday sprang to mind again as she remembered the very small gathering at the funeral—not more than 15 people allowed due to COVID-19—and no reception afterwards; the service was available to watch on Zoom so that anyone unable to be there could watch the service from their computer. What kind of send-off was that for someone who had been on this earth for more than seventy years!

However, their best friend Paul had spoken about his lifelong friend in a very moving way, his anecdotes were both very funny and very emotional, the only way one would speak of someone they have known for many years and gone through all the ups and downs that life throws up. Paul lost his wife, Sarah, only three years ago when she was diagnosed with cancer and was still coming to terms with this, as were Ma-donna and Derek—spending a lot of time with Paul when they felt he needed them. They had spent lots of weekends and short breaks away over the years and they had always been close.

Ma-donna and Derek got on with Paul and Sarah from the time they became neighbours many years ago and had children of similar ages—so went through the various stages of life supporting each other when needed.

Now Paul and Ma-donna were both widowed and their children were well into adulthood leading their own lives. Ma-donna snuggled back under the duvet having forgotten her need for a cup of tea, and began to reflect on life in general—her past life—her parents and her grandparents' lives—and reflected on where she found herself today.

Part 1

Chapter 1

Polly Dennis and Dolly Mason had been friends all their lives and left school in 1912 just before their 14th birthdays. They lived with their parents in tied cottages in the grounds of a large farming estate in Kent. Their grandparents had also worked the land on the same farm. Polly's parents were Joan and Fred Dennis, her mother worked mainly during the summer months when soft fruit, apple and hop pickers were needed—and Fred, like John Mason—Dolly and older sister Betty's father—worked on the farm all year round, in the fields and also with livestock. There were dairy cows, also sheep and pigs, hay making and harvest so always plenty of work, whatever the seasons.

Nancy Mason, John's wife and Dolly and Betty's mother would help out occasionally with farm duties but she was the local midwife so would get called out at strange times when new babies decided to make an appearance. She was very good at keeping calm in times of crisis and mums-to-be put a lot of trust in her even though, sadly, things did go wrong on occasions.

However, most of the children she saw grow up in the village were brought into the world by her and she was held in high esteem by the villagers. The magical feeling of putting a new born baby in the arms of its mother after a long and painful labour never left Nancy when she saw the mother's expression when being handed her new born child. When minutes earlier the mother's face was twisted in agony, like magic, the pain would be instantly wiped away when Mum first saw her baby.

Polly was a slight girl, quite small for her 14 years, had blonde hair and blue eyes where Dolly was a good head taller than her friend, with dark unruly curly hair and brown eyes, but they were soulmates and shared everything, as bosom pals do—although they had different interests.

They were very excited and nervous in equal parts as they were going into service at the beautiful big house on the outskirts of the village—couldn't believe how fortunate they were to be working together, having spent their early years and gone through school, always together.

The housekeeper was Jenny Armstrong, and she and her husband Jim ran Wicken Manor which was owned by Sir Charles and Lady Frances Perkins. Jenny looked after the domestic side of things in the house while Jim tended the grounds; there was a flower and vegetable garden and a copse which provided the house with firewood—there were also stables which included two shire horses, Neptune and Apollo—Sir Charles and Lady Frances enjoyed riding, and Charlie the Shetland Pony belonged to their son Frank.

Sir Charles had acquired a motor car in recent years which was his pride and joy and Jim would also look after this and occasionally would borrow it to have a drive in the countryside with Jenny, a rare treat and privilege. Jenny and Jim lived in the lodge at the entrance to the drive which led to Wicken Manor—it was a very nice two-bedroom home which was very comfortable for the couple.

There was more than enough to keep them both busy so Jenny thought it would be a good thing to have two young girls to help her around the house—Lady Frances thought that was an excellent idea as she and Sir Charles liked to entertain and would often have friends from London staying overnight, which obviously created quite a bit of work, and it would be great for Jenny to have the two girls helping at table and other domestic chores. Thus far, Jenny had always asked random people when she needed extra help but after a few mishaps she thought permanent help would work better. She went to Lady Frances with this thought and the latter agreed that it would be great to teach the girls what had to be done, and see how they coped.

Polly woke up at 5.00 a.m. and went down to the kitchen. Joan was already up having cooked Fred his breakfast. 'Good morning, Polly. How are you feeling my love, I'm so going to miss you and so glad you are not going down to London to work,' said Joan.

'I feel really lucky that Dolly and I will be together but I'm going to miss you and Dad. Still, I'll be home most Sundays for my tea after Sunday School.' She had a cup of tea but couldn't eat anything as she felt so nervous. There was a knock on the door and Dolly came charging through very enthusiastically. 'Morning everyone, it's a lovely morning, are you ready Pol, we should get on our way,' Dolly said excitedly with Nancy in her wake. 'Now think on, Dolly, do as you are told, don't argue with anyone and work hard,' her mother told her. 'Polly, try and keep an eye on her and make sure she behaves,' she added.

Polly grinned at Nancy, she'd been told this so many times then it was time to leave with their few belongings. The girls hugged their mothers in a hurry now to be on their way with calls of 'see you on Sunday' and the mothers responding with 'behave yourselves and take care!' Joan and Nancy both went into Joan's, had a cup of tea and shed a few tears at this new chapter in their girls' lives. Still, Sunday would soon come round and after the girls had finished their Sunday School classes and seen some of the younger children home, they would have tea with their families.

The girls make their way to Wicken Manor which was just under two miles away to report for duty. They were a little apprehensive as they had heard stories about how girls in service were treated, often not given enough to eat and left to sleep on uncomfortable bedding in attic rooms which were very hot in summer and extremely cold in winter.

Jenny, the housekeeper greeted them enthusiastically. 'Good morning girls, so pleased you are nice and early. Sure you'll be ready for tea and some toast and jam after that walk, then we'll talk about work.' The girls were heartened by the warm welcome and jam on a weekday was definitely a luxury. They always had jam in the cupboard but didn't have it every day.

After a second cup of tea Jenny spoke to them about what would be expected of them. They would come downstairs at 6.30 in the morning and would sort out the fires—even in summer the drawing room faced north and could be chilly—and in the winter months a few more rooms would need a fire. They would put water to heat on the stove ready for morning tea and from there the duties would vary according to the activities in the house.

They would have a half day on Thursdays, unless there was a special function in the house and on Sundays, they were free to go to church after their early morning duties. As they both helped with Sunday School on Sunday afternoons, together with Dolly's older sister Betty they were then allowed to have tea with their parents as they used to walk some of the younger children home.

Sunday School was a blessing for many parents as after a good Sunday lunch the children would be out for a couple of hours, which gave the parents a bit of breathing space before getting tea ready, and if it was a nice day, they could enjoy a pleasant walk in the lovely countryside they lived in. This often backfired and resulted in them seeing jobs that needed doing, like a broken fence or overgrown path, but nevertheless, it gave the parents a short break.

The girls settled into a routine, found Jenny firm but kind and were in awe of Sir Charles and Lady Frances—especially when they were serving at table—always conscious of not spilling or dropping anything. Some of the tureens they had to carry were very heavy and they always lived in fear of accidents. Sir Charles and Lady Frances' son Frank was a year older than the girls. He was away at school but came home at weekends and he seemed to take a shine to the two of them, Dolly in particular.

Chapter 2

Sir Charles and Lady Frances had been married some years before Frank came along, he was a well-loved and wanted son and they knew he would be an only child due to the problems Lady Frances had experienced. She was heartbroken when Sir Charles spoke about sending Frank away to school, she knew it made sense as they led busy lives, however, the thought of not seeing the child on a daily basis was heartbreaking. However, it was decided that Frank would board during the week and come home at weekends and this is what he had been doing since he was seven years old. He was quite happy with the arrangement, some of their friends had boys there so he had some pals and they would stick together when some of the older boys tried to bully them.

As he went home weekends, he could tell his parents about issues that cropped up during the week and they would deal with anything they felt was serious enough. He was a bright boy, enjoyed learning, also loved the games lessons and the activities they would have after prep and before supper. Lady Frances looked forward to Saturday when he came home before returning to school on Monday morning—usually loaded with Jenny's cakes which Frank would share with his friends, which increased his popularity and kept the bullies at bay!

Sir Charles was a physician and travelled to a big London Hospital where he would stay for two or three days carrying out consultations where surgery would follow in some cases, so he was a busy man. Apart from the financial benefits of such a profession, he genuinely cared about people and always did his best but with inevitable failures. As time went on, he realised that he couldn't help everyone and Lady Frances would know as soon as he returned home how things had gone by his face. If things had gone well or if he had made some new discovery, as he was keen to stay ahead of progress, he would come home beaming—if he had a sullen expression, he would head for his study and she would leave him till he felt he could cope with what he'd had to deal with. Not an easy job, but a very rewarding one at times, so it had its highs and lows.

The girls progressed with their household duties, Jenny taught them to bake and cook, so as they became more confident in the kitchen, she let them do more and would very occasionally have an afternoon off to give them more responsibility. However, while Polly loved all the household duties, Dolly preferred to spend time outdoors—both the girls could ride but Dolly absolutely loved it, so occasionally she would speak to Jim and offer to muck out the stables in return for going for a ride, quite often on a summer evening, or even on a Thursday afternoon if her family were busy.

She also enjoyed gardening, having spent a lot of time with her dad in the fields, if her mum was attending a birth and couldn't leave her on her own. She loved planting seeds and watching them grow, be it flowers or vegetables, and she knew which seasons certain crops and flowers grew, so really, she escaped outside whenever she could. This wasn't lost on Sir Charles and Lady Frances, they seemed to find it quite amusing, and when Frank was home for the weekend, very occasionally they would go riding together. They also realised that there was a close bond developing between Frank and Dolly, but wisely, rather than discouraging this budding relationship they thought it best to ignore it as much as possible and let it run its course.

Occasionally, Jenny would say to Dolly that she was needed in the house if they had a function on, but Jim also took quite a shine to the girl and found her a real asset both in the garden and the stables, so as long as Jenny and Polly were coping, Dolly's duties seemed divided between inside and out.

Her older sister, Betty, had gone to train as a nurse in one of the local hospitals a few miles away and she would come home at weekends if she wasn't on duty, and still helped at Sunday School when she could. Betty had always admired what her mother Nancy did, bringing new lives into the world, but also felt that she wanted to broaden her range and study different aspects of medicine, so nursing seemed the best course of action. She stayed with a friend of hers who lived near the hospital as she couldn't have gone the 15 miles there and back every day, and spent a lot of time studying when she wasn't on duty.

Also, she had to make sure she had a clean uniform whenever she went on duty, Matron was very strict and had a habit on picking on the same people, so she wanted to stay on the right side of her.

Chapter 3

It became apparent, very sadly, that war was looming. Lady Frances became very anxious as she knew that Frank was the right age to be called up and Lord Kitchener all too soon made his appeal to get young men to join the army. Lady Frances couldn't bear the thought of her beloved son being in danger, but unfortunately, she could do little about it.

Frank was due to leave school in June 1914, he was just 17—and the original plan was for him to go on to further education to study for a future career— however, this was put on hold. When war broke out in August 1914, he went out one afternoon and returned saying that he had joined the army and would await orders to be sent to a training camp. Lady Frances was devastated by the news, but accepted it and put a very brave face on, realising that Frank was doing the right thing. Sir Charles felt extremely proud of his young son, but was also very worried. Polly and Dolly, both congratulated him for making this brave move, but Dolly felt a slight sense of loss, knowing how much she would miss him.

At this point, there was no real romance, they just loved being together, and going riding, often stopping by the river and just sitting watching the water, and all the plants nearby, as well as small animals in that habitat, their love of the countryside was very mutual and they understood each other.

The girls would often chat for a while when they went to the room they shared. That evening Polly wondered how Dolly was feeling. 'Are you ok Doll?'

'Yes, of course I am,' replied Dolly, 'why wouldn't I be?'

'I just wondered, what with Frank having enlisted, and before you deny it, I know that you are very sweet on him!' Polly answered. 'He'll be fine, it won't last long and he will soon be home' said Dolly with conviction. Polly just thought to herself that Dolly was putting a brave face on things and hoped that her prediction that it would soon be over was right. All she said then was 'night-night Doll, don't forget to say your prayers.'

Over the last few months, one of the many visitors who used to come for the weekend had a daughter, Felicity, and she had taken quite a liking to Frank—her parents, Dr Hamish James, a colleague of Sir Charles, and his wife Morag enjoyed their visits to Wicken Manor. Morag watched her daughter with Frank and thought that they made a lovely couple and it would be wonderful if they had a future together. Frank enjoyed Felicity's company and while she didn't enjoy country pursuits like Dolly did, she would enjoy a walk round the grounds arm in arm with Frank.

When Dolly saw them together, she felt a very strange feeling of unease, especially the way Felicity looked at Dolly—and spoke down to her with a proprietorial air about her when she was with Frank. Dolly didn't need reminding that she was just a servant, but nevertheless Felicity reminded her of her position. Once when Dolly was weeding some flowerbeds for Jim, with Jenny's consent she heard Felicity saying, 'Frank, I thought the maid worked in the kitchen, what is she doing in the garden? I'm sure she could be doing plenty indoors, she's not very ladylike.'

Dolly didn't hear Frank's reply but he hurried Felicity along and they were soon out of sight and earshot.

The night before Frank went off to training camp, he and Dolly went for a long walk and as it started to rain, they ran back to the house laughing and breathless, and it was then that Frank took Dolly in his arms and kissed her. It was over very quickly but left her even more breathless and, despite the sad situation they were in, she felt happier than she had ever done in her life, and prayed that Frank would return safely when this awful war was over.

After training Frank was sent to France on the front line, however, there wasn't much news and it soon became apparent that no news was good news. Occasionally the post mistress would be seen on her bike delivering a telegram and everyone hoped it wasn't for their household. On Christmas Eve 1914, St. James' Church in Dover was bombed—no one was hurt, but it suddenly made the war very real to the people who lived nearby. Wicken Manor was about 40 miles away from Dover, but that still seemed too close.

Every now and then they would hear of injured soldiers being sent home with various injuries, from missing limbs to less serious wounds. All hospitals had wards set aside for these brave men and asked for volunteers to help out. Sometimes just to talk to them as they would want to explain what was happening on the front line, although many of them kept to themselves some of the worst atrocities and conditions they experienced—or volunteers needed to serve food, or even write letters to loved ones, on behalf of these brave men. Facial injuries were awful and often affected the eyes, which were bandaged and of course, the men could not see.

Betty was really busy and seldom managed to get home, as they were inundated with all these cases. She had done well in her exams and was having plenty of opportunity to practice what she had learnt. Sir Charles was spending a lot more time in London dealing with serious injuries but it occurred to him that as well as these men being injured physically, many of them were having nightmares due to the dreadful events they had gone through—many of them were still in their teens, just young lads—and wanted to see their families and try to erase the atrocities from their minds.

One night after a gruelling schedule of dealing with seriously injured soldiers, some of which had lost limbs—thus involving life changes—it occurred to him that he was missing Wicken Manor and Lady Frances, in particular. They were both very worried about Frank—but held on to the thought that no news was good news! It suddenly occurred to him that they wouldn't be entertaining and having house parties for a while while this wretched war was going on and there were several large rooms in the manor that could be put to much better use, like letting convalescing soldiers rest there for a while.

Chapter 4

When he next went home, he suggested this to Lady Frances and she reacted enthusiastically as it would keep her busy with less time to think and let her imagination run away with her. 'I feel so helpless with Frank on the front line and you in London all the time, I should be doing my bit too! I'll speak to Jenny and Jim and arrange for beds to be put and made in the two largest rooms.' Sir Charles looked relieved although he never doubted that Lady Frances would step up to the challenge. 'It would be good if we could fit ten beds in each room but we will need sheets, blankets and pillows—perhaps we can ask people in the village for any spare bedding they have to make up the shortfall and invite volunteers to come along and see what they can do to help!'

The two rooms were soon ready with ten beds in each—there was a bathroom nearby and another room was furnished with cabinets containing medicines and dressings. There was a sink in this room as Sir Charles was fanatical about hygiene, and handwashing was one of the most important aspects, in his eyes.

Jenny and Jim were very enthusiastic, thinking this was their way of doing 'their bit' and Jenny was already planning various meals she could produce and help these guys on the road to recovery! Cooking was definitely one of her passions and she never stopped thinking up ways of using produce when they had gluts of it at certain times of the year.

Although food was generally rather scarce, at Wicken Manor this wasn't too much of a problem as there were quite a few farms and smallholdings in the area, and getting hold of meat, poultry, eggs, vegetables and fruit was never a problem. The pantry was always full of preserves, jams, chutneys and bottled fruit which would last a whole year, under normal circumstances. Jenny and Polly made bread and basically all the food produced in the kitchen was all acquired from nearby farms. Also, Jim and Dolly decided that they would grow less flowers and more vegetables, as this would be a big help. They kept a smaller lawn with a few flower beds but the rest of the grounds were given over to growing vegetables.

The ten beds in each room were soon occupied by less severely injured soldiers, but most of them would suffer from nightmares and in their heads could still hear gunfire. When Nancy wasn't being called to deliver babies, she spent quite a bit of time at Wicken Manor tending the wounded, Polly was busy in the kitchen but would spend some time during the day speaking to the men, and asking them what they might like to eat, occasionally they would say that they really fancied a piece of Victoria Sponge or chocolate cake, and every effort would be made to produce it.

Dolly was helping anywhere she could—she would spend time with Jim in the garden usually digging up vegetables that went straight to the kitchen—she still helped there at times—then both her and Polly would spend two to three hours during the night making tea and talking to those soldiers who couldn't sleep, often feeling tired themselves, but a small price to pay to bring peace of mind and help a brave boy get some rest.

Dolly would then think about Frank and what he might be doing at that particular time and wondering if he ever thought about her.

As the soldiers regained their strength and began to feel better, they were encouraged to walk in the grounds and occasionally they would help with small tasks that Jim would suggest to them. Maybe some weeding or planting out, depending on the season but inevitably, those able-bodied men would soon be sent back to the front after a medical, if they were deemed fit and well. The mental anxieties they were experiencing were not taken terribly seriously, they just had to get on with it, and because it would have seemed cowardly to express such anxieties, as well as not broadcasting to all and sundry what was actually happening on the front, they stayed silent.

One young man called Thomas Morgan was convalescing at Wicken Manor and Polly spent quite a few nights speaking to him when he couldn't sleep. He would sleep for a couple of hours, and like the others who were recovering, would wake up from a nightmare and this is what Polly, Dolly and some of the other volunteers would listen out for when they did their few hours of night duty. They would go to them, mop their brow as they would often wake up in a sweat and occasionally get them a change of nightclothes. Sir Charles was very strict about hygiene, said the most common cause of fatalities weren't the injuries themselves, but infections which quite often followed, especially when they first arrived at Wicken Manor when their wounds had been poorly dressed.

Betty tried to come home most weekends and would spend much of her time tending to the soldiers' wounds—they looked forward to seeing her as she was very gentle with them, and always managed to make them smile. Nancy also did quite a bit of nursing, and the other volunteers mainly spent time trying to keep their spirits up, and doing small things to help their recovery.

Polly seemed to develop a rapport with young Thomas Morgan, he was quite a long way from home and Sir Charles had managed to save his left leg that had a small piece of shrapnel embedded within it. As it wasn't too deep he was able to remove it without severing any veins or arteries, so Thomas was recovering well physically.

However, the lads he had been among had all lost their lives, he came crawling out of the mud and stayed put till daylight, when he saw the carnage around him. He guessed it was bad as the smell was horrendous, and the realisation that the lads he had shared breakfast with were all gone came as a terrible shock to him. He dwelt on this constantly, even after he was rescued and carried on a stretcher to safety, and eventually put on a ship and sent to Dover. Once he had been cleaned up it was apparent that he wasn't badly hurt and could be treated at Wicken Manor. Polly tried to understand what he had gone through and how he felt relieved one minute as he was safe, and guilty the next minute for having survived where all his immediate unit had been killed.

When he felt a bit better, she would walk with him round the grounds when she had time, often during the lighter evenings when she had finished her chores. Then one Sunday, he said he would like to go to church, so they went together, with other members in the household. They couldn't all go, as someone had to be there all the time for the injured, Sir Charles was insistent that there should be someone with them at all times, even if it was just one person in case someone took a turn for the worse.

Polly grew very fond of Thomas, and when he was given a clean bill of health and was told to go back to the front, she was heartbroken and realised how very fond of him she was. He felt the same way about her and it was a sad farewell, but he promised that he would come back to her when this dreadful war came to an end. He knew where she was and he would write to her, and she said that she would write to him also. He said when this was over, he would very much like her to meet his family.

They lived in Birmingham but were from Wales originally—Thomas had met Polly's family on several occasions when he had gone to church with her—and actually had tea with them one Sunday after Polly had finished at Sunday School. She and Dolly took it in turns as they needed someone to stay at the manor, but that was fine.

On Friday, 25 May 1917 the German bombers attacked Folkestone killing 97 people and injuring many. The casualties were all civilians just going about their business shopping for the weekend—as well as children playing in the street. It became normal for these bombers to target the East Kent coastal towns—so Dover, Ramsgate and Margate were frequently hit.

Chapter 5

Dolly was missing Frank and often wondered where he was, how he was, and how he was coping. One Saturday out of the blue he turned up at Wicken Manor on a few days' leave. Lady Frances and Sir Charles were delighted to see him, he looked thinner and in need of a bath, but other than that, was absolutely fine. Dolly wasted no time, set to with the hot water and got a bath ready for him, she then suggested that he leave his clothes outside the door so she could arrange to get them laundered and ready for his departure, which would come round all too quickly. After he had spent time with his parents, he came to find Dolly who, with Polly, was talking about the night shift. They did this in three-hour slots so that they could still get some rest and be fit for work the next day. They were just discussing which part of the night they would do when Frank suddenly appeared and asked Dolly if she would like to go for a ride with him. She looked unsure but Polly said, 'off you go Dolly, I'll do the first night shift and you can relieve me later on, just bring me a nice cuppa' she grinned and added 'don't do anything I wouldn't do!' but secretly glad her friend was having some time with Frank.

It was evening but with plenty of daylight, so they saddled up both horses, Apollo and Neptune—Charlie the pony looking hopeful—so Frank gave him a piece of carrot and spoke to him, but told him he wasn't going anywhere. He was so very fond of Charlie as he learnt to ride him when he was a small boy, but these days, he just made a fuss of him. Obviously, Charlie had missed him and was hoping for a bit more attention.

They set off on the horses and had a great ride through the countryside and when they reached the river, they tethered them and sat on the riverbank. Dolly wanted Frank to kiss her like he had on the night before he left, this he did and, once again, her breath left her body, and she knew then that this was the man she wanted to spend the rest of her life with. They spent quite a bit of time by the river, talking about what Frank had experienced on the front, but again, he gave a very sketchy account of what was going on, but suffice to say, he was very torn about having to go back after these three days.

As he took Dolly in his arms, he said, 'It is my duty to go back and help my platoon but leaving my parents and you, Dolly, and this idyll is breaking my heart.'

Dolly held back tears saying, 'it'll be fine Frank, I'll always be here for you, just hold me.' That evening, Dolly became a woman, by the riverside in Frank's arms as dusk fell, and when they returned to the manor and stabled the horses, it was getting quite dark.

Dolly went straight to the hospital room where Polly was relieved of her duties and could go and get some sleep, but she wanted to know that Dolly had had an enjoyable evening with Frank. Over the promised cup of tea Dolly said that all was fine and they had had a good talk and catch up, but didn't tell her anymore, even though they were best friends and told each other everything. Dolly stayed up most of the night, and although she looked after the soldiers that were needing her help, she got through on automatic pilot as she couldn't get Frank out of her head. She hoped that when he came home after the war, he would certainly want to marry her, but she just didn't dare to think that far, all she knew was that she loved him so very much.

The next day was Sunday, so after church Frank came to look for Dolly and said he would very much like to spend the afternoon with her. As she was on Sunday School duty they arranged to meet before tea and he said he would like to have a walk round the grounds and speak to her. Dolly was very apprehensive, part of her hoped he would propose, and part of her was worried that Frank would say that what had occurred by the riverbank the previous evening had been a big mistake.

However, by the time Dolly returned from Sunday School she saw a car parked and realised it belonged to Dr Hamish and she had a feeling of dread that Felicity had come to visit with the doctor and his wife. Dolly headed straight for the stables and saw Frank walking arm in arm with Felicity in the garden. She thought she should make herself scarce, but not before the couple had caught sight of her. Felicity greeted her with, "Hello Dolly, have you come to muck out the horses, I know you love all that!" Frank looked very sheepishly at his feet and Dolly replied that she had already done that task earlier in the day and was just checking up on the horses that she loved!

She then hurried back to the kitchen to help with afternoon tea, that was quite a feat these days with twenty soldiers to serve the tea to—some of the more able ones would come through to the kitchen and carry the trays to the sick bays, but generally it was quite a task, especially when there were visitors. However, Jenny always had a nice piece of ham in the larder, or some potted meat to put in sandwiches, and together with scones and some fruit cake, her teas were very well appreciated. Jenny asked Dolly to take the laden trolley through to the drawing room and serve Sir Charles, Lady Frances and their guests.

Morag was just saying to Lady Frances how happy she was that Frank and Felicity were getting on so well, and hoped that after the war, things might develop. Dolly went cold at the thought and spilled tea in one of the saucers, she was mortified and quickly tried to cover up and got out of there as quickly as she could.

She hoped that Frank would come to find her later, however, Dr Hamish, Morag and Felicity were asked to join the family for dinner as they didn't appear to be in a rush to drive home. That night Dolly was on duty and then eventually fell into a very restless sleep, by the time she got up in the morning Frank had already gone back to the front. There had been a phone call late the night before cutting all leave short due to developments—not good news—and he was gone!

She confided to Polly how sad and devastated she felt at Frank's quick departure, Polly said that Frank had come to find her in case she was on night duty, Polly was there herself and offered to go and wake Dolly up but Frank said not to worry, he would catch up with her next time. Dolly thought that Polly should have come to wake her in any case, but it wasn't her fault—she just felt devastated and worried that Frank might have just used her and didn't have feelings for her but she loved him so much.

Soldiers were discharged all the time, once a week Sir Charles would have a visit from one of his colleagues, or occasionally Dr Hamish would come on his own to help check up on some of the patients, basically to see how they were doing and whether they could go back to the front, or be discharged and sent home.

Occasionally, if they were not making proper progress they would be transferred to a hospital where they could proceed with further treatment. In any event, there was quite a quick turnover of patients, they could be there from a couple of weeks to a month, but as soon as they were discharged, there sadly were always more to fill the beds. It really was an amazing thing that Sir Charles was doing, but he felt gratified that there was somewhere for soldiers with small injuries to go to—and was so very grateful to the volunteers who made this possible, including his beloved Lady Frances. They received the occasional letter from Frank which said that all was well but when she received these, she wondered how long ago they had been sent, and whether the contents still applied. She just didn't know how she would cope if anything happened to him.

At long last on the 11 November 1918, the Armistice was declared and the first World War was over! Wicken Manor, like many other places, received the news with much joy and quickly informed all the soldiers recovering in their care the very good news, which meant that they would eventually be discharged to their families instead of being sent back to the front.

Part 2

Chapter 6

Frank arrived home a couple of weeks before Christmas, he seemed well physically but was very quiet, still in a bit of shock that the war was finally over, and wondering then what he would do with his life. He had just left school when he joined up and hadn't given much thought to his future, despite the fact that he had done very well at school.

He really didn't feel he wanted to go into medicine like his father, really felt that definitely wasn't for him, although he had great admiration for Sir Charles and his achievements in the world of medicine during his long career, especially the progress made with some of the horrific war wounds he had dealt with. There were many amputees in his care who had survived their injuries and were now starting new lives, dealing with their disabilities.

Polly had heard from Thomas several times, but they hadn't met up; he had managed to get through the rest of the war without any more injuries but still struggled the mental effect of losing so many of his fellow soldiers in one battle, and the thought of Polly waiting for him to come home went a long way to help these black moods. He was hoping to be back with his family for Christmas, then wanted Polly to go to Birmingham to see him and meet his family. He assured her that they couldn't wait to meet her—they were very grateful that she played such a big part in his recovery and thought she sounded lovely. Polly said that she hoped to visit him in the spring—perhaps she could arrange a few days off work with Jenny.

Frank met up with Dolly in the stables the day after his return; it was mid-afternoon and darkness was looming, so they decided not to go for a ride and just had a talk. Frank told her how much she meant to him and how the times they had spent together were very precious, but he had to focus on finding a career now that the war was over, and would be going to London for a few days to see what his prospects might be. His father had arranged some appointments with some contacts to see what the future might hold for him. He said he would be back for Christmas and would catch up with her then. Dolly felt a little disheartened, she didn't know what to expect when Frank came home, but at this point, she felt like she was very low priority in his life.

She worried that while in London he would inevitably meet up with Dr Hamish and his family, Felicity would be very happy to see Frank, especially where she could monopolise him.

Frank was back for Christmas and on Christmas Morning everyone went to church, then Polly and Dolly returned to Wicken Manor to serve lunch, before going to their families for tea and spending St. Stephen's Day with them, returning to Wicken Manor on the 27th to resume normal duties and prepare for New Year's Eve. As 1919 loomed, Sir Charles wanted to open his home to celebrate the New Year, in a quiet way, as many families were grieving for loved ones, however, he wanted to show his thanks to all the volunteers who had helped with the injured staying at Wicken Manor, and the villagers who had ensured that there was always fresh meat and plenty of provisions available to help Jenny provide nourishing meals, especially to those who were convalescing; a healthy diet went a long way!

This meant a very busy few days for Jenny, Polly and Dolly and they were busy cooking, baking, and generally laying on a great feast for all the guests. There were over 100 villagers invited to share this event, and great fun was had by all. The food was laid out, Jim and a couple of lads from the village provided some ale, there was live music by a few people in the village who played piano, violin and penny whistle, and everyone, including the staff, were able to let their hair down and have a great party and see in the New Year.

Frank danced with everyone, including Polly, Dolly and Betty, but made sure he was with Dolly as midnight struck, and they saw 1919 in together and managed to sneak off to Frank's room and spend some special time together. As the party went on into the small hours they were not missed. He told Dolly he thought about her a lot even when he was in London trying to sort out his future, and once he had settled on a job, they would talk again. Dolly felt reassured and believed that she would be part of that future, and despite the fact that Frank would be off to London the next day, she didn't feel quite so desolate.

What she didn't realise was that Frank was staying with Dr Hamish and his family while in London, not in a hotel like Dolly had assumed, and Felicity was thoroughly enjoying having Frank around. Morag was happy for this relationship to develop, thought that Wicken Manor would suit her daughter very well one of these fine days, and was more than delighted to have Frank in their home.

Frank talked to quite a few people that Sir Charles had put him in touch with, he was very well known with good connections, so it was up to Frank to decide which path to follow. After a few weeks of thinking things over, he decided that he would go and work for a bank; he would start as a clerk and learn all about the world of banking from scratch. He had been very good at maths when at school and would pick this up really quickly, thus with the prospect of him becoming a manager in a couple of years. That meant he wouldn't need to stay in London after that, he could go to a regional branch and his thought was that he could probably go to a branch near his family home in Kent.

He went home one weekend in spring and went for a ride with Dolly, again, they spent a long time by the riverbank where he told her of his plans to work in London for a couple of years, when he would return and hopefully get a good position in a more local bank. Still, he didn't propose but again, she treasured that lovely late afternoon and early spring evening spent in Frank's arms where she truly believed that they would be together one day.

Nothing mattered as long as he knew how much she loved him and how she couldn't wait to spend the rest of their lives together. If only he would propose and they could officially be engaged! This would be absolutely wonderful. However, it was enough for Dolly to spend time with Frank and showing him how much she truly loved him.

Chapter 7

Fred Dennis, Polly's dad, became unwell in late spring. He had a high temperature and had to stay in bed and was being nursed by his wife—this was unprecedented as he had never been ill apart from a cold that he would shake off in the fresh air while working. Polly was very concerned and dashed home a couple of times to give her mum a break. Jenny said: 'Polly, you must go and see your mother and stay with her, if necessary, I'll pack up some food for you to take, Dolly can help me if I need a hand in the kitchen.'

Sir Charles was in London working for a few days, so when Lady Frances heard the conversation Jenny was having with Polly, she added, 'I went to visit your father this week and he is indeed very unwell, I will visit again today and I will tell your mother that you will be home tomorrow to help her.' Polly thanked Lady Frances profusely. After several days, Polly returned to her duties and said that Fred's fever had come down and he was beginning to recover slowly.

Sir Charles returned from London and when Lady Frances told him about Polly's father, he became very concerned, and even more so when he realised that Lady Frances had visited the patient. The reason he had spent so much time in London was because the Spanish Influenza epidemic was sweeping Europe and London had many cases. He put the thought at the back of his mind and hoped that this wasn't what Polly's dad had been suffering from!

A week later, Lady Frances became very unwell with a temperature, ached in every limb, and try as she might, she really couldn't get out of bed. Sir Charles was due home that evening so Jenny and Polly tried to make her comfortable but because of the Spanish Flu epidemic, they covered their faces when entering her room and giving her sips of water, which is all she could manage. When Sir Charles came home, he was distraught at the state he found Lady Frances in. For safety, he said that no one was to enter her room except for himself, and he spent day and night by her bedside to try and get the fever down. He sent for Frank who returned home but just saw his mother fleetingly, speaking to her quietly to let her know that he was there.

Sadly, Lady Frances lost her fight and passed away two weeks after going down with this awful flu. Everyone in the village as well as all the household were devastated, she was such a popular figure in the village and loved by all, due to her generous nature and friendliness to everybody she spoke to. The funeral was held in the local church, which was packed despite the fear of catching the flu as the large congregation paid their respects, and the burial was private with only Sir Charles, Frank and the staff of Wicken Manor in attendance.

Jenny and Jim, Polly and Dolly were very upset but felt honoured to have known such a lovely lady and thought she would be very sadly missed. Frank stayed a few more days with Sir Charles, Dolly didn't see much of him, but hadn't expected to, Sir Charles and Frank were united in their grief and spent time talking about this lady who had played such a huge part in both their lives.

Eventually, Sir Charles decided he needed to get back to work, and suggested that Frank should do the same so they both returned to London and the next few weeks summer turned to autumn—Frank came home some weekends but not as often as Dolly would have liked. Whenever he was home, they spent their evenings riding and spending time by the riverbank—where Frank would speak very openly about how much he missed his mother—and Dolly understood this as they were such a close-knit family. When Dolly was alone, she would ride to the river just thinking about Frank as this was their special place and she always felt close to him when she was there.

One weekend, Frank was home but Dolly hadn't seen him, he was spending time with Sir Charles in his study so she just went about her business. When he hadn't come to find her late afternoon, she decided to saddle up Apollo and go for a ride down to the river before dusk fell—if Frank came to find her, he would know where she was and would follow her. She rode down the drive and as she went to go round a bend, a car came charging at great speed with the driver honking the horn—this frightened Apollo. He reared, Dolly was thrown off, falling on the tarmac lane and rolling into a ditch. She was knocked unconscious and laid there for some time as Apollo took off and bolted down to the village. Eventually one of the people there caught him and brought him back.

By this time, everyone realised that Dolly was missing. Felicity was with Frank, she had arrived in her new car which Dr Hamish had bought her for her birthday, she was very excited and had wanted to surprise Frank and cheer him up as he was so down at the moment. She seemed totally unaware that she had caused Dolly's accident. If she was aware, she was certainly keeping very quiet about it, although after she had rounded the bend, she may not have witnessed the result of her reckless driving.

As darkness fell, a search for Dolly was taking place, with everyone including her parents looking for her and eventually she was found in the ditch, unconscious but with a weak pulse, so they knew she was alive. Sir Charles and Nancy took charge when they got Dolly back to the house, she was unconscious and clearly had a head injury, but what was most concerning was the amount of blood soaking her clothes. It was evident and shocking for them to realise that apart from her other injuries, Dolly had suffered a miscarriage. Nancy dealt with this professionally, medical care came first, questions would come later—she didn't realise that Dolly was even walking out with anyone!

Dolly's injuries were grave, she soon recovered from the concussion but her back injury was quite serious, her walking would be severely impaired in years to come, and the loss of the baby and the ensuing result meant that she would never bear another child. Eventually she realised the enormity of the accident and when Nancy said, 'what on earth happened, can you remember anything?'

Dolly replied, 'it all seems like a bad dream, I think something must have scared Apollo, and all I remember is falling and a hard landing! I remember a car honking its horn and I think that must have spooked him, but everything is very hazy!' She felt this might have been Felicity but couldn't be sure and didn't want to wrongly accuse anyone.

Nancy then asked her, 'Dolly, why didn't you confide in me that you were going to have a baby, feel so sad for you that you have lost this child, but I had no idea that you had been walking out with someone!'

Dolly replied, 'I didn't realise I was with child, had felt a bit strange at times and went through a period of sickness which I put down to a stomach upset—I really had no idea or I would have been more cautious and wouldn't have gone!'

Nancy bit the bullet then, 'would you tell me who you have been walking out with, and whether the young man concerned realises you might have been in the family way?'

Dolly immediately said, 'I'm so sorry to have let you and Dad down, and hopefully he won't ever find out, perhaps you don't need to tell him, please Mum.'

Nancy said that she would keep this between them as she felt that Dolly had suffered enough but she felt that the young man concerned, whoever he might be, had had a lucky escape and wouldn't need to face the consequences of his actions. Unlike Dolly who would never be able to bear a child after her awful injuries, she was certainly being punished!

Nancy, as the local midwife, came across unmarried girls who were carrying babies, and these were for various reasons. Sometimes they were taken advantage of by a family member, sometimes they were forced by whoever they were seeing and sometimes it was simply because they were in love and thought it couldn't happen to them.

Sir Charles, despite having treated Dolly for her injuries seemed unaware that she had lost a baby, he realised her internal injuries had left her in a sterile state, but never mentioned the possibility of a miscarriage. Nancy thought it wouldn't help Dolly if this news came out which is why she kept it from Dolly's father! He wouldn't have rested until knowing who the father might have been and would have literally beaten it out of Dolly. Nancy thought her recovery would be lengthy enough without making life even more complicated so the matter was never mentioned.

Dolly stayed at Wicken Manor where she was made as comfortable as she could be. If Sir Charles or Frank suspected that Felicity had been the cause of Dolly's accident they certainly never mentioned it, although it wouldn't have taken a lot of working out—but somehow everyone kept quiet about the lead up to the accident. What was done was done, had Dolly been found earlier her injuries might have not been as severe, who would know?

Polly was very distressed when she learnt the news of Dolly's accident. Ironically, she had been to Birmingham for a few days to meet Thomas' family. They were very excited about meeting her and were so thankful for the care he had received at Wicken Manor after being injured, and thought Polly was a lovely girl. Thomas didn't waste time telling Polly that he would like them to be married but would come down to see her parents and speak to them and make sure they would be happy to give their daughter's hand in marriage to Thomas. He was hoping to find work in London and they would either move there, or he would have to stay there in the week and come home for the weekends. Polly loved her job at Wicken Manor but wanted to be a good wife to Thomas and would go where they could be together.

Dolly made slow progress, her mother visited every day to check on her, her sister Betty would visit every weekend and her dad would also come and see her. Eventually, as she got a bit stronger, they took her home so that they could keep an eye on her, and Sir Charles promised to call by if her condition deteriorated. He was very kind to Dolly and to the family, he was so fond of this tough girl with a big heart who loved horses and the outdoors, as well as being a really big help in the house when needed, and he knew that she was very fond of Frank. However, Frank and Felicity seem to be getting closer, with Frank spending more time in London and Felicity playing a big part in his social life.

She would bring him home some weekends but would stay there with him before driving him back. Sometimes Dr Hamish and Morag would accompany them but without Lady Frances there would be no more house parties, and not many friends visited any more.

Meanwhile, Dolly despaired that Frank would ever come and speak to her and tell her how he felt about her, and she didn't want him to know that she had lost their baby as she didn't want him to feel pity for her. She still loved him very much and wanted him to be happy. She realised her life had changed for ever and she would need help and wouldn't want his progress in life to be held back by her. She looked upon him as a beautiful butterfly and to put him in a box meant that he would shrivel and die and no longer be beautiful, so in her head she gave Frank his freedom, and he would never know what she had gone through due to the accident caused by Felicity.

However, she felt a real hatred towards Felicity as she had always looked down at Dolly and Dolly did wonder how Felicity would feel if she knew about what had happened between her and Frank, but again, Dolly would never hurt Frank. Also, she felt that Sir Charles would have loved a grandchild and she wondered if he was aware, also thought about how Lady Frances would have felt about her bearing them a grandchild if she had still been alive. She would have treasured Frank's child in any circumstances Dolly felt sure. There was a possibility that Sir Charles did know this, but if he did, he certainly would never have told anyone.

Chapter 8

Polly came to visit Dolly as often as she could and tried not to speak about Thomas too much; she knew that things with Frank and Felicity were getting quite serious, and was aware that Dolly missed Frank more than anything. Also Felicity used to address Polly in a similar manner to the way she spoke to Dolly when requesting anything from her, be it a cup of tea or a fire to be lit. Frank did pick Felicity up on this when he heard her addressing his staff as both he and Sir Charles had always addressed them in a courteous and polite manner when issuing orders, making them more like requests, so that they were well respected, rather than feared, and this they found had worked well for years! Their staff were so very loyal, Jenny and Jim had served them for many years and Polly and Dolly had never looked for other positions. The people from the village who they requested help from whenever extra hands were needed were always glad to come along and help if they could, and this ensured that the house and grounds were well cared for. However, this didn't happen quite so much now since Lady Frances' passing, and Felicity often took it upon herself to visit with Frank whenever he came home for a weekend.

Polly and Thomas were due to get married very soon after Thomas had been down one weekend and spoke to Polly's parents, asking for their daughter's hand in marriage and they were delighted, welcoming him into their family with open arms. The wedding was due to take place in October 1919 at the village church where Polly and her family had worshipped and she had—and still did—teach Sunday School to the children.

Thomas also liked the church; it brought happy memories of his recovery and the start of his friendship with Polly. Thomas' parents would be down for the wedding, staying with another family in the village as they had a spare room, and Polly was enjoying making plans. They would initially live with Polly's parents until they could find a cottage to rent and as Thomas still worked in London, he wouldn't manage to get home every night as he tried to do as much overtime as he could to save money for when the young couple could get a home of their own.

Polly and Dolly had always promised that they would be bridesmaids to each other when one of them got married. Polly told Dolly of their plans and Dolly was delighted. She was recovering slowly and was walking very badly due to her back injury, but Sir Charles was keeping an eye on her and helping her with the pain by giving her different drugs and trying out different pain-relief methods.

More than anything, Dolly wanted to be with Polly on her big day and this became possible when Sir Charles turned up on her doorstep one day with a wheelchair. This would ensure that Dolly would make it up the aisle behind Polly and her father, and she was overjoyed and extremely grateful. Part of her used to wonder whether Sir Charles knew more about the accident than he was letting on, and whether his kindness was partly due to guilt. However, he was a kind person so this may just be his normal behaviour.

The news was broken to her by Polly that Frank and Felicity were now officially engaged—there had been an announcement in one of the newspapers so Polly wanted her to hear it from herself, rather than by some random gossip.

Dolly had already guessed that as Frank hadn't tried to see her since the accident due to spending so much time working in London, they definitely didn't have a future together, as she had hoped for so very long. She still loved him dearly and for that reason, however painful it was for her, she was happy for him to follow a different path. She felt so useless after her injuries that she didn't feel that she could cope with a relationship in any event, but thought it would have been really nice if he did visit her occasionally and they could stay friends, as this is how the road to their friendship developed through their joint interests, like loving the countryside, the change in the seasons, riding their beloved horses and the long talks and times spent by the riverside.

However, Frank was training to be a bank manager and as Felicity wasn't keen on living in the countryside it looked as though they would be staying in London, and when his appointment as manager happened, it would most probably be in the city. They had an incredibly busy social life, often out for dinner parties, then Dr Hamish and Morag enjoyed hosting parties so they would also take part in these, and generally life was a social whirl. Frank wasn't sure if he really enjoyed all the partying, as he still missed his mother and had some really low days, but found that he loved the casino.

A few of the chaps would break away from the ladies at times and would enjoy gambling. Frank really enjoyed gambling and found it was fun doing something with the other chaps in the group.

Polly's wedding day arrived and she looked beautiful and Thomas smiled all day long. One of the barns had been decorated for the occasion and could also be used for the Harvest Supper which would take place a few days later. After the church service with Dolly never far behind in her wheelchair, having taken charge of Polly's bouquet which she had arranged herself with wild flowers that she had got some of the children to pick for her, the party made their way to the nearby barn.

After a copious wedding breakfast consisting of ham salad with plenty of fresh vegetables, and apple pie, followed by afternoon tea and cutting of the cake; the happy couple were taken by horse and cart to the railway station and caught the train to London where they would spend a few days. Polly hadn't visited London since she was a child and they walked miles along the Embankment and took in all the sights, as well as some of the devastation brought on by World War 1, and Thomas took her to where he was working on the building site so she could then visualise where he might be when he returned to work.

This idyllic time was over far too soon, and they were back into a routine, Polly wanted to stay at Wicken Manor as she enjoyed her job, and didn't feel there was much point in languishing at home while Thomas was away working. They thoroughly enjoyed their weekends when they could be together and settled into a very pleasant routine. The weeks passed and 1920 loomed—but there would be no big New Year's Eve party this year—after what had turned out to be a very sad 2019. The loss of Lady Frances was still fresh in many people's minds, also Dolly's accident—where she had gone from a very active young lady to being confined to a wheelchair or hobbling very short distances on crutches—such a waste!

Frank and Felicity were due to be married in July 1920 and it seemed better all round for the wedding to take place in London. Dolly would have struggled if the wedding had been in the village, she felt very depressed at times, and was trying really hard to walk, but progress was slow.

Meanwhile, the building company Thomas worked for said they were going to build houses just outside Ashford, which was reasonably near the village. Thomas hoped that he would be asked to work there, it would suit him so well and save money as he could go home every evening, even if he still did overtime.

Polly was very thrilled at this news. She was still at the manor and Thomas had no problem with that, even when he was home every night, she would be home long before him and have a meal ready.

Things were a bit quieter at the manor, the wedding due in London wasn't involving Sir Charles obviously, Frank updated him when he saw him but even he didn't seem that enthusiastic, considering he was the groom. He would have preferred a quiet affair, but Felicity wanted her wedding to be the event of the year—rather selfish but she felt it was her special day and was used to having her own way.

The day loomed and Polly asked Jenny if she would mind if she spent part of the day with Dolly, as she knew that she would be feeling very depressed despite putting such a brave face on things. Her parents and sister had no idea of her close friendship with Frank and what had evolved from this. Jenny had an idea that they were close, and because of this, understood why Polly wanted to be there for her.

It was during the day that Dolly spoke to Polly very frankly about the depth of her feelings for Frank and how close they had been, not mentioning what the accident resulted in, or even who had been the cause of the accident. She also said that the way she was feeling at the moment she could never be a good wife to Frank, and because she loved him so much, she would have wanted to be the very best, and that could never happen, so maybe his marriage to Felicity might be a good outcome for everyone.

Polly knew her friend so very well and felt that she was putting a brave face on her situation and for that, she loved her dearly and counted her own blessings for having met Thomas when she did. They were blissfully happy despite both working really hard but Polly hoped that they would have a family soon although she didn't mention this to Dolly. She thought she would wait in case she was tempting fate.

The wedding was a very grand affair having been organised by Felicity and her mother and some of their friends. The ceremony was in a church in London and was festooned with flowers; the florist who did the bouquets also arranged the flowers in the church. The wedding breakfast was held at the Ritz before the happy couple left for their honeymoon. Frank had chosen the honeymoon venue and was driving to a village in the Cotswolds, thinking that Felicity would enjoy the countryside with stunning views; the landscape was beautiful and Frank couldn't wait to spend five days in this idyllic spot.

When they checked into the rather grand country hotel, he could tell immediately from Felicity's expression that this wasn't what she had expected. However, the suite of rooms they had did help to lift her spirits and they ordered a light supper to be served in their room as it was getting rather late when they arrived. Frank also ordered champagne and they enjoyed being together in very splendid surroundings.

The next morning, after breakfast was served in their room they ventured for a walk. The weather was beautiful and the scenery spectacular, however, after a couple of miles with Frank guiding the way with a map he had been given at the hotel, Felicity said that her feet hurt. Although she was wearing flat shoes, they were not very sturdy whereas Frank was wearing brogues, so they turned back and returned to the hotel in time for a late lunch.

They spent the rest of the day in the hotel grounds strolling round the extensive gardens—this included a rose garden and they were in full bloom at this time, and the scent they emitted was wonderful. They also had a walk in the quaint village, with a pretty stream running down the side of the road, so very peaceful, however, Frank was disappointed by Felicity's lack of enthusiasm for their surroundings.

The next morning, it was pouring with rain and to say that Felicity was not terribly happy was an understatement. Frank said, 'it might brighten up a bit later, maybe we can sit in the lounge and read or play cards.' Felicity's reply echoed what Frank had felt since they arrived. 'Not sure what made you choose this godforsaken place! There's nothing here!' And with that, she flounced down to the bar.

As it was still raining the next morning, Frank announced: I've got a surprise for you today, we are going for a drive and the weather will not dampen our spirits, I promise!'

Felicity brightened up with this statement and couldn't wait to leave. Frank drove to Cheltenham and when Felicity saw the lovely shops, restaurants and tea rooms this place had to offer she was delighted—so they had a very happy day there, but when Frank said, 'we need to get back to our hotel now but glad we've had good day' to which Felicity replied, 'do we have to, can't we stay in a hotel here for our last three days? Please Frank!'

Faced with this, Frank found a hotel that had a vacancy which he felt would suit them and Felicity wanted to go there immediately. Frank said they had to go back to the hotel to collect their things, so Felicity said she would leave him to it and stay in their new room and send for some tea.

Frank was deeply disappointed that the first hotel hadn't worked out. He so loved the countryside and really wished that Felicity could love it too. He suddenly thought of Dolly and what her reaction would have been in the same situation and he felt a real pang for the way he had treated her and because he had never been to see her since the accident. He hadn't meant not to go and see her, just hadn't done so at the time, then the longer he left it the harder he thought it would be.

He had a busy life in London working and socialising then preparing to get married so he hadn't seen her since early spring 1919 when they shared some very intimate moments before Lady Frances had passed away. He still had no idea that she had lost their child and that Felicity had inadvertently caused the accident. Such a tragic turn of events.

However, the next few days in Cheltenham passed well with a day spent at Cheltenham Racecourse, total coincidence, but Frank did love to gamble—and Felicity enjoyed watching the races. When they got there, they met up with some of their London friends who had gone for a day out, so a great time was had by all, except that Frank didn't win any money.

Chapter 9

They were back in London after their honeymoon the following weekend, and returned to Dr Hamish and Morag's home, where Frank had stayed previously when in London, except that instead of having the smaller room at the top of the house, Morag had arranged for Felicity's old room, which was huge, to be given a facelift while they were away, with an adjoining dressing room and a sitting room so that they would have their own space as newlyweds. In time, Frank was looking to find them their own home, but with all the events of the previous year, they never seemed to find the time to look at places.

Frank's biggest worry was that Felicity would choose somewhere to live that was beyond his means. He was now a bank manager, but on the bottom rung as it were, and was not earning a huge amount and he had known Felicity long enough to know that she had expectations. She also loved socialising with friends, having long lunches and shopping expeditions, which was what Morag did herself some of the time. However, she was more financially secure to do so but somehow Felicity felt that it was her right to live as she wanted.

The week after their return from their honeymoon, Frank said he would like to go and see his father as he was, quite honestly, rather worried about him. He hadn't appeared to enjoy their wedding, obviously still missing Lady Frances dreadfully, as they were so in love—and life had taken on a monochrome hue, as opposed to the colourful life he had with his wife. He still worked hard, probably more than he needed to, but it kept him busy and helping people was his vocation.

When Frank asked if Felicity would accompany him to Wicken Manor, she refused saying she had arranged to catch up with a friend who had just had a baby boy, and she wanted to go and visit. Frank said he would probably stay for a couple of nights and Felicity was quite happy for him to do this.

He actually felt happier going on his own, he would be able to relax more and spend some time with his father without worrying about Felicity getting bored. He went for a ride on Neptune while he was there and suddenly missed having Dolly near him, and all the guilt feelings returned. He spoke to his father at length that night about many things, and his father said that he should watch his gambling habit as this could easily get out of hand.

He had the downfall of friends hooked by the gambling bug, and although it was an outlet and a bit of fun, it could actually take over your life and make you spend money you hadn't got. Frank reassured his father that it was all under control and he would never let that happen. He liked the casino and enjoyed watching horseracing and an innocent little bet here and there never did anyone any harm, was his theory.

They had a companionable supper accompanied by a very nice claret and spent the rest of the time in pleasant silence. The next morning, Frank thought he would like to go to church so he and Sir Charles attended the family service. Dolly was there with her parents in her wheelchair so after the service Frank really did feel it was time, he spoke to her—he had left it far too long.

As they filed outside the church he managed to get out before she did so he was able to wait for her to emerge. She greeted him with a huge smile and he told her how sad he was to see her in the wheelchair with such limited mobility; when Nancy and John saw who she was speaking to, they hovered, initially, then Frank said he would wheel her back to the cottage when they had had a catch up. John looked protectively at Dolly but she said that was fine, so he and Nancy wandered back to their home.

Dolly asked Frank about his job and whether he was happy in London, he said that he was but he missed Wicken Manor, the countryside and his parents, especially his dear departed mother—which is partly why he was back for the weekend, but life in London was good, he enjoyed the career he had chosen and had a good circle of friends; he asked Dolly how things would work out for her, she said as far as they could tell she had made the most progress likely, yes, she could walk short distances with sticks, she spent many hours trying to improve this, but the reality was that this would be her future—life in a wheelchair or hobbling on sticks!

Her parents worried about her as she so loved outdoor life. John had built boxes in the garden which he filled with soil and placed on strong trestles so that she could do some gardening and she enjoyed growing a few flowers and vegetables, always fascinated by the part nature played in growing beautiful produce from seeds or tiny seedlings, much like nature growing a baby inside a woman's body, as Dolly had briefly experienced. The urge to tell Frank was never stronger than at this moment, however, Dolly told herself that no good would come from such a revelation so kept her secret which she would eventually take to her grave.

They carried on talking for a while, until Frank thought it was time he wheeled her home, and he promised to visit her again the next time he came to Wicken Manor.

Dolly felt better for having seen Frank after all this time, she realised that there was no way they could have a life together, as she couldn't ever see herself settling down with a life partner as she would never be able to cope, but as long as her family and friends were around her, she would be fine. However, Nancy and John were finding it harder and harder to care for her, Nancy kept very strange hours, babies came at the oddest time of day or night and with her great reputation she covered several villages—cars were becoming more popular and often someone would come and collect her to take her to a neighbouring village to help at mothers' bedsides. John was always busy but spent time with Dolly when he was able, however, he had begun suffering with Rheumatism and was often himself in a lot of discomfort.

Betty was engaged to a doctor from the hospital, Stanley Johns, a young Canadian chap who had been a medic in World War 1 and had experienced many atrocities and dealt with dreadful injuries. After the War he was offered a job at the hospital where Betty worked and the two developed a deep and loving relationship after a very short time.

At this point, he really was enjoying his time in England and had written to his family in Canada to explain to them about Betty and what their plans were, and where he was working at the moment—his father was also a doctor with his own surgery back home so understood Stan's enthusiasm and wished him well. He was glad that Stan was in a relationship with someone who would help him in his work. Stan's mother had no nursing qualifications but was a big help to his father just by being there and helping by chatting to the patients and offering moral support.

Stan and Betty decided to leave the wedding for a while, they were both busy and spent the time when they were together discussing their future and what their hopes and dreams were.

Chapter 10

Betty had learnt much during her nursing career, she was a very capable midwife having learnt from Nancy over the years and could also deal with multiple medical emergencies. Also, she read medical books so was improving her knowledge all the time, much of this she discussed with Stan and he never tired of her enthusiasm and energy.

One day, they arranged to meet up and he said he had something to show her. It was a derelict house which had been empty for a while—it was huge and was being auctioned the following week. She wondered why he was showing her this and when she questioned him, he said that he was thinking of bidding for it, to turn it into a doctor's surgery and a home for themselves. It was hard to imagine how this could be transformed and the cost involved—unbeknown to her, he had spoken to Thomas, Polly's husband, as he knew a good bit about building, and he seemed to think that if the bones of the property were sound, it would be a great project.

Betty initially felt very excited, then a bit frightened, but then felt excited again. The thought of her and Stan working together in their own surgery was very adventurous, but would fulfil their dreams. She did wonder how they would pay for such a project but Stan had some money saved, and a doting uncle said he would be happy to help out—Betty herself was a saver and being a nurse meant that long hours didn't always allow her to spend much money. She would often give Nancy money for the family, but she had savings. Also, Stan explained that they wouldn't be leaving their jobs at the hospital until the work had been done and they would carry on living in their modest digs until the building was done, which is why they postponed their wedding till the following year. A big but hopefully worthwhile sacrifice.

The day of the auction arrived and although a few people were bidding, there wasn't a massive amount of interest and when Stan outbidded a couple of people they soon gave up the idea, thinking that it would be quite a project to renovate the property for whatever purpose they had in their minds. Stan was within his budget, which delighted him and he couldn't wait to tell Betty the good news. Thomas got his boss to look at the project involved and they all had a meeting to discuss what would be needed to make this a really smart doctor's surgery—his boss recommended an architect to draw up plans, it would be an extra expense but well worthwhile to make sure that the work would be carried out efficiently and make it easier to gauge the cost.

There would be a waiting room with a reception area and a cloakroom off the entrance hall. Obviously, the doctor's surgery and a separate treatment room would be downstairs. The idea was that Betty would use the treatment room for dressing wounds, doing blood tests and generally treating people for minor ailments especially children. Betty had a wealth of experience having worked at the hospital for so long, and prior to that, helping Nancy in the village—and sometimes she could deal with matters without involving the doctor, which could prove expensive. They were there to make a good living, however, they both very much wanted to help people, be an asset to the community and not everyone could afford to pay for medical care.

At the back of the surgery area there was a bright kitchen and breakfast room and a small sitting room. There was quite a large garden which was very overgrown at the moment and would need to be dealt with. There were two further storeys with what would make a very nice lounge and several bedrooms, and a bathroom would be installed on the first floor if finances allowed it.

Thomas and his boss thought the work would take between three and six months to complete so Stan and Betty resumed their hospital work, spending every available moment making plans for their future.

They went to visit Betty's parents one weekend and were quite shocked to find Dolly very depressed and John looked unwell due to the pain he was suffering. Dolly, at 22, was confined at home most of the time and it was becoming increasingly hard for Nancy to care for her, and for John, while still carrying on as the village midwife.

Stan took Betty for a walk so he could speak to her in private and suggested that perhaps Dolly could stay with them once they moved to the surgery. She could be in the reception area speaking to patients as they came for advice or treatment, Stan and Betty had already discussed that they would need to take someone on to run the reception area also to deal with bookkeeping. Dolly was quite bright and she really needed a change and something to occupy her mind.

Betty, needless to say, thought it was a wonderful idea and couldn't wait to speak to Dolly and her parents. Dolly seemed reluctant, initially, but soon came round to the idea when Stan suggested that she could have her own room on the ground floor, with the possibility of putting what was the outdoor toilet just outside the back door, inside the building by building out a bit further. The architect's plans were not set in stone and it was something that could be done before the work was too advanced. Dolly then seemed quite excited, especially as she would have her own living space and wouldn't be under her sister's feet, she was so aware that she was a burden. However, she would be useful and felt that this was the first time in a long time that she had something to look forward to.

She couldn't wait to tell Polly so the next time they saw each other, she was excited to tell her what was happening. Polly knew quite a bit about the work involved as Thomas had explained to her what they were doing, so when Dolly told her the news, Polly felt very excited for her. It was the first time in many months that she had seen Dolly so animated, she really had lost her zest for life, understandably, but felt fortunate that she was so well cared for by her parents and her friends and felt she didn't want to grumble about her situation.

Polly also felt this was a good time to tell Dolly her special news—she was expecting a baby and she and Thomas were very happy about this. He couldn't wait to be a dad and her parents also thought that this was wonderful news. Dolly was very happy for her friend, a bit sad that she had never told her about what had happened to her so felt she couldn't tell her she understood how she must feel. Dolly herself had been excited when she realised, she was carrying Frank's child—but had put off telling anyone and would have done so eventually, when she could no longer hide the fact, however, no one ever knew apart from Dolly and Nancy and it would have to stay that way. Some days though, that knowledge really made her so very sad and this is when she became depressed.

However, with her recent good fortune and her subsequent move to the new doctor's surgery when the building work was done, she felt she had a new focus and although she was wistful about Polly's news, she felt very happy for her friend.

A cottage had become vacant in the village so Thomas was looking into the possibility of buying it; he had saved quite a bit of money and felt confident he could afford to buy the property. He spoke to Polly about it and she seemed very happy, the cottage was small but in good order, and there were two bedrooms which would be perfect for them. Thomas worked mainly in Ashford now, not often in London, and was busy with the work on the surgery with some other colleagues. They worked well and they would soon be ready to open their doors.

Both Stan and Betty felt sad leaving the hospital when they had both spent so long working there, especially Betty, and Matron was very gracious, wishing her well but saying that there would always be a job at the hospital if things didn't work out. They then decided to get married so that they could live together in their new home otherwise they would not have been deemed as respectable.

Betty was 27 now and had lived in her friend's house for years but they realised life would be so much easier if they both lived on the premises and her reputation would have been in tatters if she lived under the same roof as Stan while they were still both single. They wanted to make a good impression and hoped that the surgery would grow to have a very good reputation—so starting up as a married couple seemed a very sensible decision.

The wedding was arranged for the end of January in the village church and once again, Dolly was bridesmaid in her wheelchair and did a great job. It was a very cold day and had started with a hard frost, but the sun had shone, the snowdrops were out and it was a magical wedding. There was no huge reception, just tea and cake in the Church Hall afterwards which was well attended by all the people in the village including some older children who Betty had taken for Sunday School classes.

Sir Charles came to the wedding and gave the couple a very generous cheque despite the fact he had just spent a considerable amount on repairs to Wicken Manor, but knew that Stan and Betty would put the gift to good use. He was very impressed by what Stan had achieved with Betty and said he would very much like to visit the surgery once they had settled down. He said it would be quite difficult to start with, possibly, as gaining people's trust can be hard, however, he was sure that they would be successful and genuinely wished them well. He remembered how good Betty was during the war when the injured soldiers were convalescing at Wicken Manor, her wonderful caring manner showed what a natural she really was—he shared this information with Stan and said that he was a very lucky man, on more than one count!

No honeymoon for this couple but moving in to their new home getting the domestic side sorted and also sorting out Dolly's room ready for her to move in. Then Stan was having a telephone installed as that would help to keep in contact with hospitals and other specialists if he needed advice, also those patients with a phone would be able to ring the surgery in an emergency. They were having furniture delivered for the waiting room, the surgery and the treatment room, as well as drugs, bandages and other equipment they required.

In any event, when they were finally organised and happy with their setup, Sir Charles actually drove Dolly to her new home and took the opportunity to have a good look round the property and all the work that had been carried out. He was very impressed with the surgery and felt that it should really work well for them.

Dolly was shown into her sitting room, it was sparsely furnished making sure there was nothing for her to trip over and she could manoeuvre her chair comfortably in the space she had—or walk around on her crutches without any obstacles in the way. The room had been brightly decorated and smelled very fresh, the curtains Nancy had made and were really pretty and there were fresh flowers, so that the place was very welcoming. They had managed to build out so that what was once the outside toilet was now inside, together with a sink and hot and cold running water.

Another small room off the lounge would serve as her bedroom, again furnished with just a single bed and small wardrobe, a dressing table with drawers and again, a pretty bedspread and matching curtains so Dolly felt very welcome and thought she would be fine in her new home.

Once she had settled in, they spent a couple of days showing her how the telephone worked, as initially it would be her job to answer it, then dealing with whatever query or emergency the call was about, but Dolly was a quick learner and she would soon pick up all this new information.

The garden had been a wilderness when Stan acquired the property but with the help of Fred, John (with difficulty) and Thomas, and a few of his friends, they had cleared the ground at the back of the house and wanted Dolly to give her input and decide how to set the garden up. This was just what she enjoyed and John was going to make boxes like he did for her at home so that she would be able to plant seeds and grow flowers and vegetables until the garden was sorted; this would take some time, but good to get some growing underway. This had always been a source of fascination for Dolly and that had not changed.

A couple of months after everyone had settled down at the surgery and things were going reasonably well, news came through that Polly had given birth to a beautiful baby girl—delivered by Nancy, of course—all went very smoothly and mother and baby were doing very well. She was to be called Elizabeth and Polly promised that she would visit Dolly in her new home once she was back on her feet and in a bit of a routine. Dolly wrote to Polly with her congratulations and sent her some bootees that she had knitted rather hurriedly in pink, once she knew she had given birth to a baby girl.

Chapter 11

Things were not going too well for Frank and Felicity. At long last he had found a suitable apartment that he could both afford and was to Felicity's taste. She was quite concerned that they should be in a fashionable area of London, however, rents were high in these areas so eventually they settled in Highgate, North London where they found a very nice first floor apartment which was spacious and had a nice outlook. Then Felicity decided that she would need a housekeeper and a cleaner which surprised Frank. Morag had help in her house but Dr Hamish was earning considerably more than Frank was and they could well afford it. Felicity seemed to think it was her right to have these luxuries and when she spent an afternoon with Morag in a depressed state, Morag agreed to give her an allowance to help to pay for a cleaner and a housekeeper.

When Frank learnt this, he was absolutely furious and felt very inadequate as he obviously couldn't look after his wife in the manner that she expected—he was barely earning enough to pay the rent, plus all the socialising they took part in, and he also enjoyed spending time with his male friends down his club, which usually resulted in finishing the evening at a casino.

Felicity spent most of her days visiting friends, having lunches out, planning dinner parties which is why she needed the help of a housekeeper, but would never dream of doing cleaning or laundry so a young girl came in three mornings a week to do the chores.

Frank, in his effort to have more money, overdid the evenings at the casino and was definitely on a losing streak. Eventually things came to a head and he was almost tempted to try and take money from the bank but common sense prevailed at the last minute, and instead he took himself off to Wicken Manor for the weekend to see Sir Charles. On this occasion, he didn't even ask Felicity if she wanted to accompany him. He really wasn't feeling well disposed towards her, and partly blamed her for the problems which really were self-inflicted.

When he finally plucked up the courage to tell Sir Charles his problems, he actually got quite a shock. He always thought that money had never been an issue for Sir Charles and Lady Frances, however, this was no longer the case. Sir Charles had gradually reduced his workload, but still wanted to stay at Wicken Manor as this was where he had spent all those happy years with Lady Frances, however, the cost of running the estate had become very expensive—but he couldn't bear the thought of living anywhere else. Each room brought back its own memories and he wasn't ready to let go.

He explained to Frank that their dream had been to leave the estate to him after both their deaths, however, there had been some urgent repairs needed which had proved expensive. He had borrowed from the bank to enable this work to be done. He had also sold off their horses as he no longer rode, and as Frank was home so seldom these days, there was no point as they had to be fed and watered. Someone with stables in the village had been happy to take them and they would be used for riding. Jenny and Jim were due to retire but as they wanted to remain in the lodge which had been their home for many years, Sir Charles agreed if they paid a peppercorn rent for the privilege. They had been such a loyal couple and between them had kept Wicken Manor afloat for many years and at difficult times too.

When Frank told Sir Charles how much he would need to get him out of trouble, Sir Charles said that he would speak to his bank but would probably need to give them the Deeds for Wicken Manor in exchange for that amount of cash. The bank would have first claim when Wicken Manor was sold. Frank's inheritance was no longer existent; however, he would be out of trouble for the moment.

Sir Charles then spoke to Frank at length listening to him relating what his wife's expectations were, and how she haemorrhaged money on shopping trips, lunches and dinner parties. Sir Charles asked a very impertinent question on the subject of them starting a family, he told Frank that he thought by now there might have been the patter of tiny feet. Frank was very quiet but then said he felt that Felicity wasn't a natural mother, she would visit friends with newborn babies but always came home telling him how sweet they were until they had to be changed or threw up, and she sighed with relief when she realised that she wasn't in that situation.

When the babies started to crawl or walk, she would totally lose interest finding them a real nuisance and couldn't bear the thought of her lovely home being ruined by having a small human there.

Frank said that on the whole they had a pleasant lifestyle but he still missed aspects of life in the countryside, although London did offer lovely green areas but wasn't quite the same.

The rest of the weekend was spent in quiet contemplation on both parts, Sir Charles said he would eventually sell Wicken Manor and the bank would then take their share and anything left would buy him a modest home where he would spend the rest of his days. Frank returned to London feeling very humbled by the courage his father had shown in dealing with a difficult situation and he knew he had to be strong and do some straight talking with Felicity and explain how things stood. Although she wasn't keen on Wicken Manor she saw that as the pot of gold at the end of the rainbow and Morag had always dreamed that Felicity would one day be Lady of the manor, so she would also be in for a wake-up call.

Part 3

Chapter 12

The next few months were eventful for different people with various reasons.

Stan and Betty were busy getting the surgery established with Dolly being a real asset, and they worked as a team. Betty knew that Dolly was a bright girl and she took to her job like a duck to water. She fielded calls extremely well, knew when it needed Stan and also managed to persuade people to see if Betty could help in the first instance. She got on well with the patients and when they realised her disability, they seemed to respect her for the stoic way she dealt with her situation. She was also very sensitive and that was a good quality to have.

They seemed to be coping financially, however, it was always hard to get payments from people who couldn't really afford to see a doctor, however, Stan tried to be kind while being firm, and managed to get paid for his services most of the time, while sometimes he knew that people dragging their feet in settling the bills were often those who could afford it, but were being difficult. After some time, he got to know the patients who genuinely struggled to pay bills, and those who were just reluctant so he decided to give people thirty days to pay, and those who could manage the bills but were late paying, he would make an extra charge.

That did seem to work and after a few months' things were going very well indeed. Stan was very generous to the patients who really couldn't afford to pay very much but came down hard on those who could, and didn't. Almost a 'Robin Hood' type of attitude.

Frank had returned to London after Sir Charles agreed to sort out his gambling debts and had a real heart-to-heart with Felicity. 'Felicity, I am so sorry I have made such a mess of things, please try and understand that it was never my intention to get in so deep. I hope you will bear with the situation and stand by me while I sort this mess out, I do hope that in a few months I can then provide for you as you would wish and be the husband you would like me to be!'

Her reply was, to say the least, very disappointing. 'You must think I'm stupid, I am not hanging around while you sort out your mess, you are just weak-willed and if you hadn't been such a 'mummy's boy' you wouldn't be in this mess. I am going home to Mummy and Daddy.' The irony of this was totally lost on him as he felt very low at this point and assumed she would tell Dr Hamish and Morag all his shortcomings and he really couldn't see how this could end well. He sat in despair as nightfall came and thought about his life with Felicity, what he had achieved since World War One ended, and couldn't honestly see how he had come to such a low ebb.

Suddenly the doorbell rang and his first thought was to ignore it, however, he thought Felicity might have returned and forgotten her key in her haste, but Dr Hamish stood on the doorstep. Frank invited him in and waited for a fresh barrage of accusations at the way he had behaved. However, Dr Hamish suggested they should have a drink and discuss the situation in a calm and sensible fashion. Frank could barely look Dr Hamish in the eye, his embarrassment was off the scale—he might have preferred it if he had lost his temper with him and told him a few home truths, but in reality Dr Hamish was a gentleman, and he proceeded to tell Frank his thoughts about the situation.

He said 'Morag and I are very much to blame for the situation you and Felicity find yourselves in. We have spoilt her over the years and she assumed that when you married, she would have a similar lifestyle. Morag and I did not always have these privileges, we had to work for them!'

Frank replied 'I wanted to give her the best, but I keep getting it wrong!' Dr Hamish said he hadn't realised that Morag had been giving Felicity an allowance to pay for her housekeeper and cleaner's wages. He was quite angry about this as he felt that was a step too far. When he married Morag all those years ago, they lived a very humble life until he progressed in his career and could then afford the lifestyle they now enjoyed. Frank had only been employed by the bank for three or four years and it would be some time before he would be earning enough to have a similar lifestyle to that of Dr Hamish—or for that matter—of his own father, but that, of course, had gone slightly awry.

Frank explained to Dr Hamish that he was still grieving for his mother and missed her very much even though she had been gone for nearly three years and that when he felt depressed, he didn't have anyone to speak to. He was reluctant to criticise Felicity, but she really couldn't empathise with Frank, she was always ready to party and have a good time and felt that there were times when Frank should pull himself together and just get on with their lives.

Frank was also of the opinion that he should be stronger, after all, so many lives were lost in the Great War, most of whom were very young people—in awful circumstances, so why should he feel so bad about his mother's death when she died of the Spanish Flu, but was made comfortable and nursed with care till she passed and everything had been done to save her? Dr Hamish explained to him that grief follows a very tortuous route, it has to take its course and however much you tell yourself that there are people worse off than yourself and you should count your blessings it is never easy.

Finding solace in the casino and betting on horses was an escape and Dr Hamish said he understood how things had got to that stage. He said he would speak to Felicity when he went home, also he was happy to aid them financially to help their marriage, however, Frank was insistent that although he was happy to accept Sir Charles' help to get him out of debt, Felicity had to accept their financial situation as it stood if the marriage was going to work. Basically, if Felicity didn't accept him with what he had to offer, then the marriage may as well be over, which would be so sad after such a short time.

Dr Hamish said that he totally understood and respected Frank's wishes and he would explain this to Felicity but couldn't say how she would take it.

Chapter 13

Polly was enjoying motherhood and Elizabeth proved to be a very good baby. They were frequent social visitors at the surgery where they would go and see Dolly when she wasn't working, and she looked forward to these visits very much and found Elizabeth delightful. These visits also made her feel wistful as she knew that she would never have a child of her own. Polly asked her to be Godmother to the baby girl and Dolly was thrilled to be asked—she no longer taught Sunday School since leaving the village but she would make sure to provide guidance for the little girl, thus supporting the parents in her upbringing.

Thomas was a good builder and made the decision to start up on his own, he had learnt a lot from his boss and although it was the firm that undertook all the renovations and alterations at the surgery, Thomas did a lot of the work single-handed and he was very competent. His boss accepted his decision, the main part of his work was in London, and Thomas preferred to stay in Kent—there was plenty of work to be found and he felt that the time was right.

Sir Charles managed to sell Wicken Manor with a heavy heart, but knew it was the right thing to do. It was far too big for one person and needed lots of improvements, over the years large parts of the house had deteriorated and repairs shelved, firstly because of the war years, then losing Lady Frances meant his heart was no longer in this particular home, apart from wonderful memories. It didn't look as though Frank would ever go back there to live, so he decided to sell up. This meant he might be able to help Frank a bit more, he understood the problems he and Felicity were experiencing, and although it saddened Sir Charles, he didn't have a solution.

When the sale went through, he would buy a modest home nearer the town but the lodge was not included in the sale of the manor—Jim and Jenny could enjoy living there for the rest of their lives—or for however long they wanted. They had been so loyal to Wicken Manor Sir Charles felt he owed them that, and in later years, it would become somewhere for Frank to live, should he ever need it.

After Dr Hamish left Frank to his thoughts, he wondered how Felicity would react to what Dr Hamish would have to say, and whether she would come back to him. He became rather maudlin with his thought process so decided to go to his club, rather than have the evening stretch ahead of him in the flat. He had a nice dinner and then bumped into a couple of friends who, believe it not, were going to the casino and did Frank wish to join them. His immediate reply was that he shouldn't, however, Sir Charles had given him some money initially to bail him out with the rest to follow.

The thought of the roulette wheel with the ball spinning round, hopefully landing on the right number proved too much temptation for Frank and he agreed to accompany his friends. It started really well, with him having a few wins and the adrenalin was pumping through his veins, just the same as watching horseracing, when the horse you back is gradually creeping up into the lead, or falling behind, and the buzz Frank was getting was second to none. Although he thought he might quit while he was ahead, it was going so well that he kept on, eventually losing it all once again.

His mood plummeted and he took himself home. He realised what he had done was unforgivable, however, he couldn't see how this would ever change. He drunk a couple of large scotches which he hardly needed as he had got through a few drinks already during the evening, and he felt he had hit rock bottom. He then lost all sense of reason; his head was pounding so he took several painkillers.

Suddenly everything was very clear and he saw his way out of all this misery, a wife who he had let down and who had a low opinion of him, the father he had disappointed, and a mother he was grieving for, this could be over very, very soon. He took a few more painkillers with a couple of slugs of whisky and took himself to bed. The last thing in his mind was Dolly's face, and he realised how much this girl had loved him, and how badly he had treated her. He fell asleep with her lovely face in his mind.

The next day, Felicity phoned him at the flat but got no answer. She left it thinking he was at work and wondered whether she should surprise him and meet him from work. She waited outside the bank for a while, but when he didn't appear, she thought he must be working late, and thought she would return the next day. When one of his colleagues came out the next day, she asked him if

Frank was working late. He looked puzzled and said that Frank hadn't been to work for a couple of days and although they had phoned the flat there had been no answer. They assumed that he had gone to see his father, an emergency perhaps.

Felicity suddenly felt very cold inside, she went home and asked Dr Hamish if he would go to the flat with her, she wasn't sure if Frank may have left and gone to Kent, but felt nervous about going to the flat on her own. When they arrived, they let themselves in and everything appeared very tidy and quiet. Felicity went into all the rooms and eventually went into their bedroom. The curtains were pulled and she realised that Frank was in bed. As she went to rouse him, she felt that something wasn't right—Dr Hamish followed her into the room and told her to call an ambulance immediately.

However, he soon came to the conclusion that it was too late for any medical intervention, Frank had taken his own life. A note on the bedside cabinet just said 'Sorry.' Of course, suicide was an illegal act and anyone who survived a suicide would be prosecuted—if a suicide was successful the victim would be denied a Christian funeral. With this in mind Dr Hamish immediately removed the note without anyone seeing it, not even Felicity and concluded that Frank had died due to having too much alcohol.

Felicity was hysterical and Dr Hamish, although himself in shock thought that he must let Sir Charles know the awful news. Goodness knows what it would do to him, however, once Frank's body had been removed he decided that the only thing he could do was to visit his friend and tell him face to face the awful news. He briefed Morag and took Felicity home who was beside herself leaving Morag to deal with her while he drove down to see his dear friend to break the news to him.

An awful task for anyone to undertake but knowing how low Sir Charles had been since his wife's death, this would only bring him down even further. He found his way to Sir Charles' new home just outside Ashford and told him in as gentle a way as he could that Frank had died. He kept the note to himself promising to burn it at the earliest opportunity so no one would ever know the awful truth.

Sir Charles took the news as badly as Dr Hamish had expected. He went through all the scenarios, first, disbelief, then horror as realisation dawned on him that his friend would not be here telling him all this if it wasn't true, then in a trance, as if it was all a bad dream and he would suddenly wake up; Dr Hamish decided to stay the night with Sir Charles, he phoned Morag to enquire how Felicity was and how she was feeling and said he felt he needed to stay with his friend. Much whisky was taken and it was thought that tomorrow was another day and much needed to be done when Sir Charles finally realised the enormity of what had happened.

The next morning, Sir Charles seemed to go into overdrive, told his friend he would go to London in his own car, Dr Hamish tried to talk him out of it, but he wanted to arrange for Frank to come home and funeral arrangements could be made. Although they no longer lived at Wicken Manor, Frank's funeral would take place at the village church where they had seen so many events take place, some happy and some very sad, where the villagers would all want to pay their respects, and Frank would be laid to rest with his mother.

The funeral took place a few days later, Dolly was there with her family, Polly and Thomas, and all the families—the church was completely full. Dolly was very distraught, but showed great strength, having wept for hours when she first heard the news—however, she sobbed quietly in her hanky and Polly held her hand, while Felicity sobbed loud audible sobs, comforted by her parents, and Sir Charles looked grey and drawn, absolutely broken by these events.

After the burial and everyone were making their way home, Sir Charles looked at Dolly and smiled at her wistfully, and she knew then that he was aware of her feelings for Frank, and just wondered if for a split second if they were both thinking that had she and Frank got married, would he still be here today, and of course, they both knew the answer.

Chapter 14

Dolly settled back to work with a heavy heart, she had always loved Frank and deep down always hoped he would come back one day, so was still terribly saddened by his death—she then thought of all the young women who had lost their loved ones in World War 1 and thought that at least Frank got through the war unscathed, which made his death from choking after too many drinks even more tragic! That is what the death certificate said, and apart from Dr Hamish, no one thought anything different.

However, she was happy at work and Polly's visits with Elizabeth always cheered her. Elizabeth was a beautiful child, big blue eyes and lovely blond hair and seemed very bright. At 18 months, she was walking and talking quite eloquently, so was a joy to listen to. Dolly would sing to her and she would join in in her babyish little voice and they would both end up laughing. That was brilliant medicine for Dolly.

In 1925, at the age of 31, Betty discovered she was going to have a baby. She and Stan were both delighted, and horrified at the same time wondering how they would cope with everything going on at the surgery which was always very busy. Dolly was delighted at the thought of becoming an Auntie, she had been doing some nursing training as she was always striving to learn new skills, despite her disability, so this would be useful as Betty would need to take some time off when the baby came, then they decided that they would share the child care and may need to get someone in for their busiest time to look after the new baby.

Thomas was keeping busy with building work and had taken on a work force to help him as he had so much on. He was building some new houses not far from the surgery, there were some vast pieces of land with nothing on them, not suitable for agriculture so Thomas would buy the land with the help of the bank and sell the houses he built. He seemed to have made quite a success and although he was still a bit daunted by borrowing from the bank, his hard work was paying off.

Sir Charles now lived in this same area and he was very impressed with Thomas' hard work but was not in a position to offer to help anymore, but in his dark thoughts, felt that the money he had paid out to cover Frank's debts after his death would have been put to much better use if that same money had been given to someone like Thomas, however, it was all water under the bridge. Polly and Thomas, Betty, Stan and Dolly all kept in touch with him, and he was always happy to see them.

A baby boy arrived just before Christmas 1925, he was called Nicholas possibly due to his timing and although Betty had a long gruelling labour attended by Nancy who had been trying to retire for a while, but people still wanted her to be there when giving birth and Betty was no exception. She really trusted her mum and felt comfortable being attended by her. After a few difficult weeks of adjusting to being a new mother, Betty had a very contented baby boy who was thriving and both her and Stan were devoted to their baby son. Dolly did her fair share of baby-minding when needed and between them, work at the surgery returned to nearly normal.

However, as Nicholas got bigger and slept less it became evident that they would need some extra help with child care. It was fine when he had been fed for him to be asleep in the reception area but, of course, he got to the stage where he didn't sleep quite so much and wanted entertaining.

Around this time, Thomas had been building some more houses not far from the surgery and suggested to Polly that one of these should be for them, a beautiful new house with an indoor bathroom and three bedrooms. Polly was very excited about the new house and moving to Ashford. Elizabeth was proving to be a very bright little girl and as much as the village school had been great when Polly was growing up, she felt that she would like Elizabeth to go to a school where there would be classes for each age group, rather than the couple of classes with mixed ages which could be quite challenging for the teachers, although most of them did a really good job of this.

It was therefore suggested that perhaps Polly might be able to help out with Baby Nicholas at certain times, and Polly jumped at the idea. She and Thomas had hoped for a brother or sister for Elizabeth, but sadly this didn't seem to be happening. Life carried on in a reasonably peaceful way, Nicholas thrived and was very contented and had got used to Polly looking after him, or sometimes Dolly and he adored Elizabeth. His eyes would follow her around the room, she would play with him on the floor and the two of them would often be heard chuckling, Nicholas had a really deep laugh for such a small child!

Elizabeth was doing very well at school, was reading fluently at six years old with a comprehension beyond her years and amazed her teacher. When she started the autumn term she had a new teacher, Mrs Peters who was originally from France and had married an Englishman whom she had met during the Great War. She had settled in Kent and she was very taken with the way Elizabeth questioned everything and was so keen to learn. When Elizabeth asked her why she spoke English in a different way (meaning her French accent) Mrs Peters explained that she was French.

Elizabeth then asked if she would speak to her in French and was puzzled when what she heard was something totally alien. Mrs Peters then taught her a few French words to give her an idea of what it should sound like, and Elizabeth never looked back. She went home and told her parents she wanted to learn to speak French. After discussions with Mrs Peters it was decided that once a week, after lessons, Elizabeth would stay on for an extra hour and learn to speak French. She had a real flair for this, it turned out, and by the end of the year she was having great conversations with Mrs Peters who was very proud of her star pupil.

After the summer, Mrs Peters returned after a holiday in France, and she brought back quite a few French books for the little girl to read and she absolutely devoured these, much to her teacher's delight. Of course, Elizabeth moved up a class so Mrs Peters was no longer her teacher, but had become firm friends with the family, so they would get together occasionally and the stipulation was that only French would be spoken.

She was bright at everything she did, brilliant at art and also very good at games—she would run like a whippet! All the teachers were delighted with her and she was popular with the other children too.

One day, which had started very normally with usual routines, a telegram was delivered to the surgery addressed to Stan. He was out on call at the time and although it came from Canada, Betty thought it best to leave it till his return, rather than opening it herself. When Stan returned, he read the telegram and blanched, Betty immediately realised that something was wrong and looked at him inquiringly. He uttered four words, 'my father has died!'

Betty put her arms round him but was at a loss what to say to him; she was aware that he had been wanting to visit his family in Canada, introducing her and Nicholas to his parents and his brother but there hadn't been much opportunity with things at the surgery being so hectic. Later that evening, he managed to telephone his brother, his father had a phone in the surgery but not in the house for privacy reasons. His brother told him that his father had suffered a massive heart attack while on a call and really didn't stand a chance.

His partner had been off sick and he had been on call night and day, sleeping in the surgery and was worn out. He had a few warnings which he had kept to himself, was taking pills when he felt he needed them just to get through the days when his partner would be back at work. Stan said he would keep in touch but obviously couldn't get back in time for the funeral.

He was in a great deal of shock but soon started thinking about what they should do. He had every intention of seeing his parents after the war but then got terribly involved with setting up the surgery and there never seemed to have an opportunity for a trip to Canada. He had always thought that eventually he, Betty and Nicholas would visit his family—but they couldn't really go for less than a month, and he could never get cover at the surgery for that length of time.

There followed long discussions between Stan and Betty often long into the night out of earshot of young Nicholas, trying to decide what the next step would be. It was fairly obvious by then that Stan was seriously wanting to go back to Canada, possibly to take over his father's surgery; his brother was a Mountie so if the surgery was going to stay in the family, Stan would be the person to take it on.

After debating this issue from different viewpoints, Betty felt that a move to Canada, although very drastic, sounded quite exciting and she knew that this was what Stan really wanted to do. They decided to put a friend of Stan's in charge of the surgery, Dr Gilbert, who seemed very keen to manage it, as it stood, with the option that they may return in a few months if things didn't work out in Canada. If things did work out in Canada, then he would think about buying the surgery from Stan. They had worked together years before and, although they had not kept in touch regularly, they had a lot of respect and trust for each other.

Dolly was feeling rather bereft as the surgery was also her home—and she was going to miss Betty, Stan and Nicholas terribly. The doctor had a young family and would really need all the accommodation the surgery had to offer but was happy to have Dolly working for him in the same capacity as she had done for about ten years. The main issue was finding somewhere for her to live.

Thomas was still building houses and he, Polly and Elizabeth loved living in the house he had built for them. It had a huge garden and it occurred to him that he could build an extension like he had done on the surgery, so that Dolly could go and live there, have her independence but help when she needed it, if she had to move out of her accommodation at the surgery.

He put this thought to Polly and she was overjoyed at the thought of having her best friend so close, and also Elizabeth would be thrilled as she loved her 'Auntie' Dolly. The building wouldn't be ready for some time so they asked the new doctor if Dolly could stay where she was at present while her new home was being built. Also, they suggested that perhaps she could carry on gardening if she wanted to, as Dr Gilbert probably wouldn't have time to do that.

The day arrived when the family were ready to set sail to Canada, John and Nancy had visited the previous day to say their goodbyes, it was a very emotional parting as they didn't know if they would ever see each other again. Stan promised them that he would look after Betty and Nicholas and would make sure that they would have a great life in Canada, and if things didn't work out, they would return to Britain. Everyone apart from Nicholas was very tearful, all he could think about was the trip to Southampton to get on the boat to Quebec, however, none of the family were going to see them off there, it would have been far too upsetting for them all. For a small boy, it sounded like a great adventure.

Chapter 15

The new doctor had already taken over but hadn't yet moved his family, they didn't know much about him except that he had three children. When the family moved in, Dolly was surprised to see an older lady with the children, she expected their mother to be much younger. She waited for the introductions to be made and Dr Gilbert then explained that the children had a governess as their mother had died two years previously, after a serious illness. Dolly immediately felt very sad for the doctor's loss and also for the children who had lost their mother. The youngest child was three, so possibly wouldn't remember his mother, but the older boy aged six and the eldest child, a girl aged ten would remember their mother vividly and Dolly wondered how that must make them feel.

The governess seemed quite firm but very kind, she had been with the children for several months now, and they appeared to have a bond with her—as well as giving them tuition she also did their meals and generally shared their care with the doctor. He did try and spend as much time as he could with them to make up for the loss of their mother, but sometimes when things got busy, he was happy to let Maggie, the governess, care for them. When Maggie realised that Dolly was thinking of moving out, she said that on no account should she do so at the moment, the doctor needed all the help he could get with settling in and being introduced to patients and she felt that the building was big enough to accommodate them all without putting Dolly out.

Dolly said this to Polly so there was no hurry at the moment for Thomas to work on their house, unless he really wanted to. He was busy on other projects, it was all going well for him as he had started off small, buying a piece of land and building two homes, having sold that he was able to buy more land and so on. He didn't want to overstretch himself and have to rely on too many people to work for him, everything he did was very controlled and he was quite happy with the way the business was shaping up.

Dolly was delighted and told Dr Gilbert as much as she could about the daily routine and also that he would probably have to take on a nurse, at least part-time, to reduce his workload. He might also want to introduce changes, which he would be perfectly at liberty to do, but at the moment he just wanted to get on with the job in hand.

Dolly got on well with Dr Gilbert's children once they had got used to her, she would spend time with them during quiet periods or even to give Maggie a break sometimes; looking after three children for most of the day dealing with their education as well as their needs, such as feeding them, making sure they had clean clothes to name but a few, was no mean feat. From the beginning there seemed to be a great deal of understanding and respect from these three adults sharing a home with three children which could only be a good thing.

Dolly introduced the children to her precious garden telling them what was growing and they all seemed to respond with varying degrees of enthusiasm! The two-year-old, Steven, was more interested in running around in the open space while Simon, the older boy was quite interested in the various vegetables and fruit growing and Ruth, the oldest child, loved the flowers, especially the roses! Dolly told her what they all were and said that come the spring, there would be a lovely show of daffodils and tulips!

Sometimes if they were really busy in the surgery, she could go two or three days without seeing the children, but she made it clear to them that she enjoyed spending time with them. She really hoped that Polly would come round soon so that Elizabeth could be introduced to Ruth, she felt they would get on well once they had got over the initial shyness—neither of them were outgoing but Dolly felt that Ruth would benefit from having a friend of a similar age.

Elizabeth was working hard at school, she had just gone to senior school in Ashford where she had started learning German, her French was good and she wanted to keep that up, so Polly asked if she could do both languages, but for the French class she went with older children who had been doing French for three years.

She found being with older pupils a little bit daunting as they seemed to look down on her, and were quite resentful at first when they realised how good she was, however, they gradually accepted her and it became the norm for her to be in their classes. She took to German quite well and impressed the teachers at her other subjects too, she really was a very intelligent young girl.

Polly took her to meet Ruth and they seemed to hit it off quite well, Elizabeth had been told that the children had lost their mother and she couldn't imagine what that must have been like, and she felt sorry for the children. On that first visit they stayed to tea, Maggie put on a good spread and it was a very jolly affair. The girls both seem sad when it was time for Polly to take Elizabeth home, but she said that they would visit again very soon. It became a weekly visit which all the children looked forward to, sometimes on a Sunday they would all meet in the local park and Dr John Gilbert and Thomas would also go along.

On one occasion, Dr Gilbert spoke to Polly about the possibility of Ruth going to school with Elizabeth, he felt that she would benefit from mixing with people of her own age, and although Maggie was doing her best, she had her work cut out teaching three different age groups and caring for them into the bargain, so that would make life easier for her. Polly said she would enquire and in the event, Ruth started school in the autumn. She was very apprehensive at first, but soon settled down and enjoyed having lessons with other people, rather than on a one-to-one, and she thrived.

Elizabeth and Ruth became inseparable, which pleased everyone especially Dr Gilbert as he realised that life might be getting back to normal after having lost his wife—he missed her every day, but felt he owed it to his children to give them a more normal life where they could mix with their peers and make new friendships.

Maggie was quite happy about the arrangement, he said that there would be a job for her for as long as she wanted but it was good for life to be less chaotic for them all. Simon was the next child to go to a local primary school, so Maggie was left with keeping house, looking after Steven and taking and collecting Simon from school.

Life in Canada was going well for Stan, Betty and Nicholas, they were all enjoying life in different ways and Stan was busy in his late father's surgery, and the patients were delighted that he had taken over. Betty helped him as she always had, life was totally different, but she embraced the change and they were very happy. Dr John Gilbert agreed to permanently run the surgery as he felt it suited his circumstances perfectly.

Dolly would often spend time after surgery talking to Dr Gilbert and she found him a really nice man and easy to talk to. He told her how his wife had become ill and died after several horrendous months where he tried to keep things normal for the children while dealing with caring for her. She had a very aggressive brain tumour which had started with headaches and double vision, and had accelerated at a great rate of knots, soon causing her to stop functioning altogether, and making life extremely difficult for them all until she was finally admitted to hospital where she died a few days later. Ruth guessed that her mother was very ill but Simon wasn't aware and Steven was just a few months old so he had no clue.

A difficult time followed and Maggie replied an advert for a live-in housekeeper/nanny/governess and enjoyed the challenge. Things had changed for her with the move to the surgery and gradually her duties were less taxing but she was always very busy. She loved baking so when she had some spare time she made the most amazing cakes, and the children enjoyed coming home to the beautiful smell of fresh cakes!

Dolly gradually found herself looking forward to her conversations with Dr Gilbert and realised that she felt disappointed at the end of the day if they hadn't had time to chat. They were not necessarily heavy conversations, sometimes they would just talk about their day and different patients, and general chat about how things were progressing.

However, it always made her feel happy when Dr Gilbert was around, and she wondered why she felt like this. She used to have that feeling of anticipation when Frank was around Wicken Manor, wondering if he would come and speak to her or suggest going for a ride, and she never thought she would get this feeling again. She found that thought quite disturbing and felt that she should maybe not go down that particular road.

Elizabeth and Ruth were great friends, by now and were enjoying being at school together. They both rode bikes to school and would often go out riding their bikes at weekends, sometimes meeting other school friends but more often than not they would just go off on their own, especially during the fine weather. They would ride to the village where Elizabeth introduced Ruth to her grandparents, and they would spend time there, often coming home laden with fresh produce, eggs or cream and had to cycle back very carefully through the country lanes so that the eggs came back intact.

Part 4

Chapter 16

The months and years flew by, Elizabeth and Ruth had done very well at school, the boys were still at school, Simon was looking forward to leaving soon and getting a job, but the girls were done and were following their chosen paths.

Elizabeth wanted to do something with languages so she was at college training to teach languages and Ruth wanted to be a nurse, so she went to the same hospital that Betty and Stan had worked in, and where Stan had first met Dr Gilbert.

Dolly and Dr Gilbert had become very close and had a lot of respect for each other so one evening when Dr Gilbert said that he needed to speak to Dolly, she wasn't sure what it was all about. He didn't beat about the bush and blurted out a proposal of marriage. Dolly was just staggered but also extremely flattered, and basically, said 'yes!' The reservations she had were twofold, basically she had her disability to deal with, which she coped with very well, and she couldn't have children.

Dr Gilbert said that three children was plenty for any household and he said that her disability was barely noticeable to him. He thought she was an amazing girl and as she had previously told him all about her past when they were having a real heart-to-heart, he knew everything about her, and had nothing but admiration for her!

Maggie was delighted to hear their happy news when they told her and the children. She had relinquished her governess role as the boys were both at school now and life at home was a bit quieter so apart from helping out and overseeing their homework—which Dr Gilbert also did—her teaching days were done. However, the children had lots of friends who used to come round to the house and Maggie enjoyed baking for them and always thought that children needed feeding. Dolly and Dr Gilbert told Maggie that they would still need her as nothing would change, apart from them becoming husband and wife. They would still value her help.

In the evening, Dolly would spend time with the family before going back to her quarters and she felt she really belonged with this family and felt very comfortable in their presence. She couldn't wait to be married to Dr Gilbert and intended to be a really good stepmother to the children. She loved gardening still and produced great fruit and veg for the family to enjoy during the summer and autumn months, and the boys would often help her.

One day, Dolly received some very sad news, Sir Charles had passed away in his little house that he had settled in a few years ago, he had never got over losing his dear wife, and then Frank, however, he had made the best of the situation he found himself in, and had many friends who had stood by him, and latterly, kept an eye on him. Wicken Manor had been completely transformed and turned into a hotel and was doing very nicely and on that score, he had no regrets. Dolly felt in an odd way that this news closed a chapter in her life which had been so eventful and her forthcoming marriage would give her the chance to start a new chapter.

Polly and Thomas and their parents were delighted with Dolly's news and really looked forward to the wedding. Dolly and the doctor wanted just a simple service and a quiet wedding. Dolly had written to Betty to tell her the news and she send a congratulatory telegram with their love and good wishes. Their life was going well in Canada so Betty had no plans to come home at the moment. She would have loved a holiday in England to see all the family but it just wasn't possible. Nicholas was growing up fast and was embracing everything Canada had to offer.

The wedding took place one spring day in the village church and Dolly managed the walk up the aisle with her father at her side, who was crippled with arthritis and somehow, together, they made it to the altar. After a short service they retreated to the nearby farmhouse for tea and cake, before returning to Ashford. Everyone wished them well, Polly was Matron of Honour, as the girls had promised that they would attend each other at their respective weddings, and Elizabeth and Ruth were bridesmaids. Dolly had never expected that this day would ever come and she was so happy as was her new husband and the children.

Unfortunately, the news coming through on the wireless and in the newspapers wasn't good. There was a lot of unrest in Germany particularly, and it would appear that they were trying to force out Jewish families. Quite a few families and particularly children were being brought over to England to stay with relatives, but many were fleeing to America and Canada also to avoid persecution.

Despite political interference and involvement from various countries, the inevitable happened when Germany insisted on invading Poland, and Britain declared war on Germany on the 3 September 1939, a very dark day for everyone. Families who had relatives who had fought in the [1s]t World War could not believe that this was happening all over again, and many were angry, having been told that the Great War was the war to end all wars, not to pick up again twenty-one years later! However, Mr Churchill had spoken and that was the situation!

At this point, everyone was fearing for all the young men as they would inevitably be called up at some point. Fortunately, Simon and Steven were still quite young, but Elizabeth wondered what she might do. She spoke to her parents about doing something with her languages, she was fluent in both French and German, so she could certainly help with the war effort, or she could go and work on a local farm as a 'land girl.' Thomas made enquiries to see what opportunities might be available, but was quite horrified when he was told that Elizabeth would be a great asset in France to the Resistance Movement.

He felt that he should tell her with Polly what this option meant, and thankfully, she decided that she wanted to stay and work on the land. Rather a waste of her talents, but she really didn't feel she wanted to put herself in danger, she loved her parents and didn't want to put them through that sort of anxiety, however exciting a prospect that sounded. She felt she would enjoy life on the land and she could do quite a lot of good.

Chapter 17

Life changed for many people. Within a few months of declaring war on Germany, the Battle of Britain began and the British army soon sent troops abroad to defend and help the Allies in the hope that this would soon be over.

Ruth was getting on well with her nursing training, and like Betty a few years ago, she would get plenty of opportunity to practice her skills. Elizabeth was enjoying life on the land; they were busy in the fields and every Saturday evening there was a dance in the village hall. This was always well attended, the girls enjoyed 'getting ready,' doing each other's hair as best they could and often sharing a lipstick but they always had fun.

One evening, Elizabeth was approached by a very handsome young man called Robert, he asked her if she would dance with him, she accepted, as she always did whenever anyone asked her, but immediately she thought that this was different and they spent the whole evening together. He was a very serious young man and when he walked her home they inevitably spoke about the troubles in Europe. At this point, he hadn't been called up, he worked as a draughtsman but felt that he could get called up at any time as most of the young men were.

She asked him if the prospect frightened him, he said that his biggest worry was his mother. She was in poor health and had never got over losing his father in the Great War. It was a very tragic story as Robert had never known his father. His dad had come home for a few days' leave in the spring of 1918 and he sadly got killed on the front just near the end of the war, so when Robert was born in January 1919 his mum, Jean, was already a widow. She had been devastated at losing her husband so near the end of the war, but was thankful that they had spent precious time together before the war ended.

She had brought up Robert on her own and had done a good job, but she wasn't strong and suffered with poor health. The thought of Robert being sent away was not a great prospect and she hoped and prayed that he would not be called up.

Several weeks passed and the friendship between Elizabeth and Robert grew and they became very close. Her friends teased her as they were happy to mix with all the young men at the dances, but Elizabeth and Robert used to spend most of the evenings together and looked forward to these times.

In March 1940, Robert got his call-up papers and had to go for a medical, which he passed with flying colours. Apart from his mother being unwell, which wasn't a valid reason, he knew that he would have to go and fight for his country, as his father had done, and there was no reason why he shouldn't do this. Part of him wanted the challenge, as a challenge it would definitely be, but he dreaded telling his mother and Elizabeth this news. To be fair, Elizabeth took the news quite well as she realised that as an able-bodied young man he would be expected to fight for his country and she would think less of him if he refused, however, part of her felt devastated and very scared.

His mother was just distraught but knew that this would happen, and had been expecting it, so in the end she put a brave face on it, for Robert's sake, and just wished him Godspeed and prayed that he would return safe and sound when it was over. She remembered his father's last visit, such a precious few days, but in that short time she knew that things on the front were very bad, and couldn't bear to think of Robert going through the same ordeals.

The day came for Robert to leave and Elizabeth asked for a morning off so she could go to London with him and see him off at Kings Cross where he was leaving from to training camp for a few weeks before going abroad. It was a very tearful farewell, mirrored by so many young men getting on the train being hugged by their sweethearts, most of whom were in tears.

After the train departed and they were all left waving at plumes of smoke Elizabeth went up to one poor girl who was sobbing uncontrollably and asked her if she would like to go for a cup of tea. The girl's reaction was one of disbelief, at first, as if a cup of tea could make any difference! However, she nodded tearfully and followed Elizabeth to a nearby tea stand. There were a few tables and chairs so this girl, called Jane, went to sit down while Elizabeth got the tea.

They sat in silence for a while, stirring the strong dark tea, and Jane asked Elizabeth where she came from. She said that she lived in Kent, normally in Ashford, but at the moment she was in the village where she had been born working as a Land Girl, which she was enjoying but Saturday nights wouldn't be quite the same from now on.

Jane said that she was training as a nurse in one of the London hospitals and had just got engaged to Peter who had joined up as a medic, so would be helping the wounded in the thick of battle, and this is why she was so very upset.

He felt he wanted to give as much help to the war effort as he could, and suddenly, Elizabeth felt very guilty about not using her languages, as she could have been very useful in some areas, however, she felt that she wanted to stay near her family and that working on the land was something she enjoyed and could still be near her family.

Eventually, the girls said farewell, Elizabeth had to get a train back and carry on with her day's work, and Jane was due to start a shift. She thanked Elizabeth for the tea and said she felt much better. They both knew that they probably would never see each other again, but in that brief hour they had discussed their fears openly and honestly, and in that time, they could have talked about anything, precisely because they both just happened to be in that same place for a short time.

Elizabeth had promised Robert that she would keep in touch with Jean, she had only met her on a couple of occasions as she didn't get much time off, apart from Saturday evenings, however, she felt that was the least she could do. Robert's mother was just under fifty years old but looked a lot older. Her hair was grey and long, most of the time it was in an untidy bun as her hair was very fine, and her face was lined, due to all the sadness in her life, and she looked like she carried the weight of the world on her shoulders.

The Dunkirk Evacuation took place in June 1940 and while many troops managed to get home, some injured or traumatised, and some very lucky to escape unscathed, many were killed or captured, which was tragic. Meanwhile the Battle of Britain was raging with planes being shot down by the Allies and also by the enemy. Then September 1940 saw the start of the blitz where London and other cities were bombed mercilessly, causing the death of many innocent people; often complete families were wiped out, truly shocking. The blackout was introduced which meant that during the night no lights had to be seen which meant covering up all the windows so that in the dark targets were harder to find, however, the bombing carried on regardless destroying thousands of homes all over Britain, especially in big cities.

At this point, families were encouraged to have young children evacuated to the countryside in areas all over England where they would be housed with families, becoming part of these families while the bombing continued, and those old enough to go to school would carry on with their education in whichever village they were homed. This was extremely traumatic for parents and young children; mothers were allowed to go with babies but children from the age of 3 were evacuated without parents; some had older siblings who would help care for them but the great majority must have been traumatised and wondering what the future held for them. The outcome was that they would be safe, and this is what persuaded many parents to go down this avenue.

Dr Gilbert felt that his youngest child was safe enough in the Kent countryside and felt that this would not be an option for him as he was almost a teenager. The trauma of losing his mother in his early years was thought enough for him to cope with. They were a very happy family and Dolly loved being Dr Gilbert's wife, still carrying on her duties in the surgery with Maggie making sure that everything on the domestic front ran smoothly.

Ruth was busy at the hospital and didn't seem to come home very much these days, an odd day off here and there, but she was loving her work and was doing extremely well. She occasionally managed the Saturday evening dance with Elizabeth which she always enjoyed, and since Robert had gone to France, Elizabeth really appreciated her company.

They always got on well, but when Robert had been there, Ruth tended to leave them alone to have precious time together. She had made quite a few friends, both male and female and certainly wasn't looking for a relationship at the moment. The last thing she needed was a man to distract her from her studies and she just enjoyed the dances.

To be fair, Elizabeth hadn't planned to fall in love with Robert, these things happened and now she lived for the postman to bring the odd letter telling her that Robert was well. She did go and visit his mother when she had time, but sadly, she did struggle with this lady—Elizabeth was made to feel that she wasn't good enough for Robert but when she spoke to Polly about this, Polly said that mothers did tend to be possessive over their sons, and very few girls were deemed to be good enough. She had been so lucky with Thomas' family, the main reason being that she had helped Thomas with his recovery when he had been injured in the Great War, and kept in touch with his family before she actually met them, so had always been special to them. Polly told her not to give up on this lady and just to be kind to her and listen to her issues.

Chapter 18

Christmas and New Year came and it was 1941! The war was still raging on and there didn't seem to be much progress happening which would bring all this to an end. The winter in Kent was quite harsh, Elizabeth and the other Land girls worked with the light and got as much work done as they could during daylight hours, which were quite short, but by the end of February, they could gradually see a difference as the daylight minutes stretched out a little each week and the pressure wasn't so great as the daylight lasted longer. Soon it was spring and apart from food being in short supply, they were still better off in the countryside than in the big cities, and when the daffodils started poking through the ground with crocuses, no one would know there was a world war going on.

Dr Gilbert was having a busy time with all the seasonal ailments—mainly colds and flu—so was out on calls when he wasn't seeing patients in the surgery. Dolly kept herself busy and ensured that their stocks of medical supplies were kept in order, and obviously answered all the calls—people would phone but some would call into the surgery to discuss their ailments. She had learnt to deal with these calls, gleaning enough information and tried to sort them out in order of priority but always reported all the calls to her husband so he could also prioritise how he dealt with them.

One day, when Elizabeth went to visit Jean, she found her almost hysterical as she had just received a telegram saying that Robert was missing, but unsure what had happened to him, and they shouldn't worry just yet. A very tall order! They explained he was missing in action—he hadn't been found injured or dead and it was possible that he could be sheltering somewhere or perhaps had been taken prisoner. They said that they would be in contact again very soon once they had established what had happened.

This was little comfort and Elizabeth wished that they hadn't been told anything—no news being good news! Gosh, that saying must be the most used saying ever! Elizabeth spent the evening talking to Jean and tried to reassure her, she herself felt very anxious for Robert's whereabouts, however, until they had some definite news, maybe they really should not worry.

The news came a few days later, Robert had indeed been captured with other members of his regiment and been taken to a Prisoner of War camp in Germany. Elizabeth and Jean were devastated, initially, but at least Robert was alive and if he was going to be imprisoned till the war ended, then surely, he would be safer there than on the battlefields! It was still awful news, but not the worst news!

There were some German prisoners of war working on the land where Elizabeth was a Land Girl. They were assigned heavier tasks—and were not encouraged to mix with the Land girls, however, as Elizabeth spoke German she enjoyed speaking with them, and of course, they loved speaking to her in their mother tongue, but this was strictly discouraged. They were not allowed to go to the dances or mix with people in the village but they were generally well treated, for prisoners, so Elizabeth painted a picture in her head that Robert would be having a similar experience, and took comfort from that. She told Jean how the prisoners were treated on the farm and if Robert was being treated in this way, he was better off there than actively fighting.

The war raged on with many casualties on all sides in Europe and the Far East. Then the D Day Landings took place in early June 1944 when many boats and gliders landed in various parts of the Normandie coast in France in Winston Churchill's attempt to liberate the French. America also took part in this exercise which cost many lives but was the beginning of the end of the war with Germany suffering losses also, and realising that their attempt to win this war was failing.

However, it wasn't until May 1945 that the war ended, much to the joy of many families, but also counting the cost as so many lives had been lost, and homes, towns and cities totally destroyed, so although it was a relief to know that this was finally over, it was also a time to reflect on what happened next— obviously that was an issue for politicians to focus on.

What this meant for Elizabeth and Jean was that their darling Robert would hopefully soon be home and life could resume and Elizabeth couldn't wait for them to resume their relationship. They were still just boyfriend and girlfriend but Elizabeth hoped that they would have a future together, and that Robert would still want that too.

She also hoped that she would be able to get a job in a school or college teaching languages, as this had always been her dream, and knew that she would need to return to college herself to be a teacher. Robert would probably go back to his former job as a draughtsman, so between them, they should have a good life. Elizabeth confided in Ruth what her plans might be now that she felt she could think of the future, Ruth was happy for her but she was enjoying her hospital work and as far as she was concerned, she was happy with that for the moment.

Elizabeth also confided in Polly telling her mother what she hoped the future would hold for her—Polly said that she understood as she had hoped all those years ago that she and Thomas might have a future when the Great War ended, and she certainly hadn't been disappointed. She still pinched herself every day, unable to believe how lucky she was to have such a wonderful, loving husband. Thomas worked so hard, was doing so well and adored Polly and Elizabeth. The last few years had been awful for business as the house building had virtually stopped, but up until then he had done very well and would do so again.

Part 5

Chapter 19

Elizabeth kept in touch with Jean and visited her quite frequently as she was awaiting news of Robert's homecoming. They had heard that they had liberated the camp where he was being held and they were going through the process of assessing them medically and making sure they were fit enough to come home. They were liberated by Americans who had been assigned to the task, and they could not believe how dreadfully ill the prisoners looked. They had lost a lot of weight and this is why they were being hospitalised before being sent home, to make sure that they could cope with the journey. Some of them, sadly, wouldn't make it but Robert, although very weak, was deemed fit to return home.

He was driven home one afternoon, having been picked up at Dover and Jean agreed that Elizabeth could be there when he came back. Initially, when the military vehicle pulled up outside the house Jean looked at Elizabeth in horror saying that Robert wasn't there—the passenger alighted the vehicle with a few possessions in a small bag and as he walked towards the house, they were both aghast to realise that indeed, that was Robert. Elizabeth thought how foolish she had been to dream that Robert had been well cared for, horror stories of Prisoner of War camps had evolved over time and she tried not to listen as she found them horrific and couldn't believe that Robert would be put through all that.

Suddenly, it was evident that he had suffered but he was home and she was first to run to him and welcome him home. Jean stood back, still in shock, but rallied in time to give him a big hug and held back her tears as best she could. However, they all soon broke down and sobbed in each other arms, all supporting one another, the moment was all too much. Elizabeth recovered first and went to put the kettle on, Robert followed her into the kitchen and she had to get used to this man who was a total shadow of his former self. He had lost so much weight, that was the most obvious change but his face was gaunt, his eyes looked dead, no light in them at all, and he badly needed a shave!

They had tea, sandwiches and Elizabeth had baked a cake, and Robert, although still in a trance like state, perked up a little and really couldn't believe that he was actually home, and sitting with his mother and his girlfriend having tea! Elizabeth went home a while later to give Jean and Robert some time together, promising to return after work the next day. As much as she wanted to go to college, she wanted to stay working on the farm at the moment as she felt she needed to focus on Robert, as he would need some support to integrate himself into normal life, once more.

When Elizabeth saw him the next evening, they went for a long walk, he just loved being outdoors seeing the wide-open spaces of the countryside around him. They walked for a while then sat down at the top of a hill admiring the view before dusk and Robert said that although they had never been officially engaged, he wanted to marry Elizabeth as soon as possible and hoped that she would want that too. Elizabeth was delighted, had been hoping that Robert would ask her, but didn't expect it quite so soon. They decided that it would be a very low-key wedding, just immediate family, but Elizabeth said that she would like to get married in the village church where her parents had their wedding and her christening.

Robert was happy with that, then he suggested that they could probably stay with his mother until they found a house of their own. Elizabeth had a few reservations but couldn't see an alternative at the moment and if it meant that she and Robert could be together, then it was a small price to pay. She liked Jean and got on well with her but felt that spending the odd afternoon with her, and living with her were two very different scenarios.

Jean had had a hard life, not helped by the recent conflict in Europe where her son had been incarcerated for months by the enemy and had suffered far more than either of them could imagine. However, she was frail for her years and always seemed to have some ailment or another, but despite seeing doctors over the years, nothing physically was wrong with her. She would get very anxious about anything out of her routine, or if she had to go out somewhere and basically was like a frightened little mouse. Her physique reinforced that and she had lost weight over time worrying about what was going on in the world and not eating proper meals, due both to shortages and lack of enthusiasm.

However, being with Robert was a wonderful thought for Elizabeth and at this point, dealing with Jean would be quite a minor issue and she went home to tell Polly and Thomas her news. They were delighted and said that as soon as they had sorted out a date, they would start to make plans. Elizabeth insisted that it would only be a small affair as Robert had very little family and friends were still hard to locate. Elizabeth wanted Ruth to be her bridesmaid but other than that, had no other requests.

Robert went to see his old boss who was delighted to see him and said he could return to work as soon as he felt able, again, he was staggered when Robert walked into the office but tried not to show his shock and this was the case with everyone Robert met. He could tell that people were appalled by his appearance but hoped that now he was eating regular meals and more hearty food that he would soon be back to his old self. His biggest worry were his recurring nightmares, he hadn't told Elizabeth about these and wondered how she would deal with these, if they happened once they were married. He would wake up in a cold sweat often by his own shouts and had woken Jean up on several occasions, but asked her not to mention this to Elizabeth. He said these would soon fade with time.

Chapter 20

The wedding took place five weeks later, a gloriously warm summer's day, surrounded by loved ones and well-wishers. Elizabeth looked radiant, Thomas had given her away with Ruth behind her doing her duty as bridesmaid and loving every minute! Polly had a tear in her eye, and Jean looked very solemn and but dry-eyed—Dolly stood with Dr Gilbert, Maggie and the boys, they were such a close family and Polly was so happy that her lovely friend had eventually found love. Maggie had made a wedding cake and after the service the wedding party made their way to the village hall next door where tea, sandwiches and cakes were being served, and the wedding cake would be cut, before everyone made their way home.

The couple were not going away on honeymoon, Robert couldn't face being away from home at the moment, he really still wasn't his old self and Elizabeth wasn't worried—it was a busy time on the farm so she was quite happy to get back to work the following week, and they could maybe have a break later.

Things settled down at Jean's house, she swapped her bedroom for Robert's old room so that the newlyweds could have the main bedroom. Elizabeth thanked her profusely and asked her if she was sure, as she still felt like a guest in the house, rather than thinking of it as their home. Elizabeth, although still working long hours in the summer evenings did what she could to help with household chores and always cooked Sunday lunch to give Jean a break. She seemed to appreciate that and enjoyed meals that she hadn't cooked herself. Elizabeth would bring home fresh produce from the farm and was trying really hard to get Robert to put some weight on.

Unfortunately, he was still having nightmares and waking up shouting and Elizabeth would get up and make him a hot drink, and would actually try and ask him what the dreams were about. He couldn't really tell her, just a mixture of various horrors he had witnessed during the war years and he struggled to speak about it.

One day, Elizabeth suggested that they might go to London for the day, and said they could catch a train from Ashford. He recoiled at the word 'train' and said he was never going on a train ever again. When she asked him why, as this came out of the blue, he said that the last time he had been on a train was when he was coming home from Germany and the carriage had been packed, some men were injured and in pain, and the whole trip had been a nightmare, despite the fact he was going home.

Prior to that, and this was the real horror was the train he went to the Prisoner of War camp in, dark carriages just stuffed with people for many hours with no facilities, food or water—just a stop every six hours to stretch their legs. Many of them actually died on these trains and the German soldiers just left their bodies by the railway line. This is what being on a train meant to Robert. Elizabeth could have said to him, and he knew anyway, that nothing like this would happen on a train to London, but she just said that it was a silly idea and she shouldn't have suggested it. She still felt that a day out with just the two of them would be nice, but only when Robert was ready.

They settled into a routine with the three of them in Jean's house and Elizabeth thought it would be wonderful when they could move into a home of their own. Thomas was building again and had hinted that he would love to build them a house when they felt that they had saved some money, but he would obviously make it as reasonable for them as he could. Robert was back at work and Elizabeth was still on the farm, however, she would have loved to have gone to college or done something with her languages.

Although the prisoners of war on the farm had now gone home, she had enjoyed speaking to them in German and now realised how much better the German prisoners of war were treated here, compared to how Robert had been treated over in Germany. This made her angry, however, she couldn't imagine the people she worked with treating these chaps badly, admittedly not all the villagers were happy to have Germans in their midst and the worst they would do is ignore them.

One day, she put it to Robert that she would like to use her French and German in a teaching capacity, possibly at evening classes to start with—Robert got very angry and said that he had no problem with her teaching French, but he never wanted to hear her or know that she would be uttering any word in that filthy language! She was appalled by his reaction but understood in a small part that he would have a problem with this. She never mentioned this again for several months, except to say that whatever she did, she would not teach anyone German.

Robert seemed happy enough with this, he had been back at work for a few months but didn't seem very happy in the draughtsman's office. A few chaps had returned, sadly, a couple of them had been killed in active service which was a reminder every day although they would eventually be replaced. Everywhere they looked there were these voids where there would have been happy families just living peaceful lives. Lots of sadness everywhere, and guilt from the families that had remained intact. Hopefully, in time, things would feel more ordinary.

Robert came home from work one day to say that he had got a new job, he had gone for an interview at the local council and would be starting work as a gardener and gravedigger in the local cemetery in a week's time. He had given his notice in that day and his boss was happy to let him go, despite staff shortages, when Robert explained his reasons to him. Basically, he just wanted to be out in the open air, couldn't bear to be surrounded by four walls all day, needed to breathe fresh air and feel wind, rain, sun, whatever the weather was, rather than be indoors.

Obviously, his boss realised that he had to do this, so with regret wished him well and told him that there would always be a job in the office for him should he want to return. Elizabeth was taken aback at this news, it would mean a drop in wages, but if Robert was going to be happy, this was all that mattered.

One good thing was that once Robert had started his new job with the council, he enquired about getting a council house—his mother had lived in a council house all her married life and he explained how they lived with her at the moment, but would really love their own home. He was actually quite happy with the present living arrangements but knew that Elizabeth longed for her own home.

A few months later, they picked up the keys for an end of terrace house with a large garden so they were very excited. It meant buying furniture and everything they needed for their own home, but Elizabeth had been collecting bits and pieces for some months and stored them at her parents' place, Polly had also been looking out for second-hand furniture so by the time they were moving in, apart from a new bed and a stove for the kitchen, they had the makings of a cosy home.

Elizabeth was ecstatic and Robert seemed quite happy. Jean felt lost but was happy for them and realised that they needed to have their own home. The house was about ten minutes' walk from her house and half an hour from Polly and Thomas, so quite well positioned. Robert cycled to work anyway, so this made very little difference. Elizabeth realised she needed to earn a bit of extra money so she made an appointment with the headmistress of a local senior school and said that she would love to teach French, but had no teacher qualifications, with the war this had scuppered her chance to go to college.

The headmistress was very impressed with her knowledge, Elizabeth admitted to also speaking fluent German but said she would prefer to stick to French to begin with. The headmistress said that they didn't have a French teacher at the moment as he had returned to France when war broke out and hadn't returned so she was happy for her to do two days a week to begin with and see how it went. Elizabeth was thrilled and got out all her books and everything she needed to brush up on the French before term began.

When Robert came home, she told him her news which he had a mixed reaction to. He asked why she hadn't discussed her plan with him first, and she said that she acted on the spur of the moment and thought he would be pleased as this was something she had always wanted to do. He said it made him feel that he couldn't provide for her, so she told him that was nonsense, she just needed something to do.

Chapter 21

The winter of 1947 was brutal, snow and ice for days on end making moving around very treacherous. Robert went to work every day but digging graves was a hopeless task and made work very difficult. Also, it was dark early which made it even harder. Elizabeth went to see Jean a couple of times a week to make sure she was looking after herself properly and suggested that she shouldn't go out on her own and would bring shopping in for her. One afternoon, Elizabeth entered the house with a bag of groceries and Jean didn't appear, as she usually did. When she looked out of the window, Jean was laying on the ground outside with a broom by her side. She had obviously decided to go out and clear some snow in the back garden, had slipped and fallen. She was semi-conscious and very cold, but when Elizabeth tried to move her, she howled in pain, a piercing sound like a wounded animal.

Elizabeth got a blanket to cover her over then went to neighbours until someone responded and asked if anyone could phone for an ambulance. Eventually, Jean was taken to hospital, she was in much pain and it emerged, after examination, that she had broken her hip. She had also been out in the cold for some hours and seemed to have a fever, so Robert and Elizabeth stayed by her bedside for the rest of the evening and night.

Elizabeth had been in touch with Polly who had contacted Dolly and Dr Gilbert, and they also looked in at visiting time. Dr Gilbert wouldn't have interfered with the medical staff, just wanted to assess the situation as a friend. He was well known at the hospital for referring some of his own patients and the staff respected him. Elizabeth was always delighted to see them, she loved Dolly and they had always been close, as Dolly was with Polly.

Dr Gilbert took Robert to one side and said that his mother was a very sick lady. She wasn't strong and laying out in the cold for some time had made her very cold, hence the fever. He said that the hospital staff would take good care of her and try to get the fever down, when they would then deal with the broken hip, however, he should prepare himself for worse news. He and Elizabeth were both in shock but decided that they would stay overnight so she would see them both when she woke up.

The night nurse brought them both tea and toast just as she was going off duty and said there had been no change in Jean's condition. Elizabeth offered to phone Robert's work to say that he wouldn't be at work today, but Robert said that he had to go to work, they were getting behind with the digging and he really couldn't spare the time. Elizabeth was surprised but went along with it so she dashed home to change then returned quickly so that Robert could go to work.

Later that day, Polly popped in so Elizabeth could have a rest and get a meal ready for Robert and they would both be back in the evening. Jean woke up just after lunch, couldn't believe where she was and her temperature had gone down a bit, which was great news. She was still in much discomfort which was expected, but she had an awful cough and that also seemed to be painful. Also, her breathing was laboured so an operation to fix her hip was out of the question at the moment.

The next few days were spent in a whirlwind of hospital visits, hurried meals and snatched sleep. Elizabeth contacted the school and said that sadly she wouldn't be in for the next week but they understood and wished Jean well. However, Jean just got worse and eventually was diagnosed with pneumonia and passed away one Sunday morning ten days after her fall. No one seemed surprised as she was such a frail little lady, had gone through a lot in her life and was only in her early 50s.

There was quite a lot to sort out, obviously Jean's funeral which was attended by about thirty people, not much family but good neighbours, a few friends and Elizabeth's family and friends came to support Robert. Remarkably, he seemed to take it all in his stride showing very little emotion, and this worried Elizabeth and he seemed more concerned about clearing the house so that the council would be able to pass it on to a new tenant. They had a couple of weeks to do this, but Robert seemed to be on a treadmill and went through paperwork, some of which he kept like documents and personal letters, some of the furniture and trinkets they took for their own home, as with soft furnishings and the like, and the rest he offered to friends, disposing of anything else that was left over. He did this in a very cold, calm and efficient way.

For a while after the funeral, he was very distant with everyone including Elizabeth. He was back at work, obviously, still loving the open air, Elizabeth went back to school thoroughly enjoying her teaching sessions and the headmistress was delighted with the way the pupils responded to her.

Ruth was now working in a hospital in London but she still kept in touch with Elizabeth, they were great friends and would write to each other, but in the last eighteen months Elizabeth had taken to going to London by train meeting Ruth for lunch on her day off. She told Robert what she was doing and he was fine with it as he didn't need to go with her, and she was home before him in the evening, so it didn't really affect him in any way. Ruth was still single but loving her work and was studying midwifery which was an avenue she might explore at some point in her career.

Elizabeth told her that Nancy, Dolly's mother, had been a midwife for years and was trusted and respected in various villages in Kent where she had brought literally hundreds of babies into the world, for many years riding her bike through the country lanes to reach her patients. Ruth was impressed with this and hoped that one day she would achieve this. There was something very special about bringing new born babies into the world and to be a part of that was something that Ruth thought she would enjoy.

On the 5 July 1948, the NHS came into being. This meant that anyone who was ill would receive free health care. Many doctors were not happy about this as they felt they might lose out, but Dr Gilbert, like Stan before him treated so many people who couldn't afford to pay, and this way, with every patient he treated he would be paid by the NHS financed by the government. How amazing!

Obviously, he did expect that he might become busier, as more people would consult their doctor, however, that would mean that illnesses would be caught earlier and hopefully more people would survive. He did think at some point he might have to take on another doctor, but for now, he said that things would stay as they were.

Chapter 22

Robert's nightmares gradually became less frequent and Elizabeth began to relax a little more when going to sleep at night not worrying whether this would be one of those nights when Robert would shout out, waking them both up and needing to be calmed down. Things would trigger these nights, sometimes if Robert had a few drinks or if he met up with some friends who had been in a similar situation, they would talk about their war time experiences and somehow this would spark nightmares.

By this time Ruth had qualified as a midwife, so loved her work bringing new lives into the world and helping the new mothers through their labours. She was based at the hospital but attended home births too—she would do a home visit and make sure that everything was in place for when the birth was due. If mothers had problems or it was going to be a difficult birth, she would recommend that they had their babies at the hospital.

By early 1949 rationing was relaxed in some areas, but they were fortunate as the farm where Elizabeth had worked were very generous and often had given her extra goods in lieu of pay, also Dolly still tended her garden and seasonal fruit and vegetables were always in good supply. However, in the village where Polly and Dolly's families still lived, two tragic deaths occurred within a month of each other. John Mason, Dolly's dad had been crippled with arthritis for some years and took to his bed during early spring of 1949, basically refusing to get up as it hurt so much.

Dolly spoke to Dr Gilbert about her father, as she was so worried, and he said that permanent bed rest was not good and he should be persuaded to sit in a chair, at least, for a few hours a day. However, he refused as he said that the pain was too bad and developed a blood clot which caused thrombosis and he died very suddenly. Dolly was distraught, as was Nancy and they contacted Betty to tell her the news, which was very upsetting. However, just as they were dealing with this, Polly's dad, Fred Dennis, suffered a heart attack while having a drink down the local pub. That was a dreadful shock for Joan, Polly's mum and for all the family, Elizabeth loved her grandad and for Polly and Dolly to lose their dads within just a couple of weeks was quite dreadful.

Then, during the middle of this year Elizabeth discovered she was pregnant   she had her suspicions as she had felt nauseous in the mornings and felt generally unwell, and initially she thought it might be delayed shock, having lost her father so unexpectedly, however, she spoke to Dolly who arranged for Dr Gilbert to see her, and he confirmed that indeed this was the case. She told Robert that evening when he came home that they would be parents early in the spring of 1950. Robert seemed delighted with the news but again, took it really quietly but said it would be lovely to have a baby in the house. Polly and Thomas were delighted, longing to have a grandchild, Ruth was pleased for her friend and said she would give her any help she could and everyone generally welcomed the news.

During January 1950, when Elizabeth was seven months pregnant, she decided that she should give up teaching for the time being. The school was disappointed but wished her well and hoped that she might be able to return after the birth of the baby. Elizabeth doubted that this might be possible but said she would see how things went.

One morning, after a very cold spell, Elizabeth had got up later than intended and suddenly heard an almighty crash outside sounding like glass breaking. She opened the front door to be greeted by the milkman lying on the frosty path amongst broken glass and spilled milk. His hand was bleeding profusely so she invited him in. He seemed reluctant at first but realised he had little choice. She brought out a towel to wrap round his hand till he got to the kitchen sink then ran it under freezing cold water. She put the kettle on to make him a cup of hot sweet tea for the shock, but he seemed embarrassed to be putting her to such trouble. She told him not to worry and once his hand had been washed, she had a good look at it and it didn't look too bad. She said she would bandage it for him and hopefully it would be fine.

He was anxious to get on with his round but she told him to sit for a while and drink his tea. In the meantime, Elizabeth got a bucket of warm water to swill the front path, sweeping all the glass in a pile in a corner where she would dispose of it later.

He seemed very uncomfortable around her as he felt that she shouldn't be doing all that in her condition. She then sat down and had a cup of tea and started a conversation and he told her that he was called Freddie and his wife was due to give birth soon, like herself, which is why he felt bad for putting her to all that trouble. However, he soon got on his way, was worried about gossip, apparently milkmen were known, more jokingly than anything, as being notorious for forming dalliances with their lady customers.

A few days later, he knocked on her door and gave Elizabeth a bunch of early daffodils as a thank you for looking after him after his fall, he assured her that his hand was healing nicely and had fully recovered from the fall. He told her to look after herself in her present condition and not to venture out if there was snow or ice on the ground.

Elizabeth didn't see Freddie, the milkman, till quite some time later. She had told Robert about the incident and he seemed quite concerned about 'what the neighbours might say' and 'she shouldn't make a habit of asking him in.' She felt stung by his comments and said that he had hurt himself and was in shock, although the injury turned out to be minor, but she didn't know this at the time. She thought that Robert might have been thinking that if Jean had been found earlier, she may have survived, so she kept quiet.

In early March 1950, Elizabeth went into labour, the local midwife stayed with her throughout, Nancy had retired by now but Elizabeth was happy with Nurse Linda who was very competent and reassuring. Robert stayed at home that day making cups of tea and chain-smoking, eagerly waiting for the sounds of his new born child. All he could hear was encouraging words from Linda and just the odd groan from Elizabeth. He had walked round to Polly's earlier in the day to say that labour had started, and she and Thomas were very excited to meet their new grandchild. He assured them that he would be round once more as soon as there was any news.

Donna made her appearance into the world several hours later, kicking and screaming, very red-faced with a shock of dark hair. Linda said she weighed eight pounds, a good weight and Elizabeth was well, just exhausted. Robert took one look at the baby and felt a wave of love, totally overwhelming all-consuming love that he had never felt before, not even for Elizabeth. He loved his wife and knew she loved him but this love was different. He held Donna in his arms and the tears fell, he realised that this was something good that had come from him surviving the war; when he had dark days, he often wondered why he had fought so hard to stay alive—now he knew why!

Polly and Thomas were incredibly happy with their granddaughter and proud of their little family. They found Robert strange at times as he could be so morose and they worried about Elizabeth knowing that she hadn't achieved her potential educationally, due to the war, but now as a new mother, she would be busy for some time. Over the next few days there were a few visitors, Dolly and Dr Gilbert, and Ruth, of course, so proud of her friend.

Donna could be fractious at times, but generally settled down well into a kind of routine, but nights could be difficult. She was a very hungry baby and seemed to be hungrier during the night than in the day. She would sleep for five or six hours during the day, which meant that Elizabeth could rest herself, or get on with household chores. Polly was doing the shopping for her at the moment as going out was a performance, however, she looked forward to getting Donna out in the fresh air, it was such a lovely spring.

One day, she surprised Robert by pushing the pram to the cemetery, he looked genuinely pleased to see them and wanted to show Donna off to his fellow workers who were in the same vicinity. He was so proud of his baby girl.

His nightmares were getting less and less, would occur every now and then. Until Donna came along, they would go to the cinema if a film appealed to them, but anything that involved shooting or loud sounds, like westerns, thrillers or war films would often bring on his nightmares. However, visits to the cinema would be curtailed until Donna got into a routine and Elizabeth happy to leave her. Polly couldn't wait to look after her, and she would often have her for some time during the day if Elizabeth was meeting Ruth for lunch or wanted to shop on her own. Robert wasn't very happy about Donna being left with anyone, but on this occasion, Elizabeth said that it was good for her to get used to other people, and took this moment to say to Robert that she hoped to get back to teaching soon.

Chapter 23

She really missed the company that teaching provided and a few hours out of the house a couple of days a week should be fine. Robert obviously wasn't too happy about this so she said she would wait till Donna was a year old.

One day, Elizabeth saw an advert asking for teachers of various abilities to help run evening classes. People were beginning to get their lives back on track and learning a new skill, be it a hobby or profession, seemed quite popular. She contacted the Education Department and said that she could teach French, especially conversational French and she was welcomed with open arms as people had started holidaying in France, and a bit of basic French could go a long way! He told her to turn up one evening so they could discuss which hours suited her, and which evening.

The hard part was telling Robert; he was home every evening, seldom went out despite his workmates wanting to go out for a drink after work, or joining a darts team, he only ever just wanted to get home. Elizabeth had said to him in the past that she wouldn't have a problem if he wanted to go out in the evenings, but he was adamant that he didn't need to.

She spoke to him that evening after supper, Donna was settled for the night— at a year old she was in a great routine and always went to bed just after Robert came home, so he could play with her for half an hour or so, then she would go to bed and they would have their evening meal. Initially, Robert was quiet when Elizabeth told him, then said that he wasn't very happy about it but couldn't really stop her and would be content to look after Donna for one or two evenings a week. He again checked that she was only teaching French, nothing else, and she truthfully replied saying that for now, French was the only language they had talked about.

There was a good response to the French class, and the first evening, they just made introductions and she tried to remember everyone's name. She had ten people in her group and she felt that was a good number to start with. She looked over the people and her eyes settled on a face she recognised, Freddie her milkman! She must have looked surprised, he gave her a smile and nodded, as much to say that he also recognised her. That evening, for the first lesson, they did basic greetings and were encouraged to speak to each other. At the end of the two hours, everyone felt like they knew each other and Elizabeth thought it had gone well.

Everyone wanted to learn some French mainly for holidays, one or two had made friendships during the war and wanted to be able to communicate a little bit better, so at the end of the class it was suggested that the group should go out for a drink. Most people were happy to go along with it, Elizabeth said that maybe another night, but not tonight as she was expected home, and Freddie also held back.

She started walking home when Freddie caught up with her so Elizabeth asked him how his wife and child were, as she had been due to give birth at about the same time. Freddie went very quiet and said that he had lost them both—his wife had died in childbirth and the baby hadn't survived either. It was a difficult birth, the baby was breech and unfortunately was born dead, and his wife suffered severe blood loss, so nothing could be done. Elizabeth thought of Donna fast asleep in her cot with Robert looking after her and she felt incredibly sad and lucky all at the same time.

They walked in silence after Elizabeth had told him how sorry she was to hear this, he said life had become very hard and he hoped that learning French might help to take his mind off things, and think about something else. He had a cousin in France and hopefully might be able to visit at some point. He left Elizabeth at the top of her road and when she got home, she immediately dashed up the stairs to check on Donna. She was laying on her back sound asleep with her thumb in her mouth. When she came down, she told Robert about Freddie, he said that was sad news, but he didn't like the idea of her going out drinking with this group of people. Obviously not a lot of sympathy for Freddie from Robert.

The classes went well and, against Robert's better judgment, Elizabeth did join her class for a drink and she really looked forward to that time of the week, as well as the class itself. They were a mixed group but all got on really well, a couple of girls were hoping to be au-pairs but wanted to polish their French a little bit before going over, they would learn much more once there, but it was mainly to be more confident. A few people wanted to visit France for summer holidays, they spoke of Normandy, Brittany and the Loire Valley, as well as the Cote d'Azur down the far South, and it all sounded very exciting. Elizabeth longed to think about a holiday abroad, she spoke three languages almost fluently yet had never been out of England!

To be fair, she didn't even have a holiday in England, when Robert had a week off, they would have the odd day out, usually going on the bus but really Elizabeth would like them to get a car as this would help them get around. Polly had been driving for some time now and would drive Thomas' car, especially when he had his truck and the car was sitting at home. Elizabeth could also drive, having driven during the war when she worked on the land.

Polly had offered to take Robert, Elizabeth and Donna out on Sundays with Thomas, of course, but Robert never wanted to go. Elizabeth had been saving the money she earned teaching, it wasn't much but she was a good manager and saved a small amount of her housekeeping too, so she thought she would surprise Robert and suggest buying a car.

Donna was nearly three now, and was thriving. She was very bright and Elizabeth spent a lot of time with her, answering her many questions, and generally feeding her active little mind, as Polly had done with her.

The summer of 1953, Queen Elizabeth II would be crowned, having accessed the throne since February 1952 when her beloved father, King George VI had passed away. The country was in a grip of excitement, planning street parties and various events to celebrate the coronation. Elizabeth had spoken to Robert about buying a car, he wasn't too keen but then thought it might be a nice idea, they could drive to nearby coastal places when the weather was fine at weekends and when he was on annual leave. However, a holiday still seemed to be out of the question. He always wanted to sleep in his own bed but agreed to go on some outings once they had a car.

Elizabeth felt she was making progress—she knew that people thought Robert odd as he was quite anti-social and stuck to his routine, and when she explained that this was a result of his war experience, people's reply was that everyone had suffered in some way during the war but it was time to move on. Elizabeth was loyal to Robert and explained that it was different for everybody.

One night when they were all in the pub after class, Elizabeth suddenly came up with an idea. How about a day trip to France where everyone could practice their French in shops and cafes—how much fun would that be! Her idea was met with much enthusiasm, one chap said he could book a coach as a friend of his worked for a coach company, someone suggested it should be a Saturday, and plans got underway.

Eventually everyone drifted home but Elizabeth, normally one of the first to leave, got into a conversation with Freddie. He was doing well considering his terrible loss, but he said that he had to get on with things, and said that he would definitely try to get the day off to go to France. He asked if Robert might join them, Elizabeth said she hoped he might as she was happy for Donna to join them, so he couldn't use Donna as an excuse for not going. She said the little girl had just turned three then felt very guilty as Freddie's face clouded over, and his pain was palpable as it dawned on him that his baby boy would have been three too, had he lived.

Elizabeth was very apologetic but Freddie brushed her apology aside, then asked her if she was happy with Robert. She said she had a good life, loved her home, their child, enjoyed caring for Robert, so yes, she felt fortunate. He tried to say that wasn't what he had asked but just said that if ever she felt unhappy, he would love to make a home for her and Donna. He had admired her for a long time and had feelings for her. Elizabeth was shocked, rather flattered, but said that her life was with Robert, she had married him for better or for worse, and although he was a difficult man to live with, she had made her choice. Freddie, having realised he had crossed a line, said he admired her loyalty, hoped they could still be friends, and respected her decision. He also told her that Robert was a very lucky man.

When Elizabeth got home, Robert pointed out the time as she was later than she would usually be. He had accepted that she went to the pub after the class as she did most weeks now, but he thought she should have been home before now. She couldn't really say that she was late as Freddie had made her an offer she had to refuse, she just told Robert, quite rightly, that they were planning a day trip to France one Saturday very soon, and she hoped that he would join them so he could meet everyone. He asked about Donna and who would look after her and Elizabeth said that Donna would go with them.

He seemed appalled at that, the reason for which was unclear, as she thought it was quite exciting taking a young child on a boat and coach for the day. Obviously, anyone else with a young family were welcome, it would be good to fill a coach, would be fun, not a word Robert was familiar with.

However, arrangements were made and the day dawned when they would have their day out in France. Elizabeth had Donna with her, Polly was also joining them, but Robert had declined saying there was a lot to do in the garden, and if he didn't have to look after Donna, he could get on with it.

The coach picked them up outside the school and within an hour they approached the Port of Dover. They drove on to the boat then everyone alighted the coach and went in search of something to eat. Quite a few people had brought sandwiches and flasks to save a bit of expense, but they were all looking forward to their lunch in a French cafe. It was a lovely day so the coach drove down to the sandy beach at Calais, and the children soon got stuck in with their buckets and spades.

Donna loved playing on the beach with the other children and their laughter was infectious. The coach took some of the other passengers into town then after a couple of hours, picked up the children and parents on the beach so they could go to lunch. Elizabeth loved using her French and even more delighted when they understood every word. It was also lovely to hear the language being spoken fluently, picking up bits of conversations—the only time she did that was when she was at home on her own and listened to French radio programmes, that was the method she used for keeping up her knowledge all this time.

They had a lovely meal in a small restaurant, and some wine was drunk which they all enjoyed and it turned into a very jolly afternoon. All too soon, it was time to take the coach back to the port for the journey home. Donna had loved her day and had made new friends with some of the other children on the trip and they promised to see each other again soon, other than in class.

Robert was pacing the floor and seemed agitated when they got home, Elizabeth said that they had a lovely day, she soon got Donna to bed as the little girl was very tired, but had enjoyed the adventure, and Robert then said that he wished he had come to, but really didn't feel that he could have managed it. Elizabeth realised then that Robert had real problems, and thought a psychiatrist might be the answer, however, suggesting it was more than she dared to do, certainly not at that moment. They would have to broach this again at a more opportune moment.

Chapter 24

Polly worried about Elizabeth and Robert, wondering whether they were really happy, Robert was certainly strange, and as much as he clearly loved his family, he always looked lost, in a world of his own. This is why his job suited him well, and spending hours in their garden, but she felt that their relationship lacked what she and Thomas had, and even Dolly and Dr Gilbert, with all their work commitments, always seemed so happy together, and so very close. However, there was nothing she could do about it, she would never interfere and Elizabeth knew that their door was always open.

One day, Elizabeth asked Dr Gilbert if he could recommend a psychiatrist for Robert, she had decided to bite the bullet after a picnic out in the countryside and they were just talking generally. Polly and Thomas had taken Elizabeth and Donna and met Dolly and Dr Gilbert with Steven. Simon had better things to do these days and of course, Robert, at the last minute had decided to stay at home. Said the weeds had taken over the runner beans which Elizabeth knew was just an excuse, but she left him to it.

Dr Gilbert said that Robert was obviously suffering from what he had experienced during the war, both on the battlefield and at the hands of the Germans in the Prisoner of War camp. He had been quite belligerent in the beginning, as he felt he had rights as a prisoner, but the German guards soon knocked that idea out of him. When he challenged them, they really did lay into him and then starved him. There had been times when he hadn't been offered the meagre rations they fed the prisoners with for two or three days. He soon realised that he needed to tow the line to make his time there as good as it could be— which was not very good.

Hence his time there was still horrible and he witnessed all types of injustices on his fellow prisoners who occasionally rebelled against the system but this did them no good. He came home a lesser man and somehow had never regained confidence or trust in people, despite going through with his marriage to Elizabeth and the birth of Donna.

Dr Gilbert said that a psychiatrist might be able to help but Robert would have to be willing to do this, and Elizabeth realised then that Robert, in his own way, was quite happy avoiding all the big issues that he couldn't deal with, like sticking at his job in the office, going on a train, having holidays, and that was his way of dealing with his traumas, and as far as he was concerned, he was fine with this. Elizabeth felt that he didn't care about what she wanted, he still looked very exasperated when she suggested doing something different, and she was resigned to getting on with her life, doing things on her own or with Donna if Robert didn't want to be involved.

At this point, she gave up the idea of a psychiatrist and told Dr Gilbert this. He had already thought that this could be a long and costly road as to 'fix' Robert, a therapist would have to dig very deep to unearth all the horrors embedded in the depths of his subconscious, and this could make him a whole lot worse before making him better. In addition, there was the issue that his father had never come home due to Hitler, so his problems were severe.

Dr Gilbert was still very busy in the surgery, since the advent of the NHS, he had a lot more patients, but this was counteracted by people visiting the surgery long before symptoms became a problem, and therefore, he was often able to nip illnesses in the bud and make referrals to the hospital, as in cases of tuberculosis, a dreadful disease, but treatable if caught in good time. He was able to offer advice to parents when young children contracted childhood illnesses like mumps, measles and chicken pox so that the symptoms were controlled and made for happier patients.

This also meant that there was a regular income into the surgery account and that was a great improvement. It must be very difficult for someone in the medical profession to not care for a sick person just because they couldn't afford to pay, and this is why on many occasions doctors were not paid for seeing patients.

Donna started school after the Easter Holiday in 1955, she loved it and was a bright and popular child. Elizabeth had spent a lot of time in her pre-school years teaching her skills like doing up buttons, trying to do laces, also basic reading and number skills, and telling the time. She was quite a humble little girl and helped some of the children in her class with skills that they could not manage. She was very gentle and her teacher found her a delight. She thrived and Elizabeth carried on with the evening classes hoping that soon she might herself get a day job in school like she had done before Donna was born.

Again, she would need to talk to Robert about this and she knew what the answer would be. They had bought a car a few months back, but no progress on the holiday, just day trips, but progress none the less.

Polly called in one day and she looked very upset. Elizabeth immediately asked her if Thomas was alright, she said he was fine but Joan, her mother and Elizabeth's grandma was very ill and she wasn't going to get better. Apparently, she had been unwell for some time but hadn't consulted the doctor about her symptoms and now it was too late to do anything for her!

Polly was devastated as she wished she had known and blamed herself for not paying enough attention to Joan when she said she felt tired, and was losing weight. She really should have realised that there was a problem, and at least spoken to Dr Gilbert for advice. She had terminal cancer and would be on morphine injections for the rest of her days! Polly had suggested bringing Joan to her home so she could care for her but Joan wanted to stay in her little cottage where she had lived all her married life. She had just turned 80 and wanted to stay put.

Polly had decided to move back so she could look after her mum in her final days and wanted Elizabeth to know this and to say that she would love her to pop by and see her grandma as she had always done and to try and keep things as normal as possible. Also, she wanted her to tell Donna whatever she felt was the best thing to tell a five-year old and she should also visit when she could. Donna loved her 'little Nana,' Thomas' mum was Welsh Nana, and Donna was very fond of these older people who seemed to adore her and always brought her nice things whenever she saw them.

Ruth came to see Elizabeth one day and she could tell immediately that Ruth was excited about something. She made some tea and told her to spill the beans—she really wanted to tell her about her grandma—but didn't want to ruin the moment as Ruth had a real spark about her. Ruth looked up in surprise but Elizabeth knew her of old and could tell when something was afoot.

She told Elizabeth that she had met someone at work, had been on a few dates and thought it might be serious. She said that his name was Bob, he was a lovely man and had come over from Jamaica with his parents on the Windrush so that they would all be helping, in a small way, to rebuild Great Britain after the war. He had been here for about five years and loved his cleaning job at the hospital. Ruth really liked him but said that on a couple of occasions when they were out together people spat at them, which was awful and humiliating, and Bob wasn't sure about putting her through this. She said that he didn't know her very well and if he thought that people's bigoted and prejudiced views would stop her seeing him, he could think again.

She was going home for a few days and would talk to her father and Dolly about the situation and gauge their reactions. Elizabeth told her that as long as they were happy, she felt that her father and Dolly would be happy for them, but would obviously worry about other people's reactions, mainly for her and Bob's sake. She also said that she looked forward to meeting Bob soon.

Elizabeth spoke at length to Polly about this when she next saw her and Polly thought it was sad that if two people were happy together, why should other people have an opinion, if it didn't affected them personally. Robert had little to say on the subject although Elizabeth tried to gauge his reaction, he would have reacted more if Ruth was dating a German! Robert didn't share any views he had on any subject, even the news about Joan didn't seem to create any thoughts— apart from saying that no one could live for ever—this could be due to him losing his own mother at a relatively young age and never having known his father.

Elizabeth found life quite difficult with him at times as he was so dull to live with. However, she reminded herself of what he had gone through and chided herself for having bad thoughts. When she felt really low, she thought about Freddie and wondered if he had met anyone since she had last seen him—he had long stopped coming to evening classes and she did occasionally think of what might have happened if she had left Robert and gone with him. These really were bad thoughts and she would banish them from her mind.

The following week she arranged to meet Ruth in London for lunch so that she could meet Bob, Polly would pick Donna up from school and stay with her till Ruth got home. Dolly had offered to go and sit with Joan while Polly was out, and she could visit Nancy, her own mum, at the same time.

Joan slept all the time and it would only be a matter of days before she went to sleep for ever. Nancy had been friends with Joan for years, they were widowed within two weeks of each other about six years before, so she was very upset about Joan's condition, and she also wished that she had realised that Joan was so ill.

Elizabeth went to Ruth's flat that she had bought some years ago and prepared to meet Bob. He was very quietly spoken but had a lovely soft voice and she imagined that he could probably sing. He greeted her with a big smile and when he looked at Ruth, there was no doubt that he absolutely adored her. For a split second, Elizabeth felt jealous as Robert had never looked at her like that, but she was very happy for her friend and they had a great get-together and a good lunch. Ruth said that next time they both had a day off she would take Bob to meet her father and Donna but Elizabeth was the first person to meet him, apart from her work colleagues.

When Elizabeth returned, she told Polly how lovely Bob was and how great they were together. Polly said it was high time that Ruth settled down, she obviously had been waiting for the right person and he had finally come into her life.

A few weeks later, with everyone's blessing, Ruth married Bob and braced herself for a lifetime of happiness possibly marred by the prejudice she would encounter during her marriage. Within a year, Ruth had given birth to a beautiful baby boy, with wonderful olive skin and dark curly hair. They still lived in London and Ruth intended going back to nursing, part-time at least, doing a couple of night shifts so that Bob would be home for the baby. His parents also lived in South London so were always willing to look after baby Errol Robert, they said that when he was older, he could choose the name he preferred. They felt that the love they shared for each other and their baby boy would stand them in good stead for any future incidents which might occur due to being a mixed-race family.

Sadly, Joan lost her fight for life early in 1956, Polly and all the family were devastated, even Robert was upset as Donna was heartbroken! At six years old, the reality that she would never see Joan again was hard to take and she was very sensitive—Robert was very good with her, explained that this was the life cycle and death, sadly, came to everyone eventually. He explained this in a very kind way and tried his best to console Donna, as Elizabeth and Polly were coping with their own grief. The funeral was in the village church, very well attended and the family took comfort from the wonderful support shown to them.

Elizabeth was still doing two evenings a week teaching but felt she was ready for a day job now that Donna was growing up. She also felt she needed a new focus after losing her grandmother. She had started teaching Donna French at home remembering how quickly she had picked it up when she was younger. Donna loved it and enjoyed having this special time with her mother and looked forward to what was now an annual day trip to France so that she could practice what she had learnt.

Robert never did go with them on these day trips, being in the summer time he always felt he would be better off doing a day's gardening. To be fair, his gardening skills were very good and they would have enough potatoes and onions to last most of the year. He and Dolly would talk at length about the produce they grew and gave each other tips to sort out issues with weeds and pests.

Chapter 25

Donna progressed through school and passed her 11 plus. She was thrilled and looked forward to starting at the Grammar school in the autumn. This, like her primary school, was a mixed school and Elizabeth and Robert thought that mixed schools were a good idea, especially when children became teens. Elizabeth had seen girls hanging around outside boys' school and vice-versa so they felt that a mixed environment was much better. Donna had a few friends starting there with her so she wasn't too daunted until the first day arrived, then she felt quite nervous.

When she came home on the first day, Elizabeth was anxious to know how the day went and Donna seemed quite happy, it was a big school and none of the friends from the primary school were in any of the groups that she was in, but she seemed resigned that she would make new friends. Elizabeth explained that she wasn't the only one in this situation and she would no doubt get used to it!

There was no cause for worry, Donna joined a few extra-curricular activities, after-school clubs and threw herself into most things. She enjoyed sport and joined the netball team, she also liked running and joined in cross country, often on a Saturday morning, and started learning German as well as doing French as a regular subject.

Elizabeth cringed when Donna told her, she knew her father didn't like Germans and understood why, but hadn't been told the full horror and she felt that this would be a good thing for her to do, especially if she went travelling when she was older. They never discussed this in front of Robert and he seemed oblivious about her school work, he would ask her how she was getting on, and she would talk to him about different subjects that she enjoyed, but never mentioned the 'G' word.

He didn't join Elizabeth when it was parents' evening, he said that she was better 'at that sort of thing' so she was able to speak to all the teachers and, apart from the sciences that Donna didn't really enjoy, she was doing brilliantly at everything else. Elizabeth took this opportunity to speak to the Head of Languages and asked if there were any openings for helping with French and German.

They arranged a meeting for the following week which resulted in Elizabeth doing two days a week with the GCE classes, helping pupils on a one-to-one with any difficulties they encountered and she did this for several years. When Donna was in her first year the older pupils didn't realise that Elizabeth was Donna's mother and for that, Donna was grateful. She found the older girls daunting and wanted to keep a low profile.

In the autumn of 1958, Nancy sadly passed away; she had been fine, Dolly had seen her a couple of days previously and knew that neighbours looked in on her every day, she had seen most of the villagers being born, had brought so many babies into the world, so she was very well respected and people kept an eye on her, especially since Joan had passed. It was their postman who knocked with a large package from Canada and couldn't get an answer. He went to the neighbour who thought it was strange as she knew she was at home. She had a key for emergencies, and sadly, they both entered and found she had died in her sleep.

Dreadful shock for Dolly, and more so for Betty, she vowed to try and get a flight to come back to the UK but didn't think Stan would be able to do this. In the event, Nicholas came over with Betty and they stayed with Dolly which was a great support at such a sad time. Despite that, the sisters were thrilled to be together and Nicholas was a fine young man, he was in his early 40s and was a Mountie—a career he loved. Dr Stan had recently retired but had some health issues which meant he couldn't fly. Betty said that she would hope to visit with him again but they would sail instead of flying.

The years flew and the year before Donna sat her GCEs she took a letter home saying that they were doing a student exchange so that Donna would stay with a family in France or Germany, depending on what was available, with the idea of returning the favour by hosting whoever she would go and stay with. Donna was very excited and spoke to her parents about this and this is when Robert realised that she was learning German. He became very angry and shouted a lot, felt betrayed and couldn't understand why they hadn't mentioned this before. Elizabeth said this was the precise reason that they hadn't said anything to him, not because they hadn't wanted to, and if he had taken a bit more interest in what Donna was doing, then he would have realised.

Of course, despite all this, there was no way that they would be able to host a German student, it would make the atmosphere very uncomfortable, so Elizabeth spoke to the Head of Languages the next day and asked if it might be possible for Donna to be hosted by a French family when they were making the selection. She was seen as a valuable member of the Languages Department by now, she did explain that her husband had suffered badly at the hands of Germans during the war, and although it was now 1964, he was very unforgiving and would never agree to hosting a German student. She felt sad about this but knew he wouldn't budge. The Head of Languages was very understanding and said that she would do her best to host Donna with a French family.

The trip went well and a few months later they hosted Francine, a very nice French girl and all went well. Donna and she became pen friends and would correspond regularly between and after the visits. During Francine's visit, Robert was quiet as always, but did try to speak to the girl about her family and asked her what her father did, so he did make rather an effort, probably ashamed at his original outburst when the hosting was first mentioned.

He still wouldn't go away on holiday so Elizabeth had taken to taking Donna and they had been to various places in England, cities like York, Harrogate, Lincoln to name but a few, also day trips to London visiting museums and other places of interest, going to the theatre, and they had also visited Paris. Donna had been with Francine and her family and said that Elizabeth needed to visit as it was such a magical city, and of course neither of them were disappointed.

Ruth and Bob were still living in London, Errol Robert was growing up, he was a very handsome boy and was doing quite well at school, however, he did get into the occasional fight which caused them problems. There were a few black children at the school he went to, but somehow some of the older children would occasionally pick on him mainly because he was of dual heritage.

Ruth and Bob would go to school and speak to his teachers, and they were sympathetic, up to a point, but Ruth felt that even some of the teachers had racist views and this didn't help them much. However, they spoke to Errol at length telling him to ignore the teasing, these children didn't know what they were saying, and he should rise above it, otherwise he would be known as a trouble-maker. He said that when he was older, he would become a policeman and arrest all these people that were making his life difficult.

His parents just hugged him and said to be as well behaved in school as he could be and concentrate on learning and he would go far. His paternal grandparents Ella and Georgie were very understanding and backed up what his parents had told him. They had also experienced racism in the time they had been in Britain, and felt Errol's frustration. They had come to this country in good faith and been promised a great life and good jobs here and at times they did regret their decision. However, Georgie drove a bus and Ella was a clippie and every now and then they actually worked on the same bus, but more often than not they would be on different routes or different shifts, but they were fine with that.

In 1965, The Race Relations Bill was passed, which meant that people would be breaking the law if they passed racist comments or placed adverts stating 'no blacks,' which is what used to happen when advertising accommodation and even jobs. However, racism was something that could never be totally eradicated, and basically people had to live with this, hoping that over the years, with proper teaching, it would gradually lessen—but it was accepted that it would never totally disappear.

Dr Gilbert and Dolly adored their grandson, thought he was a beautiful boy and so enjoyed his visits. Occasionally during the holidays, he would go and stay with Dr Gilbert and Dolly and loved his uncles when they were around. Simon had joined the army just at the end of World War 2 and was still in the services—so spent quite a bit of time abroad and was based in the North of England. Steven was a school teacher in a primary school and loved his job.

Dr Gilbert felt that his children had done extremely well and was very proud of them all, the only cloud on the horizon was when Simon was sent on missions where there was conflict, and this obviously worried them all. Maggie, bless her, was still with the family although the children had gone, she had made her home with them and still looked after the house, loving the times when the family came to visit. She adored Errol Robert and would excitedly bake when she knew he was visiting and, of course, the feeling was mutual.

Part 6

Chapter 26

Life everywhere was changing with the 'Swinging Sixties' very much in full swing. The Big Band sound of the Forties had given way to Rock and Roll in the Fifties, with the advent of Bill Haley, followed by Elvis, with Cliff in the late fifties and very much in the forefront of the sixties, then of course, The Beatles and The Rolling Stones and all the groups and solo singers emerging into this amazing period in history.

Older people found the younger generation hard to understand, the boys with long hair and the girls in their miniskirts and back-combed hair! Donna had quite a few school friends and was very fond of Derek, a bright lad who was, like her, very studious. Occasionally some of the girls said that she studied far too hard and should have more fun. However, Derek wanted to go to university, as Donna did, so they ignored these comments and after they both did well in their GCEs they proceeded to study for 'A' levels which would get them into university if they did well.

They both had two years of tough work ahead of them but enjoyed the challenge, and as they were both so focused, they grew close versus the odd jibes they would receive from the other pupils. They would study in their own homes most evenings, would go to the cinema or a dance on a Saturday and would share a hot dog on the way home, or pop in to the Wimpey Bar and have a coffee or a coke, loving the easy way they could discuss all types of subjects, and loved being in each other's company. Donna loved the feel of Derek's protective arm round her as they went out and always felt safe with him.

Alternate Sundays they would have tea at each other's houses and would talk excitedly to their parents about which universities they would like to go to and which ones would be suitable for their particular subjects. Languages were definitely what Donna wanted to do, while Derek really wanted to be a chemist but needed to do well in his science subjects which was the only subject that Donna didn't enjoy and do well in.

There were a group of girls at school who still poked fun at Donna about her dedication to her studies, which she ignored. However, one of the girls, Linda, said that Derek must find her a very dull friend as she never wanted to have any fun. She said that she was holding a party one Saturday evening as her parents would be away for a few days and would she and Derek like to go along. This was in the spring about a month before sitting their exams. Donna said that she couldn't speak for Derek, but she would be unable to go. When she talked to Derek, he said that it might be fun to go along, it was just one evening after all, so they argued and Donna said that it was up to him if he wanted to be there, but she wouldn't be.

Apart from anything else, she didn't think Linda liked her so she didn't see the point of wasting an evening in her company. As the day of the party dawned, the girls were talking about what they would be wearing, also what drinks they would take with them and generally planning their evening.

She and Derek didn't discuss it any further, just agreed to disagree. On the Sunday, Derek was due to come to her house for tea and when he phoned in the afternoon, he sounded very sheepish and said that he wasn't feeling very well and he wouldn't be able to come round. Donna guessed that this was the result of the party the night before; generally they didn't drink very much, had the odd drink when they went to a dance or at home—Elizabeth did enjoy the odd glass of wine which came with her taste for France, and all things French, so Donna did have an occasional drink but not to excess, and Derek wasn't used to it either—so she guessed that he had over-indulged at the party. She just said that was fine and she would see him at school the next day.

When they met up at school, she had a feeling that the girls around her were behaving evasively and she felt that although she and Derek were on speaking terms, he seemed to be avoiding her eye. She ignored it all thinking they were all cross with her because she didn't go to the party, however, as the week went on more and more titbits came to light from various people, and the crux of the matter was that Linda had spent all evening flirting with Derek, he was drinking quite heavily and mixing his drinks and this is why he wasn't very well on Sunday. Also, the house was in a state after the party, broken glasses and the bathroom and cloakroom needed sorting out, there were cigarette burns on some furniture and generally very untidy.

Linda had spent most of Sunday with help from a couple of friends cleaning up so that by the time her parents returned that evening, they would never know she had hosted a party. Unfortunately, they could tell as soon as they came in that there had been quite a few people there, despite Linda insisting she had only invited a few close friends around and no alcohol or smoking had taken place as far as she knew. Her parents were upset at the breach of their trust and immediately grounded her.

Donna and Derek hadn't got back to their normal relationship; Donna felt that Derek was hiding something from her. The revision for the forthcoming exams intensified and they saw each other less than usual, which didn't help things. The month of June passed and one morning they woke to find that the exams were all done, it would just be a waiting game.

Derek asked Donna if she fancied a day out to the coast so they could have a catch up and try to get back to where they were before the party. Donna missed Derek terribly, visits to the cinema and sharing a hot dog or going for a drink afterwards, having tea on a Sunday and the handholding and kissing, feeling his protective arm round her, all very important to a teenager. She looked forward to this and they decided to go to Margate for the day on the train.

When they met up at the station, again, Derek looked very distracted. Donna asked him if he was alright and he said that he wasn't sure but they would have a chat once they got to Margate. It was a lovely day, and the beach was fairly quiet as the summer holidays hadn't started yet. They found a quiet spot to sit and she said that he must tell her what the problem was. They were both sitting there sifting sand through their fingers and focusing on that rather than on looking at each other.

Derek then went on to tell her that he couldn't remember what had happened at the party. He hadn't wanted to go without her but went anyway as he was upset with her. Linda made a beeline for him and sat with him most of the evening, they had a lot to drink and this is where things became vague. He must have passed out and the next thing he knew, he woke in her bed and she was asleep next to him. He was horrified, especially as he didn't know what, or if, anything had happened between them.

It certainly wouldn't have been his intention so he dashed home, feeling sick in more ways than one, and had since tried to put this out of his mind. However, Linda had phoned him a couple of days ago and told him that she might be pregnant. This hit him like a thunderbolt as he really couldn't remember what had happened. He assumed that when he passed out, she put him to bed so he could sleep it off.

Donna, obviously, was shocked and upset. Their relationship was loving and deep but they had both agreed to wait before taking things to the 'next level' as they were both young, had all their lives in front of them and would finish school first. She tried to ask him if he remembered anything and he said he didn't and he didn't really feel that anything had happened between them as he had blacked out, and the amount of alcohol he had consumed made him feel that he would have been useless to do much anyway. However, Linda's news had made him doubt himself and said that it would change his future totally if she was carrying his child.

Their day out was in tatters and they caught a train home, Donna said that she felt she needed to process what he had told her but didn't see any point carrying on with their relationship at the moment. This was a matter of trust and in the future, if either of them went to a social event alone, there had to be trust between them, and Derek had ruined that. They parted at the station on their return and Donna told him not to contact her. She went home, straight to her room, threw herself on her bed and sobbed.

Elizabeth thought she heard her come in but no cheery 'hello' and when she found her in her room, she asked her what the problem was. At first, she got the wrong idea and thought that she and Derek had fallen out, technically, they had, but it was so much worse than just a 'tiff.' Donna told Elizabeth not to worry, she would sort herself out and come down and tell her the whole story.

Elizabeth went back down and made some tea and cut some cake and waited for Donna to come down. When Donna had finished telling her the whole saga Elizabeth understood why Donna felt betrayed, on the other hand, Linda sounded quite a devious girl, especially having a party without her parents' consent. She said it might be an idea for Donna and Derek to have a break and see what happened after their exam results.

They were both due to go to university, if they got the right result Donna was bound for Bath to do languages and Derek would be going to Exeter. They had already thought that they might occasionally be able to get together at one of those places. Trust was very important and once it was broken it took time to fix.

Chapter 27

However, Derek didn't contact Donna until the day they both turned up at school for their results, along with the rest of the sixth formers who were eagerly waiting. There were cries of joy and of despair as people didn't get the results they had hoped for. Donna opened her envelope and was delighted that she had got the grades she needed for her entry to Bath. She went to Derek whose results were also good but he didn't look terribly happy. He said that she had done well and could prepare to go to university, but he would not be going—he had decided to take a job as Linda was going to have his child and he really needed to support her. He wasn't in a relationship with her, but felt he had to do the right thing and help her out financially as well as helping out at times with the child as he felt responsible for her predicament and didn't feel that it should be all down to her.

Donna admired his loyalty to Linda but realised this meant that their relationship was truly over. Despite getting the results she had hoped for, she felt very hollow inside and a deep sense of loss. It seemed such a waste that Derek was turning down his university place but could see his reasoning behind it. His parents were very upset, they loved Donna and felt that he had been very foolish.

Donna phoned Bath on her return and they said that her place was there for her and looked forward to welcoming her in the middle of September. Derek went home to make a similar phone call to Exeter, except to say that he had changed his mind about going there, they seemed surprised as his grades were good but thought there must be a personal reason as to why he wouldn't now be going. A few days later, he applied for a job in a local chemist where he might learn about being a pharmacist, and go to college locally, so that he would be earning a wage.

After all this was in place and Donna had gone to Bath, very excited despite the situation with Derek, telling Elizabeth and Robert, who were both so very proud of her that she would make new friends and this was a chance for a fresh start.

About the same time, Linda phoned Derek to say that she needed to speak with him—they arranged to meet in the local park and she told him that she wasn't actually pregnant, she had made a mistake so he was 'off the hook' as it were. He asked her how long she had known and she said that she knew a few days before the exam results had come out.

Derek was furious with her, and with himself as he had been so gullible, as she knew that he had put his life on hold so he could stand by her. She said that she had done it as she really liked him and thought they may have a relationship now that Donna had gone away. She then started to cry and he felt bad for being cross with her, but really couldn't bring himself to be anything more than just friends with her, and not close friends at that, as she had ruined his relationship with Donna and his chance to go to university, mainly out of jealousy—but, of course, he had to take some of the blame too.

He told his parents and they were relieved with his news—they would love grandchildren one day, but certainly not at the moment, plenty of time yet! They suggested he should phone Exeter and possibly try for a place there next September, in the meantime keep his job and his studies going—and this is what he decided to do.

He worked hard and soon got news from Exeter that he would have a place there for the following year. The local pharmacy was very pleased for him but also quite sorry as he was doing really well and already was a great asset to the business. He also had a lovely approach with customers and quite sympathetic as many of them delighted to talk about their problems, and he showed much empathy.

Donna thrived at Bath, enjoyed her course, and made many new friends both in the halls that she shared with several other girls but also met some lads in the social area and she really did develop a taste for alcohol. Drink was cheap in the Union Bar and it wasn't very far to stagger home. She got drunk a few times but was never totally 'legless' and although she would suffer hangovers, she kept her wits about her.

She had decided to learn Spanish, to add to her French and German knowledge and was improving on those all the time. Lots of people were going to Spain for their holidays and she felt that there might be an opportunity to use this language in the future, whether for a career or for herself if she ever visited Spain.

Donna was loving her time in Bath, such a lovely city, could get very busy with tourists at weekends and holiday times. She got a letter from Derek when she had been there for about a month, asking if they could keep in touch as friends, also telling her the news about Linda's antics—this didn't come as a big surprise to her but she hadn't realised that Linda could stoop so low, despite the fact that the two girls didn't really like each other.

She did write back to Derek and told him how she was getting on, telling him about the course as well as life at university in general, and said that she was happy for him that he would be going to Exeter next September. She hoped he and his parents were well and was happy to have some contact with him as a friend, but wanted to focus on her studies and all the new friendships she was making, as he would do next year no doubt!

Donna was home for Christmas and enjoyed seeing all the family and friends, but was glad to get back to Bath early in the New Year. Lectures didn't start for another week but she wanted to see her friends and get back to life there. At the end of June, she arranged for a friend to come and stay with her, and had been invited by another friend to spend time with her and a few of the other girls.

This girl came from Somerset and did quite a lot of fruit picking during the summer, so it was home from home for Donna and she quite enjoyed spending time doing this. Like Kent, Somerset had some wonderful orchards using their apples for cider and she managed to sample quite a lot of the local produce, sometimes resulting in a bad day the following day! The drinking was a rite of passage as all students experienced and Donna knew her limits, just didn't always stick to them.

Soon it was time to start her second year, and Derek contacted her to give her details of when he would be going to Exeter and was hoping they might meet up sometime. Donna felt she had moved on, had made some great friendships both male and female, and although she enjoyed male company, she didn't want to get into a serious relationship and that included Derek. Basically, she had grown up and had survived without him and come out the other side, so didn't want to go back there at the moment.

Chapter 28

The second year was quite intense and they were told that during this year, they would be spending some time abroad doing work experience using their languages. There were no real options, an assortment of placements which were grabbed on a first come/first served basis—Donna was very excited and didn't mind where she went and ultimately, it turned out to be to Germany. This would be for two months in the spring and she would be working in a hotel on Reception; to say she was excited was an understatement! She told Elizabeth and Robert over the Christmas break, Robert remained unimpressed but seemed to accept it and Elizabeth was delighted and said that she would like to visit while Donna was there! Robert stayed silent throughout the discussion but it was twenty-five years since he had come home and even Elizabeth felt that the scars should have healed by now. She was still understanding but with growing frustration at Robert's negativity.

He had just turned fifty and Elizabeth was heading towards her 50th birthday and felt that the time had come to move on. She had put her life on hold for many years but felt that she now needed to do the things she wanted to do. She still loved working at the school, but had long holidays and with Donna away quite a lot of the time, she did get very lonely. Any chance she had to get away, she would do so. She occasionally went to London to stay with Ruth, while Ruth was working Elizabeth would take Errol Robert out, he was in his teens now and growing into a lovely lad, beautifully mannered and loved spending time with Elizabeth. They visited places of interest in London, or would go to the cinema and this helped Ruth and Bob when they were both working.

While Donna was working in Munich Elizabeth spent ten days with her and really loved the experience. On Donna's days off they went out and explored the city, then one day they got up early and travelled to Austria, which was amazing. The scenery was wonderful, Elizabeth had bought a camera and took quite a few photos which she would share with Robert when she returned, in the hope that it might spur him to see places in different parts of the world, not necessarily Germany.

Donna was soon back in Bath finishing off her second year, she had loved the work in hospitality and this had made her think about her future. Teaching was her chosen career, initially, but after her work experience, she confirmed that it was a big world out there and it would be good to explore some of it. She could always go back to teaching in later life but she really did have the travel bug.

During the summer holiday two of Donna's friends asked if she would like to join them on a road trip. Heather and Sandra were good friends and as Heather had just passed her driving test, she thought it would be lovely to drive through England, staying in youth hostels or camping. Her father was happy for her to use his car as he wanted them to have a reliable vehicle, they would share the costs of course, so Donna jumped at the offer. Elizabeth was disappointed that Donna would only be home for a short time, but was happy for her to have fun.

The trip went well, they got as far as Scotland, via Wales and the Lake District, working their way back down to Northumberland, Lincolnshire and Norfolk. They were away for nearly a month and they had a great adventure. They all came back with a beautiful suntan but really looked forward to a bath, shower and comfortable bed on their return. The girls dropped Donna off and stayed overnight before the final leg of their journey. They were both from Somerset so would get home the next day. Heather's father would be glad to see his car returned in one piece, albeit with a few more miles on the clock and needing a thorough wash.

All too soon the holidays were over and Donna started her last year. This was quite intense and demanding—there were more lectures to attend to make sure that the entire course had been covered so more evenings and weekends with solid revision. The Christmas holiday was light relief and she spent two weeks at home, the longest time she had ever spent. Derek phoned her and asked her to have a drink with him. It was good to see him, his course was going well and he was due to do some work experience in a laboratory in the spring, and he now thought he might like to be a forensic scientist, but hadn't quite decided on his future.

They were very comfortable in each other's company and the evening sped by, however, Donna didn't feel romantically drawn to him. She'd had a few boyfriends at Uni but nothing serious and she felt this wasn't the right time to embark on a relationship. However, that was the nearest that she and Derek had got to being their old selves again, and they both went home feeling very happy. Derek felt that a line had been drawn under his previous mistake, a very silly one which caused a lot of heartbreak and he still kicked himself for going to that fateful party.

The next six months went by very quickly and Donna graduated with a First! She had excelled in her study of languages and had also done an English Literature course alongside the languages, so she was eloquent and knowledgeable. Her family were extremely proud of her and Elizabeth and Robert attended the Graduation ceremony. Elizabeth was amazed that Robert wanted to attend, and as they only had two tickets, she would have asked Polly to go with her, but was over the moon that Robert wanted to be there. The only thing was he wanted to go home on the same day, so it involved about six hours of driving, but that was fine.

The ceremony was very moving, seeing all those lovely young people who had worked so very hard to achieve their dreams was a wonderful experience and Elizabeth was very happy that Robert was there to share it with her. They had a photograph taken with Donna, and she ordered several copies to give to family and friends, despite the cost, she thought sometimes these things had to be done.

When Donna came home, she was thinking about her options and decided that travel was definitely the way to go. She went to an agency in London to see what options there were and she initially settled on working for an airline as an air hostess. She loved meeting people and this way she could also see the world and use her languages if necessary.

She went for several interviews and decided that short haul flights might suit her better to begin with, and she would be based at Heathrow. She underwent a period of training and realised that once she started work, she would need to live near the airport as the hours were not compatible with public transport and she wouldn't have time to go home if the shifts were close together.

She scoured the ads in the paper and found a room in a house share with three other girls who all worked at Heathrow. When she went to look at the room, there was only one girl in at the time, Lindsay; she said the other two girls, Dawn and Ashley were working, they all did various shifts, the two of them were desk based, checking luggage and paperwork, and Lindsay, like Donna, was an air hostess.

She said that the girls got on well but didn't see much of each other due to their shift patterns, but this resulted in the kitchen and lounge being a bit of a mess. They all tried to tidy up after themselves, but all too often they were in a rush so mugs and plates remained unwashed, the ironing board was a permanent fixture in the lounge and every now and then one of them would have a blitz and a massive tidy up.

The nice thing was they were all guilty of being untidy due to work pressures so nobody complained and basically, they all had a turn at tidying up and were all appreciative of their housemates' efforts.

Going home was a rare treat for Donna and she managed it every four to six weeks, Elizabeth and Robert looked forward to her visits but were happy that she was enjoying her work so much.

Chapter 29

Thomas had retired a few months ago, hated letting go of the business but had suffered a mild heart attack so decided the sensible thing would be to retire. He was in his early seventies but loved his work, however, both his parents had suffered chronic heart disease and had passed away a few years ago, first his mother, then his father not long afterwards, and as he enjoyed life, he decided to do the sensible thing. Polly was very relieved and had enough little jobs for him to do at home to stop him from being bored. Also, they had a few holidays planned, something that hadn't always been possible when Thomas was working, so that was something to look forward to.

Dr Gilbert was looking to retire, he had two new doctors at the practice so was gradually taking a back seat. They had converted Dolly's old quarters into two consulting rooms and a stair lift had been fitted so that Dolly could get up and down with ease. She could do stairs with difficulty, and did so with great determination, usually by going up in a sitting position and hoisting herself up backwards, her arms were very strong. However, the stair lift was a godsend and a great help and Dolly was grateful for it. They decided that they could still live in, the downstairs area was totally separate and Dolly didn't want to leave her beloved garden if she didn't need to. Early in 1970, Maggie passed away very suddenly. She was 90 years of age and active till the end of her life.

One morning she hadn't brought down the coffee, which she always insisted on doing, mid-morning for all the medical staff. Donna thought this strange, so when Dr Gilbert had seen the last patient, at about 11.00 they went upstairs to investigate. Maggie was not up and about so they went into her room and found her lifeless in bed. It was an awful shock, Dr Gilbert called an ambulance but realised it would be futile.

It transpired that Maggie had suffered a major stroke several hours previously and the saving grace was that she didn't suffer, and even if they had been aware, nothing could have been done to save her. The thought of her having lived but being in a vegetative state was too awful to contemplate, so although they were all devastated at the loss, they felt it was the best outcome for Maggie but missed her dreadfully!

She had been such a loyal member of their family, had no family of her own, the children were all devastated and they all came home, apart from Simon who was overseas, so they could share in the grief and support each other. She had been like the mother that they had lost, and had devoted her life to that family. She left a big hole in their lives, despite not having done housekeeping duties for some time, she still loved to bake and cooked the odd meal and she also helped Dolly with small chores and was very capable for her advanced years and she was well loved.

Polly was equally upset by this news, as were Elizabeth and Donna. Errol too had adored Maggie; he was desperate to leave school so he could join the police force. He had worked hard and managed to stay out of trouble, most of the time, but vowed that if and when he made it into the force, he would make sure that everyone was treated fairly, and would ensure that anyone being racist would be dealt with. That was his dream, the reality would be very different.

The years marched on and Polly and Thomas kept busy by going on coach trips all over the UK, made friends wherever they went and were thoroughly enjoying life, Thomas finally having agreed to retire; they also occasionally had Elizabeth and Robert for company on these breaks, Robert had got over his phobia of being away overnight and was happy to be away for three or four days at a time, progress indeed, and he had found Thomas a calming influence.

Life at home could be quite lonely now that Donna had moved away and was travelling all over the globe when Elizabeth wasn't there. She had been used to going away by herself and often met up with Donna if she had a few days stopover somewhere abroad. Her passport was well used, and Robert realised that Elizabeth needed to get away at times and perhaps he should see things from her perspective.

He still wouldn't go abroad but was willing to go on coach trips and when Polly and Thomas went too, they all enjoyed these.

Donna had worked for various airlines and was now doing long haul flights and loved spending time in all these far-flung places, always promising herself a longer trip in the future in those places she liked the most. Some places she wasn't fussed about returning to but she just loved seeing the world and dealing with the travelling public, most of whom were very pleasant. It had its challenges, sometimes pacifying a screaming baby while the mum prepared a feed, dealing with sick people, and serving food and drink throughout the trip.

At times, she wondered whether to quit and do teaching which is what she had always wanted to do, but for now she was enjoying what she was doing most of the time. It made it hard to catch up with family and friends, she liked to visit her old Uni friends every now and then, and enjoyed seeing Ruth, Bob and Errol, who was training to be a policeman. He looked dashing in his uniform, had got very tall and was so handsome.

Ruth and Bob were still working at the hospital, Ruth was in the Maternity Unit and specialised in looking after very premature babies, a heart-wrenching job, but one she loved full of ups and downs. Some very premature babies survived, while others didn't, and this was the heartbreaking side of it. On the whole, it was a very satisfying job and with scans available it was easier to tell if there was a problem with a pregnancy.

Again, that had its down side, at one time mothers gave birth before realising their baby might have health issues, now, as they could tell before the baby was born mothers could decide whether to carry on with the pregnancy or have a termination, again, heartbreaking decisions for couples, and often with the religious aspect, it made it doubly difficult. These were all the issues that Ruth dealt with in a day's work and would often come home exhausted. However, when she came home from shift leaving three or four happy couples drooling over their newborns, life was very worthwhile.

Bob was in charge of a cleaning team and ran the workforce, still doing cleaning himself when they were short-staffed. He was popular with most of his team but occasionally there was a bit of unpleasantness when staff members refused to co-operate. His superior had known him long enough to know that he was a great guy to work under and would occasionally intervene if Bob was having problems, but he mainly managed to sort people out and would vary the tasks so that the jobs didn't get too mundane. Between them, Bob and Ruth had a great circle of friends and had a good social life outside of work.

Chapter 30

In the late seventies on a rare weekend at home, Donna bumped into Derek, literally. They hadn't seen each other for a long time so it seemed the natural thing to grab a coffee and catch up. Donna was on an errand for Elizabeth but felt she could spare half an hour, but that flew by, she really had to go so Derek suggested they went out for lunch the next day, which was a Sunday. Donna said that would be lovely and went home to tell Elizabeth that she wouldn't be there for Sunday lunch. When she told her why, Elizabeth seemed quite delighted, she felt that they were well suited but because of the silly business all those years ago when they were both teenagers, Donna and Derek had drifted and it was good to know that they were meeting up.

They enjoyed the lunch and the ensuing afternoon when they went for a long walk and they were both sad when they had to part. Donna had to be at Heathrow in the early hours the next day so she really had to get back. She had bought a car and used to drive home, much better than going through London on public transport and messing around with trains. There was a new motorway being built round London, it would be known as the M25 and sections of it were opening in various areas, but it would be some time before its completion. Donna figured that when this happened, it would make her journey from Heathrow to Kent much quicker!

However, her friendship re-kindled with Derek, she went home a bit more often so that they could meet up. He was enjoying his job in a laboratory and was constantly working on different research projects, he opted for that option rather than forensics but could always change career course if needed. They looked forward to seeing each other and ended up speaking on the phone most days when Donna wasn't away, and gradually, her dream job became less of a dream as she really wanted to spend more time with Derek. The feeling was mutual and he would go and spend time with her in her flat, and eventually she went to HR and asked if she could change her job and go back to a desk job with more regular hours. Donna and Derek were very much in love and got engaged early in the eighties. They were both in their thirties so didn't see the point of a long engagement.

Derek had been looking at other jobs in the same field and a company in Woking approached him with a very decent package. He felt it was an offer he couldn't refuse, a pay rise and, although still in research, the work was very hush hush and this somehow appealed to him very much. Some of it was investigating old criminal cases where science had moved on, to see if solutions differed. He felt the challenge was just what he was looking for and moving to that area was the perfect location for Donna's job too! They wasted no time looking for a suitable house to buy, no point renting and lining landlords' pockets when they could get a mortgage reasonably easily—Donna had been paying rent for years now so it would be good to feel that they would be buying their home.

The strange thing was that Elizabeth and Robert had bought their council home after all these years—as suggested by Margaret Thatcher—and they were also thrilled to finally own their home in their late seventies/early eighties! Never too late for anything in this world.

Donna and Derek found a lovely semi-detached three-bedroomed house in a village just outside Woking, both loved it as soon as they stepped inside, it felt homely and just what they were looking for, so subject to survey and mortgage all being ok, this would be their new home. The next three months were a whirl of activity, making phone calls, badgering solicitors and signing various forms and finally they had the keys. Initially, Derek was still living at home but would move in the house as soon as he started his new job, but as Donna was still flat-sharing, they decided to get a new kitchen and bathroom fitted before actually moving in.

Derek would 'camp' at the house and Donna would stay there when she wasn't working. As the house was fairly empty it was very easy to work in, and the new kitchen and bathroom were completed within the first two months. The builders had keys so came and went as they needed, Donna and Derek decorated what would be their bedroom and the sitting room, and they were ready to move in! Derek had been in his job for a month by this time, he had stayed over with Donna in the flat, the girls were going to miss her!

They decided to shelve the wedding till the following summer, they were spending quite a bit on their new home and, as far as they were concerned, the wedding was merely a formality and a chance to party! They both spent their summer holiday working on the house and the garden, Robert came over quite a lot with Polly and he took over the garden, clearing it and making suggestions but also asking Derek's opinion and running it past Donna. He was old-fashioned and wasn't too sure about them moving in together before the wedding, but as they seemed so happy together, he only mentioned this to Elizabeth, and she just said that it seemed the sensible thing to do.

She had an unkind thought: if she had lived with Robert before marrying him, she might have changed her mind—however, she quickly forgot that thought, she still felt for him when she saw how he struggled to deal with things that other people took in their stride and she knew that deep down, she loved him and he loved her—just didn't often show it.

One Sunday Derek's parents visited for the day so his dad could give him a hand—Donna was cooking a roast dinner only for the second time ever and it had been a great success, to her relief, as she wasn't a natural cook but knew that she needed to learn and realised that she quite enjoyed it—just nerve-racking trying to get everything ready at once. Derek's mum gave her a few tips which she found really useful so she told her how grateful she was. Her future in-laws were very fond of her and just thought how sad it was that they had wasted years when they could have been together, however, they had made good use of that time and now both had brilliant careers!

As they were saying their goodbyes, a car pulled up on the drive next door and a young family emerged—a little girl ran up to their front door with her dad behind her, and the mother took a younger child out of his car seat. They looked over to Donna and Derek and called out a greeting and asked how they were getting on. The lady said that her name was Sarah, and Paul, her husband, had just dashed indoors with their daughter who needed the bathroom but she obviously wanted to introduce their little family and talk to her new neighbours. Derek and Donna said that they were juggling moving in with Donna working at the Airport and Derek having started a new job. Paul emerged with the little girl, Roberta known as Bobbie—and the little boy looking shyly in his mother's arms was Sebastian, known as Seb.

They had moved in the house about seven years ago, been married for five years, Bobbie was four and Seb was nearly two. They said that they liked the area, the local schools were very good and they were near some beautiful countryside—they had just returned from a picnic and worn out the children— and themselves—but would love to get to know Donna and Derek and perhaps they might go out for dinner one evening, when they could get a babysitter. Donna said that sounded brilliant and Derek thought that would be great. Sarah said they ought to go indoors and get the children bathed and ready for bed but it was great to meet them and they would see them again soon.

Chapter 31

This was the beginning of a friendship that lasted a lifetime! The two couples found that they got on extremely well, and had similar opinions and ideals—Donna and Derek got married a year after they had moved in and Sarah and Paul were on the guest list. They said they would prefer not to bring their children, Sarah's parents would look after them and they then could enjoy themselves without worrying about the little ones—Donna didn't mind either way.

The wedding was a lovely occasion, Robert proudly gave Donna away, Elizabeth and Polly shed a tear, as did Dolly and it was a wonderful day. They spent their honeymoon on one of the Greek Islands and had a wonderfully relaxing time, watching sunsets and dining in lovely little tavernas—the tourists were all made very welcome as they were very important to the economy, so everywhere they went they were made to feel special.

On their return, life picked up where they left off but as Mr and Mrs instead of Mr and Miss. Their friendship with Paul and Sarah grew, they usually went there for dinner once or twice a month, it was easier as that meant that they didn't need to get babysitters, and on occasions they all went out for a meal or to a concert, but these didn't happen often. Sarah had given up her job to bring up the children, she had done clerical work in an office after leaving university and did hope that she might be able to work part-time when the children were both at school and retrain for a career. Bobbie was due to start school in September, but Seb was a way off yet, and a couple of mornings at nursery didn't give her much time to go to work.

Derek was loving his new job, found it absorbing and really interesting. He often came home late if he got engrossed in a certain project or if police were looking for a quick result. Donna wasn't enjoying her job quite as much, desk work at the airport was very mundane compared to being cabin crew, but she loved coming home every evening and was thinking more and more about changing careers and becoming a teacher. Watching Sarah coping with her two children made her think it would be nice to have a family of their own but it looked very hard handling these little people.

Sometimes, on a rare occasion that she had a day off she would go to Sarah for a cup of tea or coffee and would find herself playing with the children. Bobbie loved singing and dancing and the radio was always on—one day, she asked Donna if she was like Madonna on the radio and could she sing like Madonna as she had the same name. Donna explained that her name was 'Donna' and not 'Madonna' but Bobbie was determined to call her Madonna, as she really liked Madonna.

They did laugh about this and she told Derek when he came home. They babysat for their neighbours occasionally if they wanted a night out on their own, Donna had volunteered as she couldn't imagine what it must be like not to be able to go out for an evening when you felt like it.

However, not long after this, Donna discovered she was pregnant. She felt excited and couldn't wait to tell Derek, but then started to think how this baby would change their lives—would certainly turn them upside down. She also thought about her job and how that would change too! She had quite a commute to work and to find someone to look after a baby would be quite hard as she sometimes did long hours, as did Derek, so she would have to think about this carefully. However, the baby wouldn't arrive for a few months yet so they had time to make decisions. Derek was over the moon and they decided to wait till the first twelve-weeks had passed before telling anyone—not even the family or their lovely neighbours.

One day, she went to Sarah's to take her in some magazines so Sarah automatically put a cup of tea in front of her. She knew she couldn't drink it as it made her feel nauseous. She apologised to Sarah and said that she had only just finished a cup before coming round so didn't really want another cup. Sarah took one look at her and asked her when the baby was due.

Donna was very taken aback but laughed and asked her how she knew—she said that she just could tell and had suspected a week or so previously when they had spent time together. Bobbie came and threw herself at Donna asking her to read to her—and very sweetly thanked her when she had finished the story. She called her Madonna all the time now so Sarah then said that it would be quite appropriate for her to be known as Ma-donna, as she would very soon be a mother!

When Derek came home, Donna explained that the 'cat was out of the bag' so they decided to tell their families the good news. They went to Kent for the weekend and, of course, the families were delighted, especially Elizabeth and Robert, and Derek's parents. Polly and Thomas were also excited to be great grandparents, although Thomas had been rather unwell in recent months, so Polly hoped that this would give him something new to focus on. They were both well into their eighties now, Polly was still in good health—as was her dear friend Dolly—despite her disability she was still enjoying life in general and her gardening which kept her going, although these days she was doing slightly less and everything seemed to take longer.

Dr Gilbert had been retired for some time and although he had carried on working for a while during his early retirement, he had now completely finished work. He found that his memory wasn't what it once was and was giving Dolly and the family concerns due to lapses in his short-term memory. He was very forgetful and often forgot where he was or why he was there. This was a big worry for Dolly but she dealt with it as best she could and would speak to Ruth about her concerns.

Ruth had moved on from midwifery and was nursing in a geriatric ward. She was due to retire very soon as was her beloved Bob, his parents had passed away some time ago, they had retired and gone back to Jamaica as they hated the British winters and decided to spend their retirement in the sunshine where they still had relatives there and were well cared for. Ruth and Bob missed them and had promised themselves a visit to see them, but sadly never managed it during his parents' lifetime.

Ruth realised that her father had some form of dementia, a terrible disease that would get worse as his brain deteriorated and he would eventually become mentally detached from the real world. She gently explained this to Dolly which distressed her greatly but she wanted to care for her husband in their home for as long as she could. Ruth said that she would help as much as possible and maybe they could get a carer to come in and help daily to give Dolly some support, as she would surely need it.

Polly was very saddened by this news but was there for her friend whenever she needed her and made a point of visiting her as much as she could. Also, she felt that the more often she saw Dr Gilbert, the less he could forget her so Thomas would go with her and sit with him just talking about the weather, or sport, to keep his dying brain stimulated.

On a warm spring day in early April, a very noisy and red-faced Charlie made his arrival in this world to the delight of Donna (now often known as Ma-donna) and Derek, weighing in at nearly 9lbs. mother and baby were doing very well, despite being a big baby Ma-donna managed a natural birth. They were home after a couple of days in the maternity ward and Elizabeth came to stay for a few days to help them settle in and give Derek a hand with the domestic chores. Robert came to meet his new grandson during this time and brought Polly and Thomas with him, they were very happy to meet this little chap with the lusty voice.

He was a very hungry baby and as long as he was fed regularly, he was very contented in between times. He thrived and by the time he was four weeks old he was sleeping through the night. Ma-donna and Derek had heard horror stories of parents not sleeping for the first couple of years of a child's life and had braced themselves for the unknown, however, as long as Charlie had regular feeds, he was a very happy baby. They couldn't believe how lucky they were and when he was six months old, they thought it would be nice for Charlie to have a brother or sister.

This baby lark was an absolute breeze—the only dilemma was that she had thought she might go back to work when Charlie was six months old but she was thoroughly enjoying motherhood, and Derek liked having her at home. This was for purely selfish reasons which he readily confessed to—also he was earning enough to pay the bills, so was happy for Ma-donna to give up her job, certainly for the foreseeable future. He guessed she would want to work again at some point, she was an intelligent woman and being a full-time mother and housewife wasn't really on her agenda, but time would tell.

They had the conversation and she contacted her employers who were disappointed to lose her, however, she admitted that she would miss being at the airport and the bustle of thousands of people travelling all over the world, which was a job she had really loved.

She knew, deep down, she wanted to spend Charlie's early years with him, watching his development and for that reason she thought it would be great to have another baby in a very short time. Derek had no problem with this, they had both been only children and the thought of a sibling for Charlie seemed a lovely idea. She told Sarah of her plans, Bobbie adored Charlie but Seb seemed to resent him a little, he was used to Ma-donna playing with him but now Charlie was there she would lay him on the floor and would tell Seb to be careful and he couldn't understand why.

She then would try and put Charlie down to sleep so she could devote a bit of time to Seb and that pleased him. She was amazed that jealousy could rear itself in such a young child, but of course, it was the change in routine as much as anything, so she would address this when she could, likewise, Seb didn't like Sarah holding Charlie—he would invariably demand a drink or a book to be read if she held Charlie—anything to make her hand him back so she could give him her full attention.

Chapter 32

On Charlie's first birthday which was a lovely celebration attended by all the family except Thomas—he really was unwell and Polly was very concerned—however, she didn't want to miss seeing Charlie on his birthday so came for a short while with Elizabeth and Robert. They hoped that Ma-donna wouldn't mind their visit being curtailed as Polly was anxious about Thomas—of course this wasn't a problem and they enjoyed their time together. As they were leaving Ma-donna and Derek took this opportunity to announce that Baby Number Two would be due before Christmas, so they were all thrilled and went home very happy.

In September, Ma-donna and Derek took Charlie on holiday for the first time, he had just started walking so they went self-catering and had a cottage on the Devon coast. Charlie loved the sand and had great fun breaking the sandcastles that they were making for him. By this time Ma-donna was well into her pregnancy which, once again, had been trouble-free and was looking forward to meeting their new arrival sometime before Christmas.

Sarah told her that it might be hard work having a new baby with an eighteen-month-old toddler and said she would help whenever she could. Charlie would go and play with the older children when Ma-donna had her check-ups, so much easier without a young child in tow, and it also gave Charlie time away from his mother which was a good thing for him to get used to. The two families would sometimes go out at weekends for picnics when the weather was good, or to some indoor play area for the children, usually ending these crazy sessions with a family meal out.

They favoured the cheaper chain restaurants that catered for children, and although it meant the table covered in crayons and colourful sheets of paper, it kept them entertained. Charlie loved his food and always enjoyed eating out. He would go in a high chair and was always very well behaved.

Baby Sam made his entrance into the world fairly sedately in early November, an easy labour this time and he weighed in at just under 7lbs, so much smaller than Charlie and a lot quieter. Everyone was delighted at the new arrival and even Charlie didn't seem too unhappy at the addition to the family. He was quite curious and couldn't understand why Sam wouldn't play with him. His parents explained that he was very small and needed to sleep a lot, which would help him grow and he would soon be able to play.

Charlie accepted this and went happily to Sarah's to play with Bobbie and Seb, quite content to leave Ma-donna with his baby brother. Elizabeth, once again, came to stay for a few days to help Derek who had taken a couple of weeks off for everything to settle down a bit. Unlike Charlie, Sam didn't feed terribly well, little and often was his motto, which meant that Ma-donna felt she was on a hamster wheel, continually feeding, changing and putting him down to sleep, only for him to be awake thirty minutes to an hour later for another small feed.

She spoke to the midwife about this, wondering why she hadn't got another 'text book' baby that would have a good feed and sleep till the next time, allowing Ma-donna to rest between times. The midwife told her the obvious that all babies were different, Sam being smaller, didn't feed quite so gustily and she assured her that this would resolve itself as he started to put on weight.

Ma-donna was fine with this, just a bit surprised as to how different she felt compared to when Charlie arrived. On top of this, Charlie also needed attention and although he has his father and grandmother, Ma-donna also wanted to spend time with him in case he felt abandoned. After ten days she decided that she would bottle feed Sam to supplement him as that would mean that Derek could also do some feeds and Sam may get a bit more nutrition and might go longer between feeds. She spoke to Sarah who said that all babies were different and trial and error were the way forward, so for the time being, while Derek was home, she let him do at least one night feed so that she could catch up on some sleep.

Needless to say, after a few days she felt very much better and by the time Derek went back to work she was in a sort of routine, decided each morning at the time that Sam woke up and how enthusiastic he was about having his milk— so totally different to how things had been with Charlie.

Sarah was excellent, doing shopping and taking Charlie to play with Seb, they got on quite well now and Bobbie was at school so the boys played nicely together.

Christmas came and went in a blur, same old routine but with baubles and presents. They decided to have Christmas on their own, they couldn't really entertain and Elizabeth and Robert wanted to spend Christmas with Polly and Thomas—who was very poorly—they also wanted to see Dolly and Dr Gilbert who had deteriorated in the last few months and Ruth was looking for a care home, initially for respite for Dolly, so that he could go in for a couple of weeks, but if he settled down and Dolly agreed, it would become his permanent home.

A really difficult decision, they had enjoyed such a happy marriage and Dr Gilbert cared so much about Dolly, as she did for him, but she had to do what was in all their best interests and his safety, with Ruth's blessing. Dr Gilbert had taken to going out of the house very early in the morning, often in his slippers and pyjamas, and would be brought home in a police car—so Dolly had extra locks fitted so he couldn't get out, but in the event of a fire or other emergency, it would take time for them to get out of the house. He also had lost his temper in recent weeks getting really angry with Dolly for no reason but this was part of the symptoms of the dementia. Dolly understood this and although it really upset her, she knew he didn't mean it!

Chapter 33

Early in the new year, Thomas passed away in his sleep, he had caught a chill and Polly was caring for him giving him hot drinks and keeping to his medication, but one morning when she took him a cup of tea, he was lying very peacefully and she realised he had stopped breathing. She called an ambulance but sadly there was nothing that could be done. Everyone was very distraught, Elizabeth got in touch with Ma-donna and everyone else who needed to be told, breaking down each time she spoke to tell someone, she could barely believe that her lovely Grandpa was gone. She had some wonderful memories of him, but then she thought about Polly and how it would affect her; they had been married sixty-five years and had been so very happy during that time so Polly felt that they had a lot to be thankful for, but just at this time, this was no consolation.

The funeral was on a beautiful sunny and frosty day, snowdrops poking through the ground to remind everyone that spring wasn't far away. The service was very well attended, and Ma-donna and Derek had left Charlie and Sam—for the first time—with Sarah. Ma-donna was concerned about her having both the children, but she said that it would be better for them to go to the funeral without children so they could have some time to themselves and with the family.

Ma-donna was really grateful when it came to it, but was anxious that Sam might be difficult and have an erratic feeding day. After a cup of tea and a sandwich they found Elizabeth and said that they should be getting back, Elizabeth said that she would be in touch and Ma-donna promised to go and see Polly soon, so she could spend a bit of quality time with her. Today was Thomas' day and everyone wanted to be round Polly, so they would visit her soon and take the little ones, which would really cheer her up.

When Ma-donna and Derek got home, they went straight to Sarah's to get the children. Apparently, they had been really good, Sam had fed reasonably well and had a couple of short sleeps, but seemed quite happy in his bouncy chair watching the other children so Sarah wasn't too fraught after caring for four children for the day. Ma-donna gave her friend a big hug, she was still feeling very emotional and told her how grateful she was.

Now that the funeral was over Polly settled into a new routine, getting used to life without Thomas wasn't easy but he had been very poorly of late so felt a bit of comfort knowing he was now at peace. She got through those early days basically not doing very much. She used to phone Dolly and have long chats with her, she was at a loose end as Dr Gilbert had now gone into a care home permanently, Dolly would visit him three times a week, but the rest of the time was her own. She and Polly would visit each other, and occasionally would go and see Elizabeth. They were both starting a new life, as it were, and as always, they spent a lot of time together, just like the old days.

Ma-donna came to see them one day with the children, just stayed for a cup of tea before going to visit Elizabeth as she didn't want to tire her gran or her Auntie Dolly, however, they were so happy to see the children and the boys were on best behaviour. Sam was growing fast, but was still quite small compared to Charlie at the same age. He was enjoying baby rice now which seem to satisfy him more than his milk did and was a lot more content and after three long months, was actually going through the night.

One lovely spring weekend, Sarah and Paul asked Ma-donna and Derek if they fancied a picnic, the weather was warm for early spring and had been really dry, so the grass shouldn't be too damp and it would be nice to get the children out. They prepared food and the men organised bats and balls and a few outdoor toys and they had a fantastic afternoon. While they were out, Paul suddenly said that they were thinking of booking a camping trip to the Lake District during the summer holiday and wondered if Ma-donna and Derek would like to join them.

Ma-donna suddenly had a vision of nappies, endless bottles with steriliser and her initial reaction was an emphatic NO. However, they talked for a while and when Sarah told her how well equipped some of the camp sites were, it could be fun, alternatively, they could maybe have a couple of caravans. Sarah said that would be a good start then another year, once the baby stage was over, they could maybe think about camping.

The Alpha Male in Paul resisted somewhat, thinking caravans were the soft option, but Ma-donna thought that the soft option sounded great. They booked for a week in August, really needed to be in the school holidays as Bobbie was now at school but that was fine, and they really did have a lovely time.

The caravan park was in a scenic spot, far enough from the water not to be a problem and there was plenty of space for the children to play; there were other families there so the children had a great time and the fresh air tired them out, so they were ready for bed earlier than they would have been at home. The two families ate together and as they were so lucky with the weather, most of their meals were outside.

They had lots of barbecues and much wine and beer was enjoyed up to a point, as they kept a watchful eye on the children, but once the children had all settled for the night the camp took on a different atmosphere, very tranquil as there were young families everywhere, and they would relax and talk about anything other than children.

Ma-donna still hoped to get back to work at some point and was leaning very much towards teaching, she would need to do a postgraduate course which she could do from home, and would like to teach languages in a secondary school. Derek would support her with whatever she would like to do. Sarah also wanted to work and thought she would try for a teacher's assistant job at the children's school—although she had a degree and could also have done a postgraduate course—when Ma-donna put this to her, she said she would think about it but felt that doing a course and looking after the family might be too much.

Ma-donna herself saw this as a pipe dream but said she would look into the course when they got home. Coping with a two-year old and six-month-old was a full-time job but she felt that she needed something extra to focus on, where Sarah preferred the easier option, just for the moment. She said she would make enquiries and maybe go for that once Seb was settled at school.

The men then got involved in the conversation—they felt that the extra income would be very welcome as bringing up a young family was quite expensive—so they said that they would happily use some of their annual holiday to do things with the children if the girls needed to do some studying. This was discussed over a couple of bottles of wine on a warm summer's evening when all the children were asleep—and from there—everything seemed possible. They eventually retired for the night all very content with their lot and feeling fortunate that they had such a wonderful friendship.

Part 7

Chapter 34

Over the next few years which all seem to morph into each other quite a lot happened. Ma-donna, Derek, Sarah and Paul enjoyed some wonderful holidays. They did a couple of caravan breaks in England, then started travelling to Europe to do camping trips visiting France and Spain and for their other neighbours it was a familiar sight at the beginning of each August to see the two families setting off in their cars with roof boxes packed to the gills. They usually managed just over a fortnight which would allow for their travelling time as it could take a couple of days to get down to the South of France or into Spain. They also went to Austria on one occasion just for a change; the children enjoyed all the walking and seeing the mountains but did miss the beach, so they decided to stick to beach holidays in future.

Most of their holidays were very successful, except for one year when the children, one by one, all caught chicken pox; there were other children on site who also had it, impossible to say where it had started but suffice to say it got rather stressful at times, smothering four children with calamine lotion several times a day in the heat. That year they were in Normandy and decided to go home a few days early, but other than that, their holidays were usually very successful and something they would talk about for a long time to come.

Dr Gilbert sadly passed away just after Charlie had started school. He had deteriorated quite considerably over time and although Dolly was devastated at the news, she had got used to him not being there as he was in the care home, and felt that her lovely husband had actually left her some time ago, and had been grieving for months for his old self, which had been gone for some time.

Ruth, Bob and Errol helped her organise the funeral and Simon and Steven were home for several days so they could also be part of saying goodbye to a man who had been a wonderful father. Dolly appreciated all their support at this time, as well as Polly who stayed with her till the family came so that she was never alone with her thoughts—Polly was still getting used to life without

Thomas—it really wasn't easy, but Elizabeth and Robert were very good to her and visited often.

Ma-donna and Sarah decided to both go for a postgraduate course to enable them to teach. When Sarah realised the earning potential of becoming a teacher, she felt she would like to try and get qualified. She wanted to teach primary children across the board, where Ma-donna would be teaching in secondary school. They often studied together at weekends when Derek and Paul, true to their word, did things with the children.

If the weather was bad, they went to the cinema, otherwise they did outdoor activities which they all loved. The girls would have time to study as well as doing a certain amount in the evenings, and also during the day although Sarah was already helping at school with listening to children reading.

This made Ma-donna feel quite guilty, however, she just didn't think she had the patience to listen to children reading—she preferred older children in her teaching role. However, when Sarah was working, she would meet the children from school and take them home for tea which would give Sarah some time to herself when she got in.

The children all got on well, with Bobbie being 'the matriarch' of the little foursome. She instigated all the games they played and they followed her, all eager to please—so whether they played 'schools' or 'mums and dads' she decided which part each child played. Occasionally they would dress up, again with her guidance and put little shows on for their parents who painstakingly sat through many of these, with Bobbie always having the star role, her reward for her input with the younger children.

They all looked up to her and of course she loved her role as organiser as she was quite naturally rather bossy when in the company of the younger children. With her own friendship group, she was very different. Somehow, being with her younger brother and little neighbours brought out her maternal instinct.

Chapter 35

Polly and Dolly were spending quite a lot of time together, were both in their early nineties and although they had health issues, they enjoyed the odd day out for tea, coffee and short shopping trips and occasionally an afternoon playing Bingo. They used to go to Bingo quite regularly about twenty years previously; they stopped when their lives changed, and when they recently talked about it, thought they would like to go on some occasions and they thoroughly enjoyed the afternoon sessions. They were known, jokingly, as the terrible twosome and this had been a label, they had carried all their lives. Their friendship had been a strong one throughout their whole lives, living through happy and sad times and always there for each other. That would only change when the inevitable happened, and as Ruth and Elizabeth used to speak about these two wonderful ladies and their friendship, they felt that it would definitely go on beyond the grave, which conjured up all sorts of images, and this made them laugh.

Elizabeth and Robert now in their early seventies loved their grandchildren, and would spend time with them, even overnight sometimes if Ma-donna had some studying to do or had to go to lectures, which she did occasionally. They would also happily look after Bobbie and Seb as the children played well together, and sometimes that would be a big help when Elizabeth was trying to organise food for them all or just wanted a quiet moment.

Robert always enjoyed being in the garden and would often play out there with the boys, kicking a ball around or playing cricket with them. Their garden wasn't set out the way he would have liked, it was mainly laid out to lawn with a trampoline and a slide, as well as a goal post and plenty of room to run around. There were a few flower beds that Ma-donna would look after, but often flowers would get broken by stray balls, so apart from a few pots at the front of the house, gardening was very much a non-event, apart from keeping the grass cut!

Derek and Ma-donna said that when the boys were older, they would redesign the garden to make an entertaining space with decking and barbecue area, but at the moment they felt that this would be a waste of time and would curtail the children's activities. They loved watching the children playing out as they felt they were safe and could keep an eye on them.

Ruth and Elizabeth still met up occasionally, either in London or in Kent. They were ladies of leisure these days and enjoyed their time together. They would meet up for lunch and occasionally go to the theatre or watch a film. Ruth was very excited on one occasion as Errol, now in his mid-thirties, had just been promoted to Detective Inspector, he had worked his way up the ranks from being a PC, had passed all his exams with flying colours and was proving to be a great DI.

He had a very good Detective Sergeant as his sidekick, a lovely Asian lady who had come over from Kenya in the seventies in her early teens when Idi Amin had thrown her family out, among many others, which meant her parents arrived here with what they stood up in plus a few pounds, but they had worked hard, bought a business with other family members which was thriving and had all lived in very crowded conditions until they could all afford their own homes.

Twenty years on, her and her immediate family had a lovely home, as did their other relatives and had settled well in this country—sadly, though, the main thing she shared with Errol was the racism, both inside and outside the force. However, they would both rise above it and felt this is why they had done so well. It still hurt at times, especially when it was expressed by their—so called—colleagues, but things were improving slowly. Errol suffered more when he was an ordinary policy constable. He didn't get the support he could have done with at certain times, and on one occasion he ended up in hospital with minor injuries as his plea for back-up in a nasty robbery had been ignored.

On that occasion he reported the incident to his superior, with a certain amount of trepidation, but fortunately the complaint was taken seriously, looked into and the person responsible was made an example of. Although that didn't make Errol Mr Popular at the time, at least he showed that he was prepared to stand up for himself, and nothing like that ever happened again. When they announced his promotion, there was a long silence as two or three people were also hoping for promotion, however, one person stood up and congratulated him and was followed by the rest of his colleagues, so however genuine or false it was, they had all wished him well in public.

He was determined to work hard and do his best, as was Aisha, his lovely assistant. She had got used to being called 'Paki' especially when apprehending a suspect but again, she rose above that. Apart from being from an ethnic minority, she was also female, so the jibes from her male colleagues varied from being racist to being politically incorrect, but again, this didn't bother her and, in the end, they had to agree that she was a good person, as was Errol and just wanted to keep people safe and help them when needed.

Errol was single and liked it that way, he had been in a couple of relationships but with his job with erratic hours, he had often been late or missed dates and eventually, after several break-ups, he decided it would be simpler to stay single. He was a very handsome lad and got on well with Aisha, she liked being single, hoped that her parents wouldn't be lining her up for an arranged marriage, still a tradition in their culture, but felt more westernised, having lived in Britain for over twenty years, and hoped that when the time came, she could choose her own life partner.

After months of studying, just before her fortieth birthday, Ma-donna passed her postgraduate certificate of education so could go out into the big wide world and get herself a job. Sarah still had a little way to go, but she was helping at the school and knew that there was a vacancy coming up in the next few months at the children's school, so felt she would be in with a good chance if she applied, as long as she graduated.

Thus, the September that Sam started school, Ma-donna began job-hunting with a view to starting after October half-term or January, depending what she could find. Sarah would be applying for a post where she already helped and that would be for a January start, she had also done well in her course.

The day Sarah passed Paul took them all out for a lovely meal to say 'well done' to both ladies, the children went too, so it was quite a noisy affair, but the restaurant were very good and made sure that the waiter entertained the children. He took them to a viewing area so that they could see their pizzas being made, and choose their own toppings while the parents enjoyed a well-deserved glass of wine.

Both the ladies got jobs starting in January, Sarah at the children's school which she had hoped for and Ma-donna at a comprehensive school in Woking. They were very enthusiastic about her knowledge of languages and they taught both French and German, but felt that Spanish could also be introduced as an extra-curricular activity. So many people were going to Spain for their holidays and even buying apartments over there so a spattering of Spanish would go a long way. She was then approached about doing private tuition, however, she felt that might be a step too far as she would already be working full-time and the boys were still quite young, but was happy for any parents to join the extra-curricular class.

Ma-donna and Sarah both made arrangements for after-school care for their children. There was an after-school club which was great, so the children were there for three evenings a week, one day a week Elizabeth would pick them all up from school, which they all enjoyed and, on a Friday, either Paul or Derek would be home in time to pick them up, so everything was very well organised and the children were very content.

That summer, they did all push the boat out and hired a villa in the South of France for two weeks, it had its own swimming pool and was in a glorious setting near the Pyrenees; it was an amazing time for them all, no more camping and cooking on a primus stove or camp fire, this had everything they could wish for and each bedroom had an en-suite, no more queuing up for showers and toilets, wandering around in the middle of the night with a torch through a field, this was 'the real deal.'

Derek and Paul were so very proud of what their wives had achieved and this was truly the holiday of a lifetime. When they eventually got home, the children as brown as berries and swimming like fish, they were able to relax and unwind while the men returned to work, and they decided that working in schools was the best idea they had ever had and worth all the hard work.

Chapter 36

Christmas 1992 was quite a lively affair and the Queen in her speech referred to this last year as being an Annus Horribilus due to various events that happened during that year. However, despite that, Ma-donna and Derek hosted Christmas with Elizabeth, Robert and Polly spending three days with them. A busy and hectic household also involving Boxing Day drinks and buffet lunch with Sarah and Paul and her parents, so very lively indeed.

Derek would have loved to have hosted his own parents over the Christmas period, however, Justin and Penelope were very set in their ways and seemed to prefer their own company. Derek and Ma-donna would occasionally take the boys over for Sunday lunch; however, the house was so very pristine that Ma-donna used to get very nervous as the boys could be clumsy at times, and Penelope had some beautiful china ornaments in her lounge. The last couple of times they had visited Charlie had spilled orange squash all over the carpet, accidently, of course, but nevertheless caused quite a fuss, then last time Sam broke a mug, so they would often pop in for a cup of tea after visiting Elizabeth and Robert, thus keeping the visits short and sweet.

They felt sad for the boys as they felt that the discipline was good for them, learning how to behave in a restricted environment, however, they couldn't act normally, and Derek felt that his parents missed out on the boys' progress as they would go very quiet and shy as soon as they entered their paternal grandparents' home.

Justin and Penelope both played golf and belonged to a club that hosted lots of competitions, which involved a great deal of their social life. Also, Penelope was Secretary of her local WI which was a very popular group, she would organise speakers for their meetings, and various lunches and afternoon teas, so their lives were very full. They always remembered the boys' birthdays and were generous with their gifts, but Derek was saddened that the boys didn't have the same relationship with them as they had with Robert and Elizabeth, and Polly, of course.

New Year's Eve was a slightly quieter occasion with the neighbours having dinner together, letting the children stay up a bit later, then when they all fell asleep in Sarah and Paul's bed, Ma-donna and Derek crept home in the early hours saying that they would collect their children a bit later.

In January when everyone was back at school and work, the weather was very seasonal and it snowed relentlessly for forty-eight hours, making roads treacherous and journeys to and from work quite difficult. Derek got home very late one evening, Ma-donna was terribly worried and when he got home, he said that he had abandoned the car and walked five miles in blizzard conditions. The children were having a wonderful time playing in the snow and the school closed for two days as the heating had broken down. Ma-donna still had to go to work but Sarah was at home so she cared for the children.

While at school, Ma-donna was called to the headmaster's office as there had been a phone call for her from someone sounded very distressed. He had taken the number down and said he would get her to return the call. Ma-donna, initially thought something had happened to one of the children, but realised it wasn't Sarah's number, it was her parents' telephone number. She went very cold, wondering what could have happened to make them ring the school.

With a shaking hand she held the receiver and dialled the number and Elizabeth immediately picked up the phone; Ma-donna was having trouble understanding her as she was sobbing and she feared that something had happened to her father. She patiently hung on trying to get Elizabeth to calm down but then Robert took the phone from her and told Ma-donna what was distressing Elizabeth so much.

Obviously, he was fine and despite the anxiety she felt, she could honestly say that was the first time she had witnessed her father doing something as decisive as this, as Elizabeth always dealt with any emergencies and was normally very calm.

Robert proceeded to explain that Dolly had a hospital appointment so Polly had agreed to go with her and they had booked taxis to take them and pick them up. On the way home, it would appear that a lorry that had skidded on ice and gone out of control, hitting the taxi head on. The outcome was that the taxi driver and his two passengers had all died at the scene. The lorry driver survived and was in hospital, however, the lifelong friends that had been through so much together had both died in the crash, and processing this was too much for any of them to bear in that moment.

When Ma-donna was able to explain to the headteacher what had occurred he immediately told her to go home and deal with anything that she needed to, and to return to work when she felt she could. He would get a supply teacher in to cover her classes for the rest of the week and they would go from there. He understood her distress and offered to drive her home, as she had travelled on the bus due to the snow, rather than risk the drive. However, she was in no fit state to go on public transport and meekly accepted the kind gesture, just grabbing her coat and bag and leaving it to the headmaster to explain to her colleagues the situation on his return.

When he pulled up outside her house, she saw that Derek's car was there, he had obviously collected it from where it was left and had managed to get home. The children were still with Sarah, Derek appeared at the front door and seemed very surprised to see her, and assumed she was unwell. The headmaster made a hasty departure when she alighted from the car as he felt she needed to tell Derek the dreadful news.

Derek could see that she had been crying and when he asked her what the matter was, fresh tears flowed but she managed to say that her poor gran and her friend Dolly had been killed in a tragic accident, most probably caused by the weather. He was stunned, then phoned Sarah and asked if she would mind having the children for a little while longer while Ma-donna phoned her parents again and could have another talk with Elizabeth. She sounded more composed but dreadfully quiet, they really didn't know what to say to each other, so Ma-donna spoke to Robert and just asked him to keep an eye on her mum and let her know if she could do anything. She said that when the weather improved in a day or two, she would come to see her, and he said that would be nice.

The rest of the day passed in a blur, she went to Sarah and brought the boys home amid much protest, but she needed to explain to Charlie and Sam in simple terms what had happened to their great grandmother and her friend and not to worry if people around them were feeling sad, it was a normal thing to happen.

The boys sat quietly while she spoke to them and then asked if they could go out and play in the snow. Derek went out with them and built a snowman, then they had a snowball fight; Bobbie and Seb hearing the commotion asked if they could come over and Paul, who had just come home from work, decided to join them.

He had been briefed about the tragedy that had occurred that morning and felt very sorry for the whole family. The only consolation was that they had gone together, if ever any friends needed to be together till the end of their days, it was Polly and Dolly, however, it was still heartbreaking for them all.

Ma-donna spent time with Elizabeth in the next few days helping to arrange the funeral. Nicholas was over from Canada, he adored his Auntie Dolly and although his parents had hardly been over during the years since they had emigrated, Nicholas had been over to London several times and always visited his Auntie Dolly and Dr John, as he called him. He had come over a while after Dr Gilbert had passed away and Dolly always loved his visits. He was now retired from the Mounties, had been happily married for many years, they had three children and five grandchildren.

Betty and Stan had passed away a few years ago, two years apart. Stan had lung cancer, partly due to many years of heavy smoking and Betty had emphysema, again, aggravated by cigarettes, but they both felt that although they eventually realised the dangers of smoking, the damage was already done and they didn't see much point in the change in lifestyle. Nicholas would tell them, at times, as would his children—how bad for one's health smoking was, however, all they said was what was done was done.

Nicholas was obviously very distraught at losing his Auntie Dolly and Polly, of course, of whom he was very fond. He felt that the circumstances were horrendous and should never have happened. He spoke about the roads in Canada being virtually impassable for several months in the year, but somehow, they had ways of dealing with it, and couldn't understand why a cold snap lasting under a week could create such carnage.

Elizabeth let him go on, as it seemed to make him feel better and they proceeded to arrange the funerals. They jointly decided that the friends should share the service as they had shared so much throughout their lives, and that the service should be in the village church where they were christened as babies, taught Sunday School to younger children and were themselves married there. However, the village had changed considerably over the years. Some of the cottages had been knocked together to make bigger living accommodation with much modernisation in a sympathetic way, keeping some of the character—and some of the cottages were now holiday lets, and very popular they were too.

However, the church was still there, as was the village pub so it was decided to hold the wake there after the service, and both friends would be interred in the graveyard behind the church, as were their parents before them.

Ma-donna and Derek, after several mind changes, decided that they would take the boys to the funeral as they had explained to them what had happened and that people would be sad, so although they were only six and nearly eight, they felt that in a small way, the boys would cheer Elizabeth and Robert up. Sarah said that they could have stayed with her which would have worked equally as well, but Ma-donna wanted them to understand that they were part of a family and it would be nice for them to be there and say their goodbyes also, as this is what Ma-donna told them funerals were about.

In the event, it all went very well, Robert delivered a beautiful eulogy for Polly which included much about Dolly and Nicholas did the eulogy for Dolly which obviously involved Polly too. Tears and laughter in equal measures for these two legends and a deep sense of peace seemed to come from the thought that they were back where they had started nearly one hundred years ago.

Chapter 37

Ma-donna was very concerned about Elizabeth, she was obviously grieving for Polly as they all were, and for Dolly too, but Elizabeth had been so very close to her mum all her life, and her mum understood a lot about her relationship with Robert, which wasn't quite like Polly's relationship with Thomas.

Although Polly understood that Elizabeth wasn't as happy as she might have been with Robert, she never judged him and always treated him as a well-loved son-in-law, putting his issues down to the way he was treated during the war, and also his upbringing, having never met his father, so all in all, Elizabeth knew she could talk to Polly about her problems, and Polly would never interfere despite feeling sad for the way Elizabeth's marriage had turned out. However, Robert had got better over the years, as Elizabeth had never pressurised him but he still wouldn't go abroad, and of course, Elizabeth had dealt with that by travelling on her own or with Ma-donna; Polly was going to leave a massive hole in all their lives.

Ma-donna had understood her father's problems over the years as she was growing up, however, she didn't know how badly he had made Elizabeth feel in the early years of their marriage, but she knew that her mother was a very special lady, and right now, she was very concerned about her. Her Grandmother had been a rock to her mother, understanding the difficulties she had faced with her marriage to Robert. Ma-donna knew that life hadn't always been easy for her mother but Elizabeth loved Robert and had always been very loyal to him. Ma-donna thought that she would try and see her mother a little bit more often, on a one-to-one, to make sure she could open up if she needed to. This wasn't easy with two lively young boys but Ma-donna felt that she would make a point of doing this, however difficult.

Soon, it was summer once again and Bobbie had finished her first year in secondary school, she was really enjoying it and was growing up fast. These days she found the boys a bit tedious at times and would often let them go and play football or other games without involving herself, preferring to go out with friends of her own age.

Seb and Charlie both liked school, but Sam struggled at times, he would far prefer to be at home. He was a very bright boy and Sarah had suggested to Ma-donna that maybe he was too clever and found school boring whereas the other two lads quite enjoyed their classes. The boys all had activities outside the school, they all played for their local boys' football club but were all in different age groups.

They also belonged to the Cubs and hoped to become Scouts when they were old enough. Sam enjoyed these activities; it was just school that he wasn't keen on. Sarah had covertly checked at times to make sure he wasn't being bullied, as she worked there, or whether there were other reasons why he wouldn't enjoy school, but couldn't find anything out of the ordinary.

The two families still went abroad on holiday, the villa having been a great success, this had now been repeated a few times. Sarah kindly asked if Elizabeth might like to join them with Robert, of course, if he felt he could as this villa was huge and there were plenty of rooms. The boys, from past experience enjoyed sharing one room, which gave them a spare en-suite room so Sarah suggested this to Ma-donna knowing how worried she was about her mother.

At first, Elizabeth said she couldn't possibly gate-crash their holiday but was persuaded in the end that this was an invitation, and, of course, Robert didn't really want to come. He said he wasn't feeling very well, couldn't pin-point anything specific, just felt out of sorts.

The holiday was a great success, Ma-donna managed some good quality time with Elizabeth, and Elizabeth was happy to stay at home in the evenings if the adults wanted to go out. Most of the time they all went out together, but on one occasion they took advantage and the four of them went out for a very luxurious meal, again, a change from Pizza and Burgers! Elizabeth cooked for the children and herself on that occasion and she was very happy to make herself useful.

Christmas was upon them again and Elizabeth and Robert spent it with Ma-donna and Derek, Robert was fine staying overnight with the family as he felt at ease there. It was their first Christmas without Polly and Dolly so it had its moments but all in all it went very well.

However, they were all concerned about Robert's health, he had said before their holiday that he didn't feel right, and he had several episodes where he would feel very anxious and become disorientated; fortunately, he usually stayed home if he was feeling under the weather, so the doctors couldn't find anything really wrong with him. They put the episodes down to urine infections and treated him each time with antibiotics. He was fine over the Christmas period, but once again, in late January, he was very unwell and was talking gibberish so Elizabeth took him to A and E and they admitted him for tests.

A few days later, Elizabeth was called in to see the consultant who had been carrying out tests and he broke the news to them both that Robert was suffering from prostate cancer. This was a huge shock, but explained why he had felt so ill at times. Obviously, Elizabeth and Robert were very upset and told Ma-donna as soon as they could, said that he would be undergoing chemotherapy treatment to reduce the size of the tumour, followed by an operation. This was a lot to take in and they all felt that Robert did not deserve this, however, he took it quite well considering, and said that he would get on with the treatment as soon as he could, to get rid of this 'monster' invading his body.

Chapter 38

Robert coped with his treatment and everything that went with it with great courage, but sadly lost his fight over the next three years, and finally passed away in 1996 at the age of seventy-seven. He had never grumbled during that time accepting the chemo, the operations and the constant knock-backs, each time he thought he was getting better, this monster would pop up in another part of his body constantly attacking him, and in the end, he passed away at home with the family round him.

Elizabeth didn't want him to go to a hospice, and although the work load for her was unrelenting, she wanted to look after Robert herself, which she did with help from cancer charity nurses, who were absolutely brilliant. They would make sure she managed to get some sleep, always had the kettle on if she was having a low moment which enabled her to keep Robert home until the end.

Ruth came to stay with her a few times which was a great help and she felt she could speak openly with her, and not burden Ma-donna and Derek too much, who were being as supportive as they could be. The boys were also there when their grandad passed and they accepted it as the normal course of events. Sam asked Elizabeth if she was also going to die, and she replied that she would at some point, but not yet, and he wasn't to worry about it. Charlie seemed to accept it and didn't have too many questions.

Charlie was now in secondary school with Seb who was a couple of years ahead of him, and Bobbie had started at sixth form college after doing well in her GCSEs. Sam was still in primary school and seemed to be enjoying it a little bit more as he was getting older. He liked helping other children who would struggle with either maths problems or spelling, he was a very bright lad and one teacher had actually realised that by getting him to help others, he had something to focus on and he really was liking school a lot more than he had previously.

Ma-donna had Sarah to thank for that as she had persevered to find out why Sam was bored on a good day, and disruptive on a bad day as she knew he was a good lad having known him all his life and she tried really hard to get to the bottom of the problem, eventually realising that helping others made him feel useful and gave him a focus.

Sam went on to do extremely well at secondary school, was in the top stream in every academic subject, played football and cricket for the school, and his teachers really challenged him so that he could never be bored.

Ma-donna was concerned about Elizabeth, she wasn't coping as well as she hoped she would after losing Robert, the garden was getting her down and she knew he would have hated the way it was looking at the moment; she had never been gifted with 'green fingers' despite Dolly's efforts over the years spending time with Robert discussing the seasons and the progress of their various crops. It took her all her time to do the weeding, Derek had gone over a few times to help out but had suggested that she might need to take on a gardener once in a while, just to keep it under control.

However, the thought of someone other than family tending Robert's beloved garden was not something she could think about—Robert's garden was so much more than just a garden, it was his place of safety, somewhere he could process all his insecurities and where he would hide from the real world when life became too much for him, as it often had.

Ma-donna tentatively suggested to Derek that perhaps Elizabeth might think about moving house—Derek had been thinking about re-doing their own garden—their boys were growing up and the days of ball games were now behind them—they needed a much bigger space now—and he had visions of creating an entertaining space with flower beds here and there and a summerhouse at the bottom of the garden. He then wondered if it might be worth building an extension at the back of the house which would suit Elizabeth where she could make her home with them, having her own bedsitting room with an en-suite where she could be independent while sharing her life with the family when she felt she wanted to.

Chapter 39

Again, the years flew by—the Millennium was looming with all the concerns about technology and how everything might crash as 1999 became 2000! Bobbie went to university to study law, Seb wanted to be a PE teacher so he would be off to Uni after his 'A' levels and Charlie was doing GCSEs. Sam was going to start GCSEs the following year as some of the teachers thought he would do well in certain subjects—so he would be able to put more effort in the remaining subjects the following year! Ma-donna and Derek were proud of their boys but did wonder where Sam got his brains from. As Elizabeth told them many times, his parents had done well so why shouldn't he? Charlie thought he would like to be an electrician, he liked figuring things out and had often thought about how all the appliances at home worked, so felt college might be the way for him to go after his exams. He really didn't want a desk job, he wanted to be active, he detested paper work, but his parents did explain that if he became an electrician, he would need to do a certain amount of paperwork to survive.

Sarah and Paul were also proud of Bobbie's and Seb's achievements and the two couples often felt they needed to count their blessings when they heard of other youngsters going off the rails through truancy often followed by shop-lifting or drug-taking—they would often see young women about Bobbie's age pushing prams and whether it was their chosen path or whether it had been thrust upon them, they all felt there was so much more to do in life before settling down and having a family.

Derek knew only too well how things could go very wrong in a heartbeat with the experience he had with Linda all those years ago. He often felt he was so fortunate to have been given a second chance—he and Ma-donna were great together so he was thankful that everything had worked out for them.

When he suggested his plan to Ma-donna about Elizabeth moving in with them, albeit with her own space, Ma-donna felt very moved and thought again how fortunate she was to have such a thoughtful husband. They talked over all the issues this situation could bring up—the boys were growing up and were far from quiet, the house often noisy with their friends popping in and out, sometimes it was like Piccadilly Circus and how would Elizabeth cope with this as she was getting older. She was very tolerant and adored the boys but she wasn't used to the chaos that reigned at times.

Also, if she became unwell, with both of them at work all day she would be alone, however, that would be the same as if she was on her own, but it would be a big responsibility on Derek and Ma-donna's shoulders, but again, they would cope.

They spoke to Charlie and Sam, saying what they were planning including building an extension and plans for the garden. Charlie said he was cool with all that and he loved his grandma and missed his grandad terribly, so thought it might be nice—Sam said that if his grandma came to stay with them, she might not die yet and that seemed to please him.

When they went to visit Elizabeth and told them of their plans—just a suggestion—initially her reaction was that she couldn't possibly leave the house that had been their home for most of their married life—however, they explained the benefits of living under their roof—while keeping her independence—so she said that she was very touched by their suggestion and would definitely give it some thought.

They also said that they had talked this over with the boys who were both enthusiastic about having her with them, and as she would have her own space, she could take herself off whenever she felt the need, while they would share the kitchen—that would be the only issue—but again, they would be flexible with this. She re-iterated how very touched she was that this suggestion was being made and said that she would think long and hard about this possibility and everything it would involve, but would let them know her decision very soon.

She phoned them three days later to say that she had spoken to an estate agent who had valued the house, it seemed it was worth a lot more than she had ever imagined. Robert and Elizabeth had paid a very reasonable price for their house, which had been a council house, and because it was on a corner plot with a huge garden, it was now worth a lot of money. After the crash in the early '90s, things were picking up nicely in the property market so it would appear that this would be a good time to sell up.

The estate agent could sense Elizabeth had reservations about selling the house, she had lived there a long time and had lots of memories, so he refrained from saying what a wonderful buy it would be for a family as with all the land, they could build a massive extension and still have a big garden. It would appear to be the wrong thing to say and he really wanted to have this house on his books as he felt it would sell very quickly, but experience told him that sensitivity and tact were needed. Some of his younger colleagues would have gone into this house raving about all the possibilities, but this wasn't the way to go. He left Elizabeth with a rough figure of what the house might fetch and suggested she should think about it and give him a ring if she wanted to go ahead.

Elizabeth told Ma-donna how she had got on with the estate agent and was thinking of ringing him back to tell him to put it on the market. However, she wanted to speak to the family again, so Ma-donna suggested she came down for the weekend so that they could discuss everything at length. Derek had made a rough plan of what the extension would look like but needed her thoughts on all this.

Only if she was happy with their plans would she put the house on the market. Ma-donna met Elizabeth at the station, she still drove locally but didn't do long drives anymore as she found the motorway a bit daunting with the way everyone drove so fast, so she was happier to travel on the train, and use her car for short journeys.

The boys welcomed her with enthusiasm and Sam said that he was looking forward to her being with them all the time. She warmed to this young lad, he was so very full of love for her and very openly affectionate. Charlie was also very fond of her but didn't wear his heart on his sleeve like his brother did. They had a lovely family supper full of chatter and laughter, then Sarah popped round to ask if the boys would like to go out with them for the day on Sunday to give Derek and Ma-donna chance to speak to Elizabeth without getting interrupted.

They were good lads but could be quite a distraction when wanting food—which was almost every hour of every day—or help with homework, or a lift to friends, so it would be lovely to have a few hours to iron out issues for both parties.

To be fair, it all went well. Elizabeth told them how much she would get for the house—far more than any of them imagined—and with that she insisted that she wanted to pay for some of the building work that they would undertake. They would need planning permission as they thought they would extend right across the house and some way out to give Elizabeth a decent sized room, together with an en-suite shower room and at the same time they could also extend the kitchen, which would give them more space to move around if they both needed to use the kitchen at the same time.

That sorted, Elizabeth said she would contact the agent when she got home and Derek would get an architect to draw out plans and get some estimates. They assured Elizabeth that should the house go through before the building work was done, she could move in anyway then she would be on hand to put the finishing touches to her new quarters. Obviously, she would have to get rid of some furniture, however, they told her that she could bring anything she wanted and all her things could be stored in their spare room and garage, if the house sale went through quickly.

The boys were very excited when they were told it was a done deal and said they couldn't wait for Grandma to stay with them all the time—Ma-donna explained that she would need some peace and quiet so they were not to assume that they could barge in her room whenever the fancy took them. Elizabeth said that they would sort out some ground rules when the time came, but she was also looking forward to seeing more of all of them, as well as their lovely neighbours and she said she was feeling positive for the first time since losing Robert.

Part 8

Chapter 40

The Millennium happened with lots of celebrations, parties and fireworks and technology got through it all without a hitch. Despite all the horror stories of what could possibly go wrong with microwaves, computers and mobile phones, to name but a few, the pessimists were very disappointed—and life carried on as before.

Elizabeth, at the age of seventy-nine, moved into her new residence within her family's home. The sale of her house had eventually happened, unfortunately there were a few hitches, people wanting the house but unable to get a mortgage while convincing her that things were imminent, she really wanted them to have it but ultimately, it didn't happen—instead of which it went back on the market and another family came along, having already sold their flat, so in the end it all went through.

The extension was nearly done by this time so there was no problem for Elizabeth to live in with the family while the finishing touches were put to her new quarters. She was able to pick tiles for the bathroom and paint for the walls, and enjoyed making it her own, while having family support, and of course, able to help them in return. The boys didn't need babysitting these days, but if Derek and Ma-donna went out, it was good to know that Elizabeth was there in case they needed anything.

Quite often on these occasions, they would happily go and sit with her and they would watch a film together, and although said film wasn't Elizabeth's choice, she enjoyed sitting with the boys and found their enthusiasm quite infectious and realised she understood their humour and could laugh with them; these were moments that she treasured.

Within a few weeks, the extension was complete and there followed a busy time organising the new bigger kitchen, Elizabeth rooms, a cosy lounge and a bedroom with en-suite. Derek spent his spare time putting up mirrors and pictures, and Ma-donna enjoyed buying new things for the kitchen. They had a new range fitted and had kept the original cooker at the other end of the kitchen so should Elizabeth wish to cook at the same time as Ma-donna, they would not get in each other's way. It was working really well and Elizabeth would bake during the day when the family were out which went down very well with the boys. They would come home from school, often starving, so this made them very happy.

As summer approached, Derek got busy sorting the garden out, he had a summer house built at the bottom, had quite a large decked area around it, and the rest was given to lawn and flower beds with all ball games strictly prohibited. The boys were not too fazed, they had long taken to going to the local park with Seb to have a kick around and as they all played in teams, it wasn't necessary to use the garden. When this work was completed, Derek and Ma-donna arranged for Sarah and Paul to spend a jolly evening with their children, Bobbie happened to be home for the weekend from university and they all had a very happy and at times raucous evening.

Derek tried out his new barbecue which was a great triumph and much alcohol was consumed. This started a summer of spending lots of time in the garden when the weather permitted which all the family found very enjoyable. Elizabeth seemed very happy with the family, but one evening when they asked if she wanted to go on holiday with them—they were going to a villa in the sun with Sarah and Paul—Elizabeth said that she would pass this year, and stay at home and enjoy some time on her own.

She was hoping to go to London to see Ruth and was also going to have a look round the area and see if there were any clubs she could join. Up until now, family life had taken up a lot of her time, which she loved but now she felt settled, she thought she might look into the area a little bit more.

By the time the families returned from holiday, Elizabeth had joined a book club, a choir and a French speaking class. She still loved her languages but was very rusty. Occasionally Ma-donna would spend an evening with her and they would call it a 'French evening' or a 'German evening'—drinking wine from the appropriate country—but as Ma-donna was teaching all day, it didn't happen often.

Elizabeth had a lovely day with Ruth and told her that she would have to visit her next time. Sadly, Bob had suffered a stroke and really wasn't at all well and needed lots of care, however, Errol would happily stay with his father to give Ruth a break. He had never settled down with a partner, he was very fond of

Aisha, as she was of him, however, a couple of years ago she had been promoted and transferred to the Midlands. Both of them were very committed to their job and realised that to commit to a relationship was very difficult—so they had remained great friends—and both were destined to remain single.

The children all had busy lives, Bobbie at university working on her law degree—it would be six years before she would be a fully-fledged solicitor, she was into her third year, enjoying it and resigned it would take that length of time. Seb had sat his 'A' levels the previous summer and was having a year off, debating what to do in the future and in the meantime was working reasonably long hours in a local supermarket, which made him financially independent in as much as he could pay his way on nights out and short break with friends and didn't rely on his parents for pocket money.

They were helping Bobbie with her living expenses, she had suggested finding a part-time job, however, her studying was intense and Sarah and Paul said they would prefer her to focus on lectures and reading, rather than trying to fit a job into the equation. They told Seb that they would give him similar support depending on what his plans were for the future. He was quite happy with that and at the moment was liking doing the casual work, having a break from education and generally enjoying life.

Charlie was going to do his GCSEs in a few months' time so was well into all the subjects he had picked, apart from English which he wasn't very keen on but was mandatory—he was good at maths and enjoyed the sciences. He still thought he would like to be an electrician and that would mean him going to college after his GCSEs, which was a daunting thought for Derek and Ma-donna, the years were flying past and these little lads were almost men!

Sam was enjoying school and particularly loved sport and would be choosing his options soon. He had already decided that he wanted to be a PE teacher. This would involve a four-year university course but, again, Derek and Ma-donna wanted to support whatever he wished to do—as they would support Charlie with his choices.

Elizabeth always kept a low profile when the family were discussing the boys' futures—she was very proud of all of them and would support them whatever they wished to do, as long as they were happy. After all, her dear Robert had found his niche as a grave digger when he had originally started out life as a draughtsman. He would have had a more comfortable life in that job than he had working out in all weathers and spending most of the time seeing people burying their loved ones, but he chose that road and Elizabeth supported him all the way.

The outdoors was where he was at his happiest and where he best managed his demons. She often wondered how different their lives would have been if there hadn't been a second world war. Robert's career would have been totally different, of that she was sure as he was very intelligent, however, in the end she was just glad that he got home, as so many of the other lads never made it. The fact the war experience completely changed him and his personality and made him very bitter was a small price to pay!

Chapter 41

Elizabeth thoroughly enjoyed her new found interests. The choir she had joined met up one morning a week and they occasionally held concerts in a local church. They raised funds by having a raffle once a month and charged a small membership fee to keep afloat.

The book club met once a month and was a lively group made of about six to ten people and they would take it in turns to meet in each other's houses. Ma-donna had said that Elizabeth was more than welcome to use their lounge as it was more spacious than her cosy little lounge so they all enjoyed their meetings there as Elizabeth would always bake before a meeting, so tea and biscuits was actually tea and a choice of cakes, of which the boys would polish off when they came home from school. The members told Elizabeth that she was very fortunate to live with her family while retaining her independence and she did feel very blessed.

As for the French speaking class, that was also once a month and they met in a local pub, it was only for a couple of hours but they would enjoy an afternoon tipple, often ending with riotous laughter, but she thoroughly enjoyed those afternoons.

Elizabeth felt she had enough to keep her occupied and felt that her life was full. She encouraged Derek and Ma-donna to go away for the odd weekend and she would keep an eye on the boys and as she still had her car, she could take them to their various weekend activities. She was gradually driving less and less, mainly locally, but that suited her and she felt that she could cope.

She reflected on how things had changed from when she was growing up; she and Ruth would cycle everywhere they needed to be, but then when Ma-donna was growing up she was very protective when she had to go anywhere, and so was Robert, until she got into her teens—however, these days children got lifts everywhere they went if it was further than a few minutes' walk.

Christmas came and went—albeit a lot quieter than previous ones, mainly because the boys didn't wake up at the crack of dawn anymore—although they still loved their stockings at the end of their beds—and everything was much more relaxed. Drinks and dinner with Sarah and Paul, but dinner was much later in the day—as breakfast was so late—but always silly games and definitely no television after the Christmas meal. Everyone joined in and Ma-donna did tell Elizabeth that no one would mind if she wanted to go back to her room and spend a quiet time watching television, however, she loved joining in their games and wouldn't hear of it.

Boxing Day was even more relaxed when everyone felt they could come and go as they wished. They went to Sarah and Paul's for an afternoon buffet, and this was the day when they traditionally talked about the following year's summer holiday and where they should go. Bobbie suggested Croatia as she had been there with friends for a long weekend and said it truly was beautiful; everyone said it would make a change from Spain, France, Portugal or Italy, places they had all picked in the past—and they would definitely look into it.

Derek and Ma-donna had been discussing Elizabeth's forthcoming eightieth birthday. Derek had already suggested to Ma-donna that she should take her mum away somewhere that they would both enjoy. He wondered if the Easter holidays might be an option, he would take a week off to be with the boys and Charlie would be very busy revising for his GCSEs which would be imminent.

At this point on Boxing Day, Ma-donna presented Elizabeth with an envelope telling her it was an early birthday present but felt she would enjoy looking forward to a trip to Vienna, which is why she wanted her to have it now. Elizabeth was overwhelmed and shed a tear, and everyone hugged her and said that she deserved it and they would have a great time, just the two of them. Elizabeth couldn't help but remember the wonderful time she had in Vienna when she spent time with Ma-donna during her work experience.

The day ended on a high, although Sam cosied up to Elizabeth saying that he didn't want her to be eighty as that was very old, and he wanted her to live for ever. He was such a sensitive soul. Elizabeth once again told him she had no plans to go anywhere, apart from Vienna with his mum.

The trip was a great success, they had four nights in Vienna in the same hotel that Ma-donna had done her work experience all those years ago, and as well as exploring the city they did a couple of coach trips which were very enjoyable. It gave them a chance to speak German and Elizabeth thoroughly enjoyed the experience. She said she was a very lucky lady to have such a thoughtful family—obviously included Derek in this as he gave up a week of his annual holiday to be with the boys, but he really didn't mind at all.

Charlie's exams were over by the end of June and the families were looking forward to school being over so that they could go on their annual jaunt. They did decide on Croatia with lots of jokes with Bobbie, saying that if this trip was not up to their usual standard there would be big trouble. Bobbie assured them they would not be disappointed and, to be fair to her, they all had a wonderful time. Again, Elizabeth was happy to stay at home and enjoy some quiet time, which was fun for the first week, but by the second week, like the previous year, she started to miss them all, and the noise that went with them, however, she always managed to keep busy.

She baked for the freezer and got a few jobs done like weeding the flower beds as weeds grew faster than flowers especially in the warm summer weather. She wanted the house to look perfect when the family returned—it was always so chaotic just before they left, so she restored order where she could.

Results day came and Charlie had done very well, so there was a family meal out that evening. Everyone was proud of him, he had worked very hard, however, as he wasn't keen on returning to school he would probably start college in September to learn about electrics. He had already taught himself basic skills like changing plugs and fuses and was very keen to pursue this as a future career. The electrician who did their house extension had taken quite a shine to Charlie as he had been very interested in the work that was being done.

Derek now thought that he might have a word with him and ask which direction Charlie might take, and also ask if he might be looking for someone to take on as an apprentice. He didn't mention this to Charlie as he didn't want to raise false hopes, but wanted to help him on the road to his future.

After a lot of soul-searching, Seb had decided he would like to be a chef and had just joined a big hotel in London to start training. He would stay there during the week, coming home at weekends. It wasn't the best paid job in the world but he was thoroughly enjoying learning to cook and loved seeing how people behaved when they were out for meals! He would come home with some really funny stories so Paul and Sarah were delighted that he had, hopefully, found what he wanted to do.

Bobbie was still doing well, finished each academic year with great success and couldn't wait to qualify so she could help people with legal problems. She just had two more years to do and was as dedicated to her studies as she was when she first went to university so her family were very proud of her. She would occasionally have an evening out on the town with friends but was mainly focused on all her lectures. She had been to a couple of solicitors' practices for work experience and felt she had learnt a lot and loved the diversity of it all.

She had always wanted to do criminal law, however, one case that was going on when she was doing work experience involved one of the solicitors defending a criminal who was clearly guilty—she had to question her conscience asking herself if that was ethical, however, the solicitor concerned had a job to do, which was to find this criminal not guilty. She questioned this, and was soon told that jobs were handed out and you got on with it.

The idea was to win a case, but when it was blatantly obvious that the defendant was guilty, they would suggest that they pleaded guilty, that way, the judge might show leniency, and basically that was how it played out. Bobbie thought to herself that she might just act for a plaintiff rather than a defendant but life, sadly, wasn't that simple. However, she wasn't put off by this, she still wanted to be up there doing her bit to help people, but because that meant locking up criminals, she might have to think about how to go about this when the time came. In the meantime, she carried on learning.

Derek had always enjoyed his job in the lab as a chemist, and a lot of his work included a certain amount of research. He loved looking at new formulas for flu jabs, for example, also there was continuing progress searching for new remedies for AIDS which had gripped the world in the eighties, and which people were much more familiar with and didn't live in fear of being in close proximity to some who was HIV positive.

Derek also did his normal work which included police forensics and this was a great part of the job that he really enjoyed, but would also study different drugs and antibiotics, looking at ways to make improvements. He would meet up with other scientists and chemists once a month and they would discuss various ideas and would try out new formulas. Sadly, this meant experimenting on rats and mice but sacrifices had to be made and he had to look at the bigger picture, especially if it meant saving lives in the future. He didn't discuss this part of his work in any detail, except to tell Ma-donna when he might be away for a conference, or late home after an evening meeting.

Ma-donna never questioned his work as she knew that parts of it could be considered controversial, and maybe a little bit unethical even though it would ultimately save human beings.

Charlie's electrical course was going well and Derek had spoken to the guy, Richard, who had done their electrics and he remembered that Charlie showed a keen interest in his work. He said that when he had been at college for a couple of terms, he would be happy to take him on as a trainee, and he felt sure he would do well.

Charlie was very happy when Derek told him, however, Derek emphasised that it would be very basic jobs and everything he did would have to be double-checked by Richard so wouldn't be very well paid, as initially it would slow him down, but that was the way to learn. Charlie was thrilled at the thought of going out into the real world. After a few months, Richard kept his word and took Charlie under his wing. Charlie was also learning to drive and that was going quite well, so he really felt that he was a 'grown-up' and his family were very proud of him.

Sam did extremely well in his GCSE's and had started his 'A' level course—he was still keen to go to university to become a PE teacher. He did plenty of sport and kept himself fit, also had a good diet, and this was reflected by the fact he had great skin with very few spots, where Charlie suffered from acne and often had spots. This wasn't totally due to diet but Sam believed that a healthy diet was helpful when dealing with spots. He was also very particular about his appearance and loved smart clothes.

Chapter 42

One day, the doorbell rang, everyone was out apart from Elizabeth and she answered the door to Errol. He looked visibly upset and as he entered the house, he told her that Bob had passed away during the night. He had died at home, very peacefully, but Ruth was totally distraught and in a terrible state. Errol wondered if Elizabeth could go back with him and stay with Ruth while arrangements were being made, he didn't want her to be on her own. Elizabeth was immediately taken back to the time Robert had passed away, and although it wasn't unexpected, it was still a shock when it happened.

Elizabeth understood totally, made Errol a hot drink and told him she would need to make a couple of calls to re-arrange her day and would pack a few things, but this wouldn't be a problem. She left a note on the kitchen table telling the family briefly that she had gone to Ruth's, would be gone a few days but would ring later that evening.

In the event, Ma-donna guessed what had happened, and when she spoke to her mother, she told her to stay with Ruth for as long as she needed to. She would go up at the weekend to take her anything she needed and she hoped to be able to attend the funeral, depending when this might be.

She went on the train with a suitcase for Elizabeth and really wanted to see how Ruth was and tell her how very sorry she was for her terrible loss. Elizabeth seemed very at home at Ruth's and had basically 'kept the home fires burning'— Ruth was still in shock; Errol was terribly upset and Elizabeth had just been making tea for visitors and making scratch meals and persuading Ruth that she should eat something. Errol was off work for now, his colleagues were very supportive and Ruth was facing the dilemma with funeral arrangements and where Bob's ashes would have their final resting place.

She was torn between putting them in the graveyard where her parents were, and where she ultimately would like to go, or whether they should be sent to Jamaica to lie with his parents. Errol said that he would support her whatever her decision but she was struggling to ensure she did the right thing. When the funeral was over, after Errol told Ruth that he would be happy to be laid to rest in Kent, she decided that was where Bob's ashes would go, which would also give her somewhere she could visit when she felt up to it.

In the autumn of 2003, Sam was off to university after some excellent 'A' level results. He toyed with the idea of having a year out but decided he would like to crack on with his four-year course, he was very much looking forward to it. Ma-donna and Derek were getting their heads around him leaving home, certainly in term time where he would be in Halls of Residence, and thinking that the house would feel very strange without him.

Charlie was still at home, there was a girl in the picture now that he had been seeing for a few months, which was quite something as he had quite a few previous girlfriends but nothing very serious, however, he was spending quite a bit of time with Joanne and they seemed very happy together. Joanne was a beautician and she always looked immaculate. She loved her work and when she had finished her training and got her diploma, she really hoped to start her own business. She was employed at the moment by a lady who had several beauty salons and so Joanne was getting a lot of experience quite often working in different places. She was encouraged by her boss telling her that some customers were asking for her specifically, especially for massages, and that made her very happy.

Charlie was quite smitten with her and they were enjoying each other's company. She would often stay over at weekends with the family, likewise Charlie would stay at her parents' place, and everyone seemed fine with it all.

Sam came home that first Christmas, he said that everything was going very well and he was thoroughly enjoying the course. Everyone asked if he had made some new friends, he said he had, but didn't expand and they didn't press it, except for Ma-donna to say that anytime he was coming home, he would be more than welcome to bring a friend with him.

Bobbie was now a fully-fledged solicitor and had been taken on by a law firm in London and was thoroughly enjoying her work, just a bit frustrated that she was under someone's wing at the moment and felt she wasn't being stretched. When she explained this to Sarah and Paul, they said that she couldn't run before she could walk, and she should make the most of it, as suddenly being on her own could be very daunting. Her opinion was that it would happen at some point, and the sooner the better as far as she was concerned.

Seb was now working in a London hotel as a trainee chef, along with a couple of other lads with the idea that one of them might be offered a permanent position, if the chef thought them suitable. Seb struggled a little but enjoyed the challenges and the pressures in the kitchen and was getting used to chef shouting orders at them all, sometimes using colourful language, but he stood up to it very well and accepted that this is how it was and the old adage came to mind, 'if you can't stand the heat, get out of the kitchen!' and at the end of each working day he felt he had learnt something new, which he was very encouraged by.

Needless to say, he didn't get home till Boxing Day as he worked Christmas Eve and Christmas Day. Due to this, Sarah and Paul carried over their Christmas Day to Boxing Day which meant that Bobbie spent Christmas Day at her boyfriend's house, they worked together and had been out a few times and out of the blue he had invited her over for Christmas lunch if she could manage it. Paul and Sarah accepted that things would change as the children were growing up and they would tailor their family celebrations to suit.

Ma-donna had invited Ruth and Errol to spend the Christmas period with them as she had done ever since Bob had passed away. Errol was now retired as a Detective Inspector but worked in the community, which he had always done in his spare time going round schools and youth centres generally talking to youngsters about the merits of joining the police force even as a Special Constable and discussing racism with young people and basically explaining to them what toxic situations could be created by the hate and venom spouted by racists.

Errol had a certain presence about him and was very intense when explaining situations and case histories that had occurred during his career, and he seemed to earn a lot of respect from his various audiences. He also admitted that racism would always exist but he felt that any progress he made in his campaign, however small, was progress indeed.

Of course, the summer holiday arrangements all changed for the first time for as long as the families could remember. The thought of all of them trying to get time off at the same time was definitely a step too far, so the families agreed, for the first time ever, to have separate holidays.

Ma-donna and Derek had always wanted to visit Canada, The Rockies and Niagara Falls. Sarah and Paul fancied South Africa, so it was agreed that they would make their own arrangements. Elizabeth was happy at home and she would keep an eye on both houses when the couples were away.

However, the friends promised themselves a weekend away at a luxury hotel and spa so they would get away together, but just for a short time and again, Elizabeth was asked to accompany them if she wished, and she accepted as it sounded relaxing and would be fun.

Charlie eventually passed all his electrician's exams and was fully qualified. He was very thrilled and everyone was very proud of him. He carried on working for Richard who was more than happy to keep him on as he was trying to reduce his workload, and felt happy that Charlie was capable of tackling any job, and was also great to work with when they had bigger jobs to do.

The beauty of Richard training Charlie was that Charlie could read Richard like a book and they worked extremely well together. They were a great team but Richard knew he could trust Charlie and for the first time for several years, he felt happy to go away for a holiday, leaving Charlie in charge, and put him in the good books with his family.

Chapter 43

After Sam had been at university for a couple of years, with two more years to go, he was on track to do well, his grades were good and he had been on work experience in a couple of schools for the best part of a term. This reinforced his wish to become a teacher eventually as he enjoyed encouraging young people to reach their potential, especially the pupils who didn't like sport and needed help, with the reward that they were more able than they thought they were. As much as it was great to teach pupils who were very keen, it was equally rewarding to achieve results with the less able pupils. As well as teaching physical education and games, he also had to teach other classes, and as he had done so well in most subjects at school, he could turn his hand to anything, which would put him in good stead eventually when he finally qualified.

When Ma-donna and Derek spoke to him about friendships at Uni, he could be quite evasive and yet didn't seem unhappy, he had never brought any friends home, but he said he had a circle of friends he had the odd night out with, but no one special and he might surprise them one day and bring a friend home. When he was home, he often went out with old school and football friends, and caught up with them all.

Elizabeth had heard the conversation and knew she had always been close to Sam, she loved both boys very much but Sam was the one who would spend more time with her, especially now when he was home, and she felt he had something on his mind.

Before he went back to Uni, Elizabeth asked him if he wanted to watch a film with her as this was something they both enjoyed and he said as he had nothing much on, he would like that. After the film which was a World War II movie, they chatted initially about the futility of war and got on to other subjects like various prejudices, then talked on about Errol and what he was trying to achieve. Then, suddenly, Sam blurted to Elizabeth that he thought he might be gay—said he had never told anyone and was really worried about telling his parents.

This came as quite a shock to Elizabeth, but in some ways, it did explain quite a lot of things including why he had never brought a girl home. She asked him to explain and he said that he liked girls but not in a romantic way, and had had a couple of relationships with guys at university which confirmed his sexual orientation.

He wasn't in a relationship at the moment but had just met someone and it was early days, but he felt that this could be really serious and he really needed to speak to his parents. Elizabeth felt for him and suggested there was no time like the present. Sam suddenly looked very scared but agreed that there would never be a good time. Elizabeth went through to Ma-donna and Derek and asked if they would like to come to her lounge as Sam needed to speak to them, and she would go and put the kettle on.

They walked in the room looking really worried and Sam's eyes filled with tears, and they didn't know at all what to prepare themselves for. Various thoughts went through their minds: was he giving up on Uni, had he got girl problems or was he ill—the best way to find out was to ask him to tell them the worst. When he told them, they relaxed while taking in this revelation; when Ma-donna and Sarah had conversations about the children they both felt that they would know if one of their children were gay, obviously, that theory had just gone out of the window.

Questions followed like, was he sure, how did he know, but they emphasised that as far as they were concerned, he was and always would be Sam and they loved him dearly and whatever happened, they would always support him—all they wanted was for him to be happy. Elizabeth walked in at that point with a tea tray and some biscuits she had made earlier, and after a few tears, they said that life might get difficult for him at times, as homophobia, as well as racism was still a big problem in society, but they would always be there for him. Obviously, they needed to speak to Charlie and Sam was more than happy for them to tell Sarah and Paul in their own time.

Charlie and Joanne took this news in their stride, Joanne said that she had friends who were gay and it should never be an issue. Sam was a great guy, very genuine and Ma-donna was delighted that he had told them and, to be fair, she was not expecting that revelation and the only thing that made her sad was that he had told Elizabeth, his grandma who was in her eighties—rather than speak to them first—but was so happy to know that Elizabeth totally accepted this, unlike some elderly people who were brought up in the days when homosexuality was a crime—and for this Ma-donna was truly grateful.

When the news drifted to Bobbie, she said that she had guessed a long time ago that Sam might be gay so wasn't at all surprised. Sarah, Paul and Seb all accepted this as 'the norm,' so when Sam went back to Uni it was with great relief that he felt he could follow his heart knowing that his family had accepted the way he was.

Charlie and Joanne had bought a flat, moved in together and seemed really happy. She was enjoying her job as a beautician and was quite keen to set up on her own, however, premises and overheads could be expensive, and with Charlie being self-employed, although he and Richard were busy, he needed to make sure that there was enough money coming in to pay their mortgage, as sometimes they had to wait for clients to pay their bills, and it was always the biggest jobs that took the longest time to pay.

Charlie said perhaps in a couple of years when they were more settled, she could maybe look for a work base, or they could move on and get somewhere with a spare room where she could see clients, or, of course, she could become a mobile beautician, but that would involve expenses travelling—so it was a bit of a conundrum—but for now she would stay with her employer at the different salons. Of course, she did see friends and relatives in her own time and gave them treatments, but these were few and far between and would not generate serious income.

Ma-donna, now in her mid-fifties, found that her contemporaries were looking forward to early retirement, she knew she could retire at sixty, however, as she had only been teaching for just over fifteen years, her pension pot would be slightly larger if she worked for a few more years. At the moment, she was happy to go down that road, Elizabeth was still busy with her hobbies and very capable, loved being independent within her family so felt very fortunate.

Derek's parents who they didn't see very much these days—although now the boys were grown up, it shouldn't have been a problem—they just loved their own hobbies and friends and had never got overly involved with Derek and Ma-donna, as Elizabeth and Robert had. They had contacted Derek recently to say that they had sold their house and had bought a property in a retirement village on the East Coast and were looking forward to 'living the dream'—they likened it to being in an up-market holiday resort where they were many facilities like gyms, swimming pools, golf courses, restaurants, cafes and pubs, and as some of their friends had already moved there, when a property came up for sale it was too good to turn down. They were due to move in a few weeks, so if Derek wanted anything from the family home, he should go and visit them very soon and take whatever he felt he would like.

He was a little bit taken aback at the news, tried to think of any books or items in his childhood home he might like, but he felt happy for his parents and hoped the move would work out for them. They were in their mid-eighties, still extremely active and loved their busy social life, so it was the perfect time for them to move.

He had a strange relationship with his parents, he loved them dearly, had been well brought up, a happy childhood and lots of support during his adolescent years but since he had made his way in the world and had his own family, his parents had become almost detached and carried on with their own lives, which involved great holidays, entertaining and being entertained.

Although Derek and Ma-donna had always invited them to the children's birthday parties and family celebrations, while they came to a few they also turned down many, usually because they were otherwise engaged, whereas Elizabeth kept dates clear when there was a birthday imminent and she and Robert embraced the family celebrations.

However, reflecting on all this, Derek thought that his parents had done nothing wrong, just followed their own path in life; they had always been generous with gifts for birthdays and Christmas and this they all appreciated. However, he decided that he would visit his parents very soon with Ma-donna, mainly to find out exactly where they were going and to wish them well—if he did think of anything he might like from the family home he would ask them then.

Chapter 44

Sam graduated with a First and everyone was very proud of him, he had been home a few weeks ago, after his final exams and had introduced the family to Roger, his partner for the last eighteen months. They took their relationship very slowly after they had both been hurt previously, Roger had experienced abuse which had left him very traumatised and Sam had been a bit too full on in earlier relationships, so they had both learnt to take time to know each other—if it was meant to be it would work out—and this is why they had only just recently introduced each other to their families.

It seemed a little strange but Derek, Ma-donna and Elizabeth welcomed Roger to their family, Charlie and Joanne came for dinner, and Sarah and Paul came for Sunday lunch, a very jolly and noisy affair, as their gatherings always were! Bobbie was away and Seb was working, however, they were often on social media together so they were up to date with everything that was happening, and they both sent Sam messages wishing him and Roger well, and glad they were happy, and they would hopefully meet up soon.

Sam and Roger had just got their first jobs, Sam as a physical education and science teacher in a London Comprehensive, and Roger as a primary school teacher, also in London, so they would be looking for somewhere to live possibly in North London where rents were slightly cheaper with good transport links. They had decided not to buy at this time, again, taking their time and if all went well, they could follow that path in a year or so.

The family genuinely liked Roger, he was a very pleasant chap with a good sense of humour and really cared about Sam, which is all they wanted. They appreciated that Sam and Roger were not rushing to buy a home together, but certainly hoped they might do so if their relationship continued to thrive—it certainly looked promising.

Roger's previous partner George had been insecure and very jealous so Roger had become quite paranoid when speaking to anyone which he knew would result in an argument, and often with physical abuse. He had been to A&E with broken ribs, also to the dentist with a broken tooth, and always made excuses for George, usually blaming his own clumsiness and telling people he had walked into a door or fallen over. This resulted in low self-esteem and after yet another nasty incident, Roger realised that he needed to get away from George. He had seen Sam in a bar the students all went to and Sam had got talking to Roger, picking up on how nervous he was.

A couple of days later when Sam saw Roger, he had a black eye and he then admitted that this was a result of their conversation—the first time Roger had told anyone that George was responsible for an injury.

Roger then said that he knew he should end the relationship with George, but until he had met Sam, he hadn't found the courage to do so. George was distraught at the break up and, like on previous occasions made all manner of promises but Roger had had enough, and as it was the end of term, it was a good time to call it a day.

This was a few months ago and Sam and Roger were now moving into a flat and starting their careers, so it was an exciting time and their families were very happy for them. Roger's parents liked Sam, they had never taken to George, and although his father was still struggling with accepting that his son was gay, he could see how happy he was with Sam so wished them both well.

They started their new jobs on the same day and both faced challenges, Sam coping with classes of twelve- to eighteen-year-olds, and Roger with primary children in Year 3. He was the only male teacher at the school which meant he would be assigned with one or two other tasks, as well as teaching his own class, but he was prepared for that and happy to start this new chapter. He looked forward to going home in the evening to their flat where he and Sam would talk about how the day had gone, and discussing all the different aspects of their work—and they enjoyed sharing this while having their meal or relaxing with coffee after dinner.

Chapter 45

Bobbie was doing well, had at last been given her own cases to deal with and embraced this new phase with such energy and enthusiasm, surprising the partners of the practice and her colleagues.

She had won her first two cases despite locking horns with an older and much more experienced solicitor, so this gave her added confidence, without making her too cocksure, as she knew how these things could work out.

She had recently split up with Michael, her boyfriend in the practice after being together for nearly three years, they decided to part after she found him rather controlling, not in a nasty way, but he was highly critical of certain things she did—she got on well with all the girls in the office and would occasionally go out for a drink with them after work—he thought that was totally inappropriate and wasted no time telling her this.

She felt he was unreasonable which is why she had been reluctant to move in with him, something he had asked her quite a while ago, but she preferred to live in a house share with three other people. They didn't work with her, but she got on well with them and was happy there, she felt that Michael would suffocate her so she had gradually pulled back—he wasn't happy about this, and his parents were very fond of Bobbie, as Sarah and Paul were of Michael, but they didn't really understand what he was like.

When she eventually explained that their relationship had not worked out, they felt sorry, but understood and were proud of her making such a decision. She enjoyed her single status and felt relieved that she had made this difficult decision but knew it was for the best. She enjoyed her nights out with the secretaries in the office and was always discreet, never discussing work issues, after all, the idea of going out for an evening was to forget about work!

After a few months, Michael decided to move on and got another position at a different law firm and that really meant that Bobbie could draw a line under that particular relationship.

Seb was enjoying his work as a chef, he had won a couple of competitions and had come across some very prestigious chefs along the way, and learnt a lot. His dream was to have his own restaurant but that was a little way off, he spoke to his parents about this and they said that they would be prepared to help him when he felt that he had found the right time and location—he had some brilliant ideas for menus and different types of evenings, he really wanted to experiment and Paul said that he was very welcome to cook for them next time they had a dinner party.

He jumped at the chance when Paul invited some of his work colleagues and their wives for supper, and instead of taking them out he invited them into his home, with Seb doing the catering. He had run menus past Sarah which she approved of, and they had a wonderful evening. Paul's team had done quite well in the last few months, resulting in them receiving a bonus and in previous years Paul always took them out to celebrate.

All the guests were impressed with the quality of the food and out of the ten people Seb cooked for, three of the wives asked for his contact details so that they might hire him for future celebrations they had planned. They realised how relaxed Sarah was as their hostess with Seb working in the kitchen, and thought what a brilliant idea this would be. Seb was very happy with this and wondered if he might have a career as an outside caterer.

This could work very well, but he needed a bigger kitchen especially if he was catering for a lot of people, but he would give it some thought, wondering if he could rent some premises which he could use for food prep and storage—rather than running a restaurant when he would need to employ staff—doing it this way he could get casual help which would reduce his overheads and would give him a lot more experience, apart from dinner parties, he could do weddings and birthday celebrations, catering for any occasion, thus suiting any budget depending on what was required.

Seb became very excited about this and talked about it eagerly to his parents and Bobbie, she was always very encouraging when he had plans and could point out the pitfalls. She said that when he did find suitable premises, she would get someone she worked with to look over the lease to make sure it was sound and would not leave him with hidden costs, and for this he was very grateful.

He said he would wait for a few months, possibly using Sarah's kitchen initially, if she didn't mind, and perhaps he could get a second-hand freezer to put in the garage for storage and see how things worked out.

Seb's business really did take off, after doing three more dinner parties his phone rang constantly, praising the food he produced and asking him to take future bookings and how available he was. Initially, he accepted and fulfilled every booking as he was trying to build up his reputation, however, within six months Sarah was afraid to go into her kitchen not knowing what was going on in there as he was so very busy, and occasionally she and Paul would phone for a takeaway, or would pop in to Derek and Ma-donna's as the kitchen was a 'no-go' area.

Seb realised he needed to find premises sooner rather than later, so within three months he had a beautiful unit on a local industrial estate, fitted out with an industrial cooker, massive stainless-steel worktops and a huge fridge freezer, which meant less wastage.

He was absolutely cock-a-hoop with this and the business just grew. He had a group of people he called on to help, and occasionally Bobbie volunteered her services waitressing and serving drinks, it made a pleasant change for her and she loved how everyone raved about Seb's culinary skills.

Chapter 46

Ruth and Elizabeth still kept in touch, they were both in their late eighties—Elizabeth would go and visit Ruth in London, and Ruth and Errol came down every Christmas or at some time over the Christmas period. The friends loved meeting up and sharing memories, often reminding Ma-donna of her beloved grandmother Polly and her dear friend Dolly—however, Ruth had problems with her eyesight and was struggling trying to get about, so Elizabeth would visit her at her home and would spend a few hours with her but it upset her to see her friend struggling so much trying to perform the smallest of tasks.

However, Errol still lived with Ruth and was so very supportive basically looking after the house and doing shopping, or taking her shopping to make her feel that she was still in control of the household, he really was a most amazing son.

Elizabeth herself was having problems with her eyes caused by cataracts but was confident that when the time came, a small medical procedure would sort her out, unlike her friend with advanced glaucoma, which would eventually leave her completely blind. Elizabeth had stopped driving a while ago, her car still sat on the drive and basically was used by anyone in the family who needed it. It was old but in very good condition with low mileage so seemed very silly just to get rid of it. The boys or Joanne would use it occasionally and it came in jolly useful.

One evening, out of the blue, Charlie and Joanne called in looking every excited and told Ma-donna and Derek that they were engaged. The news was met with much joy with hugs all round—Charlie had carried out the age-old custom of asking Joanne's father if he could marry his daughter and both her parents were very happy about this. To be fair they had been living together for some time, but it was exciting to think that they were going to be husband and wife.

Of course, the rest of the evening was spent discussing the wedding plans, such as they were, and Joanne said that her parents would like to get together with Ma-donna and Derek to discuss everything. Later that night Derek jokingly said to Ma-donna that the wedding could cost them dearly, however, he also said that they would, of course, make a contribution towards the big day.

The happy couple had very set ideas about their wedding ceremony, it wouldn't be a church wedding as neither of them went to church and they looked at several venues where the service and reception would take place under one roof. However, the prices were eye-watering and as Joanne's parents had a large garden, Joanne thought an autumn wedding with a marquee might be the answer! Her father had beautiful flower beds and their house backed on to farmland with lovely views of the North Downs in the background, and Charlie asked Seb if he would consider doing the catering.

He had been reluctant to ask him as he wanted him there as a guest and to enjoy himself, but Seb liked nothing more than a 'busman's holiday' and was over the moon to be asked. Basically, all the guests would be there for the ceremony, followed by buffet, speeches then disco, and there would be in the region of seventy people.

Seb thoroughly enjoyed spending time with his friends suggesting various menus, there would be hot as well as cold food and on the day, he would bring in people to serve the food and drink. He had recently acquired a licence which meant he could supply drinks and run a bar if people had to buy drinks. The days of a 'free bar' were over, at most occasions.

Drinks were served before, during and after the meal for 'toasting' the bride and groom and the bridesmaids, then people bought their own drinks during the evening, however, as Seb was running his own bar, he made the drinks ridiculously cheap just covering his costs so as well as being a wonderful wedding, it didn't run into thousands of pounds, as weddings these days often did. Seb also made the wedding cake which was his present to the happy couple.

Of course, Seb strategically left a few flyers here and there during the course of the evening in case some of the young guests, possibly thinking of their own nuptials, might use him also. He advertised wherever he could, and still did private dinner parties for his father's colleagues where this very successful business had begun. He had quite a lot of regular clients considering the sort of business it was, and was extremely busy most of the time.

One evening soon after the wedding, Sarah and Paul came for dinner and Elizabeth joined them as she often did. They all spoke about the wedding and how well it had gone, and what a wonderful job Seb had done with catering for the occasion. They also spoke about some of the guests, quite a few people they had never met, and the conversation carried on in this vein with lots of laughter and frivolity, as was normal for their times together.

The conversation then turned to holidays they had enjoyed over the years with the children, and although they had not been away together in recent years, apart from the odd weekend, they thought it would be really nice to have a holiday together after doing 'their own thing' in recent years. A quick look at the internet, and within a couple of hours they had booked a villa in Italy for the following August, so the evening ended on a high.

They told Elizabeth that she would be most welcome to join them and she instantly agreed. She hadn't been abroad in recent years, preferring to stay at home keeping an eye on things, but that wasn't necessary anymore and she thought it would be great to see if she might pick up a bit of Italian, she still loved languages and had never visited Italy! She was nearly ninety but thought that one was never too old to learn.

Christmas soon came and went with the usual chaos, but much fun. For Boxing Day, it turned out that all the children were at Sarah and Paul's. Bobbie and Seb were both at home, both single—Bobbie had a new man in her life and as he came from Norfolk he had gone home to his family; they both felt it was early days and it would be nice to meet each other's families in the New Year when things were quieter.

In the meantime, they had arranged to meet on New Year's Eve at a colleague's party, which should be great. Seb was single as he was always so busy but did have lots of good friends and wasn't short of admirers but enjoyed these family occasions and being able to relax.

Charlie and Joanne had spent Christmas Day with her parents as Sam and Roger had spent it with his, so it was great for all of them to be together on Boxing Day with their family and friends.

Chapter 47

Ruth and Errol didn't spend Christmas with the family as they had done for years, Ruth's eyesight had deteriorated and Errol said she was behaving very strangely. Elizabeth's mind went back to Ruth's dad who developed dementia in his later years, and she was really worried that Ruth may be suffering from the same awful disease. She told Errol she would visit her friend in the New Year if the weather was fine, in the event Ma-donna decided to drive Elizabeth one Saturday as she was worried about her travelling on trains during the winter when it was cold and she knew her mother was very concerned about Ruth.

They both got a shock when they saw Ruth but didn't say anything to Errol, they waited for him to tell them how she had been. To be fair, he said that she was having a good day and when they saw Ruth, she greeted them both warmly. She could barely see them but while Errol made tea and plated the cakes that Elizabeth had brought with her, the friends chatted animatedly.

Ma-donna sat back and let the friends chat, then spoke to Errol about Ruth and asked him how he coped with her care and if he was getting any help. He said that he had been in touch with Social Services mainly to see what might be available to help Ruth and suggestions to make her life easier. Since his retirement from the force, he had been doing a lot of voluntary work but he had put that on hold now so that he could look after his mother. The only thing he had help with was her personal care.

A carer came in most mornings to help Ruth wash and dress and several times a week she asked for a shower, so this is what they helped her with. Errol was very grateful for this and was happy to do everything else that needed doing in the house. In recent months, Ruth had become very critical of his efforts which was quite demoralising for him and totally out of character for her, so he put it down to frustration at losing her sight and her independence and took her criticism in his stride, although he found this very hurtful.

Ma-donna really felt for him, she didn't really do much for Elizabeth while she was still so very independent. She couldn't imagine what it must feel like to help a loved one but not be appreciated as Elizabeth was always grateful for anything anyone of them did for her. The visit went well except when Ruth at one point burst into tears as she told Elizabeth that she hated her life and what she had become and was scared at times when she felt she couldn't remember things.

Elizabeth hugged her friend and told her that she also forgot things at times, and she was very lucky to have Errol who looked after her so well. She said she knew that but felt that she was stopping Errol living his life, but Errol, catching the end of the conversation assured her that she was his life, and nothing else mattered, as long as she was alright. He said they had a lovely home, enough to live on and each other, so life was fine.

Time flew and soon the friends were in Italy for their summer holiday and had a great time, Elizabeth thoroughly enjoyed it and was so very grateful to have such a caring family and good friends. She picked up a little bit of Italian, to the delight of waiters when they visited restaurants and cafes and it was great fun. However, Ma-donna felt that Sarah wasn't her normal self and seemed distracted at times, Paul hadn't picked up on this, in fact, she felt that she was the only one who thought Sarah was rather quiet at times and that came from having been friends for such a long time.

When they had been home for a while, after Derek and Paul were back to work, Ma-donna popped round to Sarah to see how the preparations for the new term were going; quite a lot of planning went into how the class would work with the new intake, and teachers' jobs were far more demanding than anyone could imagine. The perception that teachers turned up for work then went home to put their feet up was totally false. They often went into school during holiday periods to prepare their classes ready for the new term and thought about the challenges that lay ahead with each new class.

Sarah was on the computer when Ma-donna went round and the conversation soon came round to their recent holiday and talking of their children and how they were all progressing in their various career paths. Sam and Roger were in Europe on a three-week tour of various capital cities and were having an amazing time. Seb was far too busy for a holiday as was Charlie, at the moment, although Joanne was hoping for a break later in the year, and Bobbie had been away with a couple of the girls she shared the house with, and had enjoyed getting away from work for a couple of weeks. Her new relationship with Jason was going well and Sarah felt that they might be moving in together soon, however, Bobbie enjoyed her house share and didn't want to rush into anything, but was very fond of Jason and loved being with him.

However, the holiday with the girls had been booked many months before and she felt that it wouldn't hurt for her and Jason to be apart for a week or so.

Ma-donna bit the bullet and asked Sarah if all was well as she had noticed her distraction at times while they were away. She wondered if she and Paul were alright, amazed as she would be if they were not, then Sarah, uncharacteristically just burst into tears. Ma-donna was very taken aback but immediately went to hug her friend and waited for her sobs to subside and waited for her to say what the problem was.

It would appear that Sarah had found a lump in her breast a few weeks ago, had waited till after their holiday before going to her GP expecting him to tell her that it was just a cyst, nothing to worry about. However, he seemed very concerned and had immediately referred her to the local hospital to see a specialist and she had an appointment the following week, before term started. Sarah said she was just very frightened and was imagining all sorts of scenarios.

Ma-donna asked the obvious question: did Paul and the children know—to which Sarah replied that they didn't as she hadn't wanted to worry them. Obviously, she would have to tell Paul, at least, about the appointment but Ma-donna said she would accompany her if Paul wasn't able to; Sarah then asked Ma-donna if she would take her for the appointment and she promised she would tell Paul after this—Ma-donna was reluctant as she felt her loyalties were divided as this meant that she couldn't tell Derek either, or Elizabeth, however, as it was only a few days away, she tentatively agreed, but with the proviso that whatever happened, she would need to tell Paul after the hospital visit.

It was easy for the two of them to go off for the afternoon on the pretext of a shopping trip and they headed for the hospital. The consultant was very thorough and did a biopsy there and then which was rather a shock but felt that they needed to know what was going on sooner rather than later. Obviously, Sarah was rather shaken by the procedure and was in some discomfort, so when they got home Ma-donna waited for Paul to get home so that Sarah could speak to him.

An hour or so later, Paul came round to see Ma-donna by which time Derek had come home, and Paul was very upset that Ma-donna had gone along with the secrecy and felt hurt that she could keep something like this from them all. Ma-donna was in floods of tears by this time, Derek hadn't got a clue what was going on and Elizabeth went to put the kettle on.

Derek suggested they should all sit down and discuss this situation and work out exactly what Ma-donna was being blamed for. Emotions were running high; everyone was upset and all Ma-donna had done was to be a good friend to Sarah.

Eventually, Paul calmed down but was visibly shaken by the thought that Sarah might be ill and didn't know how he would cope without her by his side, as she had been constantly for nearly forty years. He apologised and Derek suggested they might go down the pub to wind down and talk about things, if this is what Paul might like to do. Ma-donna put Elizabeth in the picture, she was upset for them all, then Ma-donna went back to see Sarah to assure her that Paul had calmed down and they had gone to the pub but would be back for supper, which could be at their house, as that might help the evening along with everything out in the open.

During the evening Paul was very quiet, still in shock with what might be in store as a result of the biopsy but calmer and had the grace to apologise to Ma-donna and thanked her for being such a good friend. They agreed that it would be best to wait for the result before speaking to the children.

They didn't have too long to wait and the result was the dreaded one: Sarah had breast cancer! This was followed with an appointment with the oncologist with Paul at her side, eagerly listening while the diagnosis was explained to them both and what the options were. The oncologist explained that the best option was for Sarah to have the affected breast removed, followed by a course of chemotherapy and possibly radiotherapy, depending on how the cancer reacted to the treatment. The oncologist was very optimistic and said that the odds of a full recovery were very strong.

Sarah asked him about work, the new term had started ten days ago and she was just getting used to her new class, as they were to her, and felt that this would be a bad time to be away from school—however, the oncologist said that it was far more important for her to be treated as soon as possible. She would need to tell the school that she would be away for a few weeks to begin with; once the treatment was underway, if she felt well enough, she would be able to go in for a few hours but the treatment could be harsh and she might find it exhausting. Having said all that, the oncologist said that she was a fit lady with no other issues, so the prognosis was good.

When Paul and Sarah left the hospital they went straight home, Paul had suggested they go out for lunch but Sarah felt they had a lot to process and preferred to be at home to do this. Paul did them a sandwich and made them a drink, she bristled as she felt he was already treating her like an invalid, however, she felt that was rather unreasonable and just smiled gratefully at him.

They finally decided they should tell the children so they arranged for them to come for lunch on the following Sunday, Seb was free that day after a wedding on the Saturday; Bobbie asked if Jason could come too and after a short hesitation, Paul thought that Bobbie might need him for support so said that would be fine.

When Bobbie arrived on Sunday, she saw that the table was laid for five, and wondered why Ma-donna and Derek were not joining them, and began to get a slightly anxious feeling about all this. However, after Seb arrived and Sarah had made coffee for them all, she told them that she had been diagnosed with breast cancer and would be going in for surgery any day. Obviously, they were horrified at this news and in total shock, initially. Sarah and Paul took it in turns to explain that the prognosis was good but the treatment would be brutal, worst-case scenario.

Bobbie immediately offered to move back home so she could support her parents, she was thinking of leaving the house share due to her progressing relationship with Jason, however, he immediately agreed that Bobbie should do whatever she felt was right for them all, and if it meant her commuting to work and spending less time with him, he would totally understand. He loved that she was so committed to her family, as he was to his in Norfolk. People didn't always realise how important family could be and would sometimes make derisive comments if Jason chose to go home for a weekend rather than go to a party.

Seb took the news very quietly and just gave his parents the biggest hug with eyes filled with tears. Sarah went on to say that she had a hospital appointment the following Friday after school and would then get a date for her operation. They then proceeded to have lunch a bit later than planned so the beef was slightly overdone, but no one mentioned that like they might have joked about this on previous occasions, blaming the pre-dinner drinks for an overdone joint of meat.

Sarah made a quick call to Ma-donna to tell her that they had told the children, so she was now free to tell Charlie and Sam about Sarah's illness and her forthcoming operation. The boys, understandably, were upset—it felt like the unit they had been part of all of their lives was disintegrating and nothing would ever be the same again.

However, Sarah's operation went ahead and was successful, as far as anyone could tell and this was followed by regular chemo; this wasn't so good as the side effects were horrendous, Sarah was often ill for a couple of days afterwards and Elizabeth, bless her, took it upon herself to stay with her so that Paul could go to work. Bobbie was there in the evenings but commuting took its toll, she was out for twelve hours a day, however, she would get home and rustle up supper for them all and would tempt Sarah with tasty nibbles when she didn't feel she wanted to eat, and having Bobbie home was a great comfort.

Seb called round often, but they were all grateful for Elizabeth's support, for her advanced years she was an amazing lady and was always very calm in a crisis. Sarah knew that she wouldn't be back at work till the New Year at the earliest, and then, would be off when she was having treatment. The school were very understanding and had supply staff when necessary. However, her oncologist warned Sarah that her immune system might be compromised and she should be extremely careful if she wanted to go back to work as a simple cold could turn into a nasty infection.

Chapter 48

Christmas was organised by Ma-donna and Derek, with Elizabeth busy doing mince pies and sausage rolls and they were happy to host the whole of the Christmas period, with Sarah dipping in and out as she felt well enough. Between the chemo treatments, she wasn't too bad and enjoyed having the family round her without having to do any of the work. At times she felt a fraud, but of course, no one else thought that.

One big surprise this Christmas was Sam and Roger announcing that they would be getting married as soon as gay marriage became legal in March 2014. They were very happy and had set a date for April 2014. The ceremony would take place in the local registry office with an evening reception in a hotel. They were both so very happy and hoped that everyone would be able to attend including Sarah.

She said her chemo should be over by then and if all was well, she would return to school after the Easter break. She said she couldn't wait and in an emotional moment when they were all there, she thanked everyone for all their support and said she couldn't have got through her ordeal without them.

The second surprise was Charlie announcing that he and Joanne had sold their flat and put an offer on a new house; it had been built about five years ago and it had a lovely extension on the rear with a utility room which would be ideal for Joanne to see clients at home. They could get in from the side so they wouldn't have people walking through the house. They were hoping to get the keys in February, everyone was thrilled but Ma-donna, fleetingly, had hoped they would be announcing the arrival of a grandchild. However, she soon recovered herself and added her congratulations with the rest of the family and friends.

Ma-donna knew that Charlie would love to have children but Joanne obviously wasn't ready for motherhood, and knowing the challenges of being a parent, one had to be totally committed as it was a mammoth task, therefore it would be wrong for them to take such a step without both of them really wanting this.

Soon the festive period was over and everyone was back at work. Sarah woke up one morning and found a heap of hair on her pillow and realised the chemo was having some effect and hoped that it was working in other ways too. She waited till Ma-donna got home and asked her if she would shave her head—it would be so much better than losing bits of hair every day with the same eventual outcome. She had a beanie she would wear and no one would be any the wiser. Ma-donna, again, did what Sarah asked of her but said that she didn't want Paul to be cross.

Just before Easter Sarah had her last chemo, followed by a scan and a week later, her oncologist told her that she was cancer-free! She was over the moon; she had got her life back and could go back to work after Easter. He said that they would call her in for regular checks to make sure she stayed clear. She was very excited as they had Sam and Roger's wedding to look forward to, the first gay wedding that any of them had ever attended, so were very much looking forward to that occasion.

Sarah got in touch with the school and said she would very much like to return for the summer term. They were delighted but said that if it got too much for her, she would need to tell them.

Easter Sunday, they had a celebratory dinner provided by Seb—a lovely spring roast dinner. Ma-donna and Derek said they would call in later for cheese and biscuits to give them some family time. While they were waiting for dessert Jason suddenly asked Paul and Sarah if he and Bobbie could get engaged, he had waited until Sarah had recovered as he didn't want Bobbie to commit to him while she was so pre-occupied with Sarah's illness, but now she was clear, he thought this might be a good time to propose.

Bobbie had been expecting this as they had discussed their future but not there and then. She was overwhelmed and said that Jason made her very happy and she was looking forward to a future with him. She had met his parents and they seemed very fond of her which meant a lot to both of them. Sarah and Paul were delighted, Seb was thrilled as he liked Jason, and Sarah joked that she would need yet another wedding outfit as mother of the bride this time!

One afternoon, Elizabeth got a call from a very distressed Errol. Ruth had got up before daylight and gone out in her dressing gown. Errol realised as soon as he took her morning tea that she wasn't in the house. He went out looking for her but couldn't locate her, so had called the police and explained that his partially sighted mother had gone walkabout without her stick and he was very worried about her.

Errol was well known to them, although that made no difference, they immediately called out their search volunteer team out and sent every officer they could spare. She couldn't have gone very far so they concentrated their search locally and found her in the local park. She had fallen but was partly hidden by bushes so no one had seen her, it had been a wet morning so apart from a few dog walkers, there hadn't been many people about.

An ambulance was called and she was taken to hospital, she was unconscious and A and E thought that she had a broken femur, but couldn't be sure until they had carried out X-rays. She had been admitted to intensive care where her condition was being monitored. When Elizabeth told Ma-donna and Derek, they immediately offered to drive her to the hospital to see her friend—Derek said he would drive her so after a quick bite to eat, they set off. The journey into London wasn't too bad as the rush hour traffic was going in the opposite direction and soon, Elizabeth was at her friend's bedside. Errol was very distressed, blaming himself for her condition but Derek told him that it wasn't his fault, and now that Elizabeth was there, Derek suggested that they went to find him some refreshments.

A nurse kept popping in and checking on Ruth but the look on her face told Elizabeth that her friend's condition was serious. She had got very cold and was in shock, so the situation was grave. She held Ruth's hand and spoke to her but there was no reaction. Ruth had definitely gone downhill in the last couple of years. Elizabeth had spent a few days with her at different times but Ruth had got very paranoid, all part of her dementia and had accused Elizabeth of taking her purse, stealing her jewellery and other irrational wrongs that Elizabeth was supposed to have done.

Errol told Elizabeth not to take any notice as she couldn't help it and he was always being accused of doing bad things—he said it was quite hurtful, which is how Elizabeth felt, however, she still visited her friend mainly for Errol's sake. He really had been brilliant looking after his mother.

When Derek returned with Errol, Errol said he would be staying overnight by Ruth's bedside. Elizabeth felt she would like to stay but he said he would keep her informed as to Ruth's progress and she should go home with Derek and get some rest.

However, the next day the call came to say that Ruth had passed away during the night without recovering consciousness. Errol was understandably very distressed but as Ruth had a broken femur, she would have needed an operation, and being in her nineties, it would have been a massive ordeal for her. He just blamed himself for her going out without him being aware. Everyone said it wasn't his fault and, deep down, he knew this.

Chapter 49

Ma-donna and Derek were discussing their future, she could have retired four years previously but chose to keep working, however, what had happened to Sarah made them realise how short life really was sometimes, and they felt they would enjoy retirement. Derek wouldn't get his state pension for a couple of years, but Ma-donna had been receiving hers since her 60th birthday—being one of the very last women to get her pension at 60—and she also would get a good pension from work, and Derek thought he had enough in his private pension pot for them to survive for a while. They decided that the following Christmas would be a good time to retire, also it meant that Ma-donna could spend more time with Elizabeth. She was amazing for her age, but at ninety-four they both felt that she could do with a bit more support. She was still very independent, not so active in the community, but enjoyed everything she did and felt so very thankful to be part of such a loving family.

Elizabeth had been to Ruth's funeral, Ma-donna and Derek went with her, they were amazed at the number of people supporting Errol, which really made them thankful. He was such a lovely guy and had a lot of friends and they were all there for him. That really pleased Elizabeth and when they went home Ma-donna and Derek said that he must visit them soon and not be a stranger. He promised he would once he had got through the next couple of weeks.

Ma-donna and Derek were amazed at how Elizabeth was dealing with Sam and Roger's forthcoming wedding, she just accepted that they were two people who loved each other and wanted to spend their lives together. To be fair, she was the one who realised that Sam looked troubled before he 'came out,' so they never thought she would have a problem with the couple—but they had found that the older generation were not so open minded—after all, they had been brought up when times were so very different and as much as it was good, it was strange to some people that what was a crime when they were growing up was now perfectly acceptable.

Derek had a very different experience when he visited his parents, for some reason he said to Ma-donna that he would prefer to go alone and she was happy to occupy herself on a Saturday. He was keen to see this wonderful retirement village his parents had moved to and wanted to tell them in person about Sam and Roger's forthcoming wedding. He didn't know what to expect, thought they might be unenthusiastic at best, however, he wanted to let them know that they would be most welcome to attend the ceremony.

When he finally arrived after a three-hour drive due to problems with his satnav and he'd had a cup of coffee, while listening to his mother enthusing about how busy they were and would he be staying for lunch, he told them the news about Sam and his relationship with Roger which had developed over the last couple of years, and both his parents were speechless, and looked totally horrified.

They couldn't understand how Derek and Ma-donna could have let this happen, surely it was just a phase he would recover from in time! Derek felt at a loss and thought there were not enough hours in the day to explain to these two about homosexuality, and, worse still, didn't feel he had the energy.

He said that he felt by their reaction that they would not wish to attend the ceremony and maybe he might just skip lunch and grab something on the way home. They both sat there in silence, and Derek took that as his cue to leave.

On the long drive home, he felt very emotional, anger, disbelief and heartbreak for Sam—while people like his parents existed what chance did Sam and Roger have—however, he shed a few tears and pulled into a layby for a cup of tea and a bacon sandwich in order to calm down—he would play the meeting with his parents down with Ma-donna and just say that they were struggling with the concept so would not be attending the wedding, but they wished them well—which was a lie, of course, but he loved his family too much to put them through the anguish he felt at his parents reaction.

The rest of the drive home was uneventful and he had a big smile on his face when he returned. Ma-donna had cooked them a really nice meal as she'd had time and there was a bottle of Chablis chilling in the fridge. She didn't question his trip, had guessed what his parents' reaction might have been but thought he would tell her anything he would like her to know. The visit was never mentioned again.

The wedding took place on a beautiful spring day in late April, the hotel had lovely grounds and the photos were amazing. Sarah looked great, she had invested in a wig that she only wore on rare occasions as her hair would start to grow soon, and Ma-donna looked lovely too. Both Derek and Paul talked about their wives and what lovely strong women they were, and how fortunate they were to have such wonderful families.

They valued their friendship which had lasted for over thirty years and were all proud of how well their children had done. Errol also enjoyed the wedding, despite his sadness at his recent loss, and was very happy for the couple. He had known Sam all his life and was very fond of the whole family, in fact, he felt part of this family as they had always been so very kind to him.

Bobbie and Jason were to be married the following summer; they were settling down in Jason's flat but were hoping to buy a house soon.

Derek and Ma-donna forged ahead with their retirement plans, the school said they would be sorry to lose Ma-donna but understood her situation and said that she may be able to do a bit of private tuition near exam time, which could be quite useful for students and would bring in a bit of income too.

Derek's news was not received quite as well, his boss was concerned as they had been short-staffed for some time, not many youngsters were coming into their field, Ma-donna could back that up as the school had noticed that when it came to 'A' level studies, science subjects were not as popular as languages, technology or media studies.

Derek was such a vital staff member as he was so experienced in all fields. He would work in forensics or in research—he was very clever though generally very modest—but some of his research had gone to big drug companies and had helped with various vaccines needed all over the world—however, he didn't get a lot of credit for this and just enjoyed the satisfaction of doing a great job.

His boss couldn't stop him retiring, however, he said he would ask human resources to advertise once again for graduates aiming at the universities where they specialised in the sciences particularly chemistry then they may have some new members of staff for training before Derek went. His boss also asked him if he might be willing to help out when they were very busy after his retirement. Derek said that if he was able to, he would be happy to do so.

Chapter 50

Bobbie and Jason started house hunting initially just to see what was available but could see that prices were rising all the time. They made the decision to put Jason's flat on the market so they could start to look for their future home. It was a very exciting time and Sarah and Paul enjoyed hearing about their plans. The wedding arrangements were still in their infancy—the young couple wanted Bobbie's parents to meet Jason's mum and dad and this was arranged for a Sunday when Sarah and Paul were on their way home from holiday.

After such a fantastic holiday in Italy last year after which so much had happened to Sarah, this year holidays were going to be quite low-key in comparison. Sarah, despite having been back to work for the summer term, still got very tired so Paul suggested that the two of them get away to Yorkshire staying in the moors in a really nice hotel where Sarah could do as little as possible, if she so wished. There were some lovely walks from the hotel and all they wanted was some nice dry weather. On the way home they would stay overnight in a hotel in Kings Lynn before visiting Jason's parents for Sunday lunch and to discuss the forthcoming wedding.

It was a very pleasant week and they both looked forward to meeting Sue and Ted, Jason's parents. Bobbie and Jason had gone for the weekend on Saturday morning by train and would get a lift back to London with her parents. They arrived at midday and when the introductions had all been made, Ted asked them whether they would like coffee or something stronger. They said that coffee would be lovely and Sue said she would put the coffee on as she had to check on lunch anyway. What struck Sarah and Paul was the delicious aroma coming from the kitchen, and said as much. Ted said that they were having roast beef which would hopefully be cooked to perfection.

Sue soon returned with the tray of coffee and they all sat down chatting about the journey, the weather, asked them if they had enjoyed Yorkshire and how Sarah was. They were obviously aware of what a difficult time she had had, and all hoped that this was behind her now and it would be great to have the wedding to look forward to next year.

Bobbie then said that they had almost decided on a venue, it rested between two places—one was an old manor house with a great ballroom where the ceremony and reception would take place and beautiful grounds, and the other was a hotel which wasn't so grand but where everyone could stay overnight. The manor house was in the middle of nowhere and everyone would need accommodation which meant either booking a coach to take people to accommodation in that area and ensuring that everyone could be catered for, or having the wedding in the hotel which was very nice and where there would be enough space for people to stay if they so wished.

Unfortunately, the parents were less than helpful saying that it was their big day and the choice had to come from them. However, it would make sense to have accommodation where the reception was just to make life easier for everyone, but the young people had to be happy with their decision.

They then sat down to a beautiful Sunday roast, the beef was succulent, the potatoes beautifully crunchy, everything was absolutely perfect. By the time they had finished Sue's apple pie and custard they thought they wouldn't eat for about a week. They had also enjoyed a nice Merlot with the meal and all they needed was a cup of coffee to round it off before going home.

Paul had asked Ted about his work, he was a butcher and all the meat he sold was locally sourced, hence the delicious beef. Sue had her own florist shop and had already said that she would do the flowers for the wedding, if Bobbie wished. Bobbie and Sarah thought that was an excellent idea and the rest of the time was spent talking about wedding arrangements—all they had to do now was to await Bobbie and Jason's final decision for the venue and on that note, they said it was time they got back home.

They thanked their hosts profusely saying that they had very much enjoyed meeting them, what a lovely guy they thought Jason was and how he made Bobbie so very happy, and Sue and Ted reciprocated by saying it had been lovely to meet them at long last, and they hoped to meet again soon once more plans were in place!

They had a good drive back with a few little hold-ups, customary on a Sunday evening with traffic going towards London, they dropped Bobbie and Jason off then had a trouble-free drive home. Sarah felt absolutely worn out by the time they got back and went straight to bed, glad of the summer holiday so she would have quite a few days to unpack after their holiday and do the laundry.

Paul said what lovely people he thought Jason's parents were and what a happy day they had with them, finishing off their week very nicely. The next day, Ma-donna went to have a cuppa with Sarah and wanted to know all about their holiday and also the wedding plans. She and Derek had been away ten days before Sarah and Paul went away so they really needed a good catch up. They had spent the time in Wales with very mixed weather, but nevertheless had a great time. They also stayed in a hotel and it was really lovely.

Elizabeth had stayed at home, she was doing fine, Errol had been to see her, he was grieving for Ruth and couldn't get over the fact that her fall could have been avoided if he had made sure the door had extra locks, but always felt that in the event of a fire, a quick exit was needed. Ruth had never left the house on her own before! Elizabeth kept telling him it wasn't his fault and he should stop blaming himself, but he was still struggling. Also, the boys had called in to see their grandmother while their parents were away, so Elizabeth felt fortunate to have so many people looking out for her.

Chapter 51

Summer drew to a close, Sarah and Ma-donna were back at school facing new terms, and in Ma-donna's case, her last term as a teacher, which felt very strange. She was introduced to the new languages teacher who would be joining the staff full-time after October half-term so that Ma-donna could work with her, liaising and handing everything over and, especially with the 'A' level classes so that the new teacher would know the students, and what their needs might be. These were all Ma-donna's 'chicks' and she was very protective towards them, wanting the best result possible for them which is what made her such a brilliant teacher, however, instilling that into a newly qualified teacher was quite hard, when, quite rightly, her job was to teach languages! However, she seemed to understand what Ma-donna was explaining to her and said that she would do her very best to get their pupils through the various exams.

Ma-donna felt that Miss Jones would do very well, she was keen to do her best so she told her that once she had retired Miss Jones would feel that the Language Department was her own and she would thrive. Miss Jones felt encouraged despite still feeling in Ma-donna's shadow while she was there.

Derek had a couple of young qualified chemists at his disposal to show the ropes to, and he initially felt daunted by this as he had been used to working on his own and found it quite hard explaining to other people what he was doing, but do this he must otherwise he would never be able to retire.

Christmas soon came round and there were retirement celebrations as well as the seasonal festivities. Sarah insisted on doing Christmas as she had missed out the previous year leaving it to her lovely friends to organise, so Seb was very prominent helping his mother in the kitchen—or the other way around—as he didn't want Sarah wearing herself out. Paul and Bobbie were grateful for his help and consideration to his mother, and Bobbie then roped Jason with the clearing away and making coffee. She wanted to let her brother know how much she appreciated all he had done to provide the family and friends with such delicious food while taking the pressure off his mother.

On Christmas morning, Derek handed Ma-donna an envelope with her other presents and she opened this, not really sure what it could be. The envelope contained two tickets for a Mediterranean cruise with a flight from Gatwick to Tenerife, where the cruise would begin, and they were off on New Year's Day! Her immediate reaction was shock/horror, how could they go away in less than a week, but Elizabeth asked her what on earth was stopping them and she agreed that it was wonderful; Derek said that he had wanted to get them a joint retirement present and that was the most appropriate gift he could think of. It meant that they wouldn't be around when they would have been due to go back to work and Derek thought it would be good to be away then.

Bobbie and Jason had finalised their wedding arrangements, in the end they decided that the manor house, although beautiful was not practical and the hotel they had as second choice they really were not sure about, so in the end they had gone for a country club that had many rooms with a spa, pool and gym in the grounds, together with a couple of large self-catering cottages, so enough accommodation for all the guests to stay on the premises with time to enjoy the facilities. The views surrounding the country club were stunning, so all they wanted was a beautiful sunny day and everything would be perfect.

Seb had offered to cater for their wedding but Bobbie refused purely on the grounds that she wanted Seb to have fun on the day and not be spending most of it in the kitchen. He reluctantly but could see that this made perfect sense, so went along with it. However, he wanted to see what menus they had chosen and who was doing the catering so Bobbie included him in their plans so he could offer some useful pointers.

Early in the New Year, Bobbie and Jason moved out of Jason's flat and moved in to their new house, juggling decorating with wedding plans, and work, so very hectic but great fun and they were loving every minute.

Meanwhile, Ma-donna and Derek had returned from their cruise, and it had truly been wonderful visiting resorts in the winter sunshine in early summer temperatures knowing that at home temperatures were barely above freezing. They were now settling into their retirement, leisurely walks when the weather allowed, pub lunches, also long-awaited decorating projects, so this new life wasn't so bad having begun with a lovely holiday.

Charlie and Joanne were loving their house, had been there for a while now and although they were both extremely busy with work, they had made a beautiful home. Ma-donna wistfully thought it would be so nice if they were planning a family, they would love a grandchild but it would only happen when Charlie and Joanne felt they were ready. As it was, Charlie has broached the subject with Joanne, he would love a family but Joanne enjoyed the life they had; she had three siblings and although she had a very happy childhood, she knew the sacrifices her parents had made to give their children the best life, and Joanne felt she wasn't ready to make that sacrifice.

Charlie agreed they had a great life, good holidays and a reasonable disposable income so obviously hadn't mentioned it anymore, hoping that Joanne would let him know when she had a change of heart. She used to look at Charlie when they were visiting friends with children at how he played and related to little ones and her heart melted with love for him—however, it still didn't make her feel she wanted a baby of their own. Maybe in another year or so!

Chapter 52

The wedding plans were going along nicely and Stag and Hen nights were being organised. It was decided that they would have two each, Bobbie wanted to have a Hen weekend with all her girlfriends which her chief bridesmaid was arranging, and was promising to be on the wild side, but she felt she wanted to have a hen night with her mum, Ma-donna and Elizabeth, and Joanne was also welcome to join them but she would be included in 'the wild one!' Bobbie also invited Sue, her future mother-in-law to join them, but she was up to her eyes in 'wedding season' and sadly declined the invitation, but hoped they would have a wonderful 'girls' weekend.' Joanne was busy with clients that weekend but she was looking forward to 'the wild one'—which was a long weekend in Ibiza, and that was also where the stag-do was being held, but on a different weekend, which was a total coincidence.

The girls settled on Brighton for their weekend staying overnight on the Saturday. The weather was kind so they had a lovely walk along the pier enjoying the slot machines, as this reminded them of their childhood—Bobbie loved to indulge them, she adored all these ladies, her dear mum who had been through so much, lovely Ma-donna that she had known since she was small, and Elizabeth who was one of the strongest and nicest people she felt fortunate to have in her life.

They had fish and chips for lunch, then went shopping, first of all they went to the huge Churchill Square indoor shopping area, only to find that it was filled with chain stores that they could find in any high street, so they hit the lanes, and had a wonderful time. Spent a long time looking in all the quirky little shops, beautiful boutiques and lovely antique jewellers. They were mainly window shopping but had a lot of fun, stopped at a tea shop for a reviving cuppa, unable to resist the cakes on offer. Bobbie reminded them that they had an evening meal booked and would need to work up an appetite for this.

They appreciated this, but explained to Bobbie that this weekend away was all about the 'here and now'—might just have to be a salad later rather than a big main meal, but this was great and they were loving it. Bobbie agreed this was what they all needed, relaxation and enjoying the moment.

After the shopping trip, they went back to their hotel to relax for a while and get changed for dinner in a nearby restaurant. By the time they met up in the bar for a drink before setting off they all felt quite peckish and thought it must be the sea air doing its magic! They enjoyed their meal and after a short walk along the front to help their digestion, they made their way back to the hotel.

The next morning, after a leisurely breakfast they loaded the car with their luggage, had a final stroll and Bobbie drove them home. They had had a wonderful time and Bobbie enjoyed being with them and not thinking about the actual wedding plans for a little while. Everything was coming together and now it was a case of sitting it out until a few days before when flowers would need to be sorted and all the last-minute touches would take place.

Paul and Derek had spent the weekend in Norfolk with Ted and Jason having their own 'Stag-do for the Older folk,' they had visited a Brewery and sampled the goods and had a good meal out before returning to spend the night at Sue and Ted's. Sue had been up to her eyes in weddings both on the Saturday and Sunday so they saw very little of her, but she cooked them a lovely brunch before their return on Sunday afternoon. Her job was done, she had been up early decorating the local church and the adjoining hall for that day's wedding so was now free for the rest of the day.

The three men departed, Jason giving his mum a big hug and saying that the next time they would meet up would be for the wedding, so it was all very exciting. Paul and Derek thanked Ted for a great weekend seeing some of the Norfolk sights, mainly the inside of various hostelries, but great fun. This was the first time that Derek had met Ted so it was great to make his acquaintance before the big day.

The next few weeks flew by with Stag and Hen weekends in Ibiza where it all went well, as far as anyone could tell, the old saying that what happens on these weekends stays on these weekends but to be fair everyone said they had a great time. Charlie, Sam and Roger and Seb all went with Jason and some of his other friends, and Joanne went with Bobbie and some of her old work colleagues. It all seemed quite civilised.

Sue and Ted would be down a few days before the wedding, they would come in Sue's van and she would go to the flower market early one morning to get all she would need for the bride and bridesmaids' bouquets, buttonholes, corsages for some of the ladies, also the table decorations and to decorate the room for the ceremony. Bobbie was happy to leave the choice to her, just gave her the colour scheme and left her to get on with it. Sue was in her element and was up in the early hours to drive into London.

On her return, it was a frantic unloading of her purchases without damaging any and finding the coolest place in the house to keep them. They should be absolutely fine but Sue felt more nervous about this than she would a paying customer—she really wanted Bobbie to love her work and would be putting a lot of herself into this. She was happy that Bobbie trusted her to get on with it and she couldn't wait to see her reaction.

The flowers were all left in the garage, which was remarkably cool and when Sue was happy with everything, she called Bobbie over to have a look at her work. Bobbie was overwhelmed, loved her simple bouquet, peach roses to match the bridesmaids' dresses and the men's beige cravats and the rest of the flowers all looked stunning.

Sue had asked what colour Sarah was wearing, also Ma-donna and Elizabeth, she knew how close to the family they were so did their corsages to match their outfits. In the morning she would drive over to the country club with the rest of the arrangements for the room and the tables and, by this time, she started to calm down thinking that it was all going to be absolutely brilliant.

There were heavy rain showers during the night which kept a few people awake worrying about the next day and thankful the wedding was being held inside; however, it was hoped that some photos would be taken outdoors to include the beautiful setting and by the sound of the rain, this would make the grounds very wet.

However, the day dawned bright and sunny and by lunchtime everything had dried up nicely. The flowers in the grounds looked stunning, refreshed by the overnight showers. The wedding was wonderful, went without a hitch, Bobbie looked radiant, Jason had a huge smile on his face, the bridesmaids were beautiful, Sarah was stunning in her lovely outfit and it was a wonderful day. Lots of people taking photos as well as the official photographer, especially in the rose garden which was at its best and the smell of the roses was intoxicating.

The rest of the day was very relaxed and enjoyable, lovely food which Seb insisted on overseeing, finally it was one of his friends that organised the catering, under Seb's guidance and everything was lovely. The day ended with a disco with the happy couple starting the dancing with 'their' song, followed by all the other couples taking to the floor, a few tears shed by Sarah and Ma-donna when things got a bit emotional.

Elizabeth was one of the first people to retire for the night, and all she had to do was find her room; she had loved the day but found it very tiring, however, she wouldn't have missed it for the world. She went to find Bobbie and Jason and told them what a marvellous day it had been and how happy she was to be there. They both gave her big hugs and told her to sleep well, they would all meet up for breakfast the next morning.

Once the dancing was over people drifted off to bed while a few lingered in the bar for one last drink. A few people were slightly the worse for wear but there were no problems or unpleasantness, just lots of laughter.

The next morning, the majority of the guests were there for breakfast before finally packing and checking out. Bobbie and Jason were off to the airport to spent a few days in Croatia and Sam and Roger were dropping them off on their way back.

Chapter 53

After the wedding things seemed very calm for a week or so, Ma-donna and Derek were thoroughly enjoying their retirement but keeping busy with various jobs, and Derek had been at work for a few days here and there to cover for holidays. He was selective when agreeing to various dates, however, he did enjoy being in work especially when he knew it was only for the odd day and he wasn't actually responsible for anything.

They planned to have a few days away in September and it would be nice to get away once the schools were back, for years they had to take holidays when it was the most expensive time to go, so it was a pleasant change to see what was available during term time, and how the money went further.

Sarah and Paul had got away for a few days in Scotland after the wedding, it had really taken it out of Sarah but she had enjoyed every minute, as had everyone else. They had also been invited to spend a weekend with Sue and Ted at some point, they found they got on really well and Sue had made a wonderful job with the flowers for the wedding. She was obviously very professional and had a real flair, and very conscientious. She really wanted to do Bobbie and Jason proud. She showed them all how they could preserve their flowers if they wanted to keep them, and they all thought that was a lovely idea.

Sam and Roger were visiting Ma-donna and Paul one day, they had recently moved into a house, having sold their flat and said they had some news for them. They had spent their summer holidays getting their new house straight, it just worked well that they moved in at the beginning of August. They were now back at school but wanted Ma-donna and Derek to be the first to know that they had applied to be foster parents.

They really wanted to have a family but didn't feel they wanted to go down the surrogate route with a mother having a child for them then handing it over. They were not comfortable with that concept, also, both being teachers, they could appreciate how many children out there needed good homes, so they decided that fostering older children would be the route to go down.

They had several appointments with Social Services and had been found to be suitable prospective foster parents. Ma-donna and Derek were very excited for them, they could see how enthusiastic they both were—Social Services had asked them about a couple of brothers they had in care, aged nine and seven. Very sad, as all these stories were, the boys' mother had fled from the family as the father was abusive, and despite loving both the boys, explained that she was unable to stay with them, but couldn't take them with her, but when she finally relocated somewhere she would send for them.

However, this was over a year ago—the mother had given the older boy a phone which she would top up so the boys could ring her once a week, but they shouldn't tell their father. The father was totally out of his depth, was a lot older than his wife and really couldn't cope with everyday household chores. The teachers noticed that the boys were looking quite scruffy so kept an eye on them, then, one day the older boy came into school and appeared to be in pain.

His teacher asked him what the problem was and he said he had fallen over. She took the liberty, with another teacher, to examine him when they were changing for games, and the boy's slight body was a mass of bruises. The boy got very agitated and said that his father had beaten him up as he had found a mobile phone he was hiding in his room, and wanted to know where it had come from. When he refused to say that it was to phone his mother, he got a serious beating.

Social Services and the police were called, the father was arrested and the boys were immediately placed in care. They had coped very well but would fare better in a home environment, and it was felt that Sam and Roger were ideal candidates. The boys were due to stay with them the following weekend, and if all went well, they would go and spend half-term with them, and take it from there.

Ma-donna's heart went out to these two little lads who had such a sad beginning, and felt so very happy and proud of these two lovely men who wanted to give these boys a much better life. In her head, she was already planning Christmas, but when she voiced these thoughts to Derek, he told her not to get ahead of herself, if it didn't work out they would all be so very upset. She loved the thought of having children in the house once again.

Two or three weeks before Christmas, Charlie and Joanne popped in to see Ma-donna and Derek and said they had some news and Ma-donna held her breath and wondered if this is what she had been hoping for such a long time. Joanne pulled a piece of paper from her handbag and handed it to Ma-donna, it was a grainy picture but clearly it was a scan and the shape of a tiny human. Both Charlie and Joanne had big grins on their faces and said they had wanted to wait for the first scan before announcing their news.

Ma-donna was in tears at this point, and went to get Elizabeth, she came in the room wondering what disaster had befallen the family now, only to be told that she would, in the next few months, become a great grandmother. Tears all round by this time and Derek decided that they could all do with a drink, then realised that Joanne probably couldn't have a drink! Chaos ensued for a few moments when they all settled for a cup of tea and a cake that Elizabeth had baked earlier.

It turned out that Joanne and Charlie had suffered a few disappointments on the baby front when they had both agreed to start a family, so this was a much-wanted baby. Joanne had been getting upset as she felt she had missed the boat, as it were, and was now delighted that they were going to be parents. Ma-donna was so glad that she had never mentioned to the couple that it was time they started a family. That sort of interference never did work and just caused animosity; Joanne had been reluctant to think about a baby until she felt that her career was well established but then panicked when it didn't happen immediately! Of course, she would be able to work from home once the baby arrived, not immediately, but in due course thus saving a fortune on nursery fees.

She felt that she might find a local childminder for a couple of days a week, also her own mother had offered and she felt that Ma-donna might be happy to look after her grandchild on occasions but didn't want to presume, and there was plenty of time to discuss all this.

Sarah came to see Ma-donna to say that she had got a call from Bobbie and—although it was only ten days before Christmas, Bobbie decided that she wanted to host her parents and her in-laws for Christmas lunch—she was quite nervous about the whole thing, but Seb said he would be there if needed and Jason also said he would help which made Bobbie feel that she could cope.

Sarah had graciously accepted the invitation and said she couldn't wait and it would be lovely to have the meal cooked for her. She would freeze what she had already ordered and they could have it at a later date. As they always had Christmas with Ma-donna Sarah hoped that Ma-donna wouldn't be upset.

Ma-donna thought that was lovely for them to spend Christmas at Bobbie's—also Ma-donna had the boys with the two foster children for Christmas—this was going really well—they had met up with them a couple of times but were leaving them to settle with Sam and Roger as it was a learning curve for them all. However, they were very excited about spending Christmas with them and Ma-donna had bought rather too many presents for them but felt that they deserved to be spoilt! Charlie and Joanne were going there on Boxing Day which would be their big family day, and they would celebrate with Sarah and Paul at New Year.

It all went very well, the two little boys Hari and Suni had a wonderful time once they had got over their shyness, and Elizabeth enjoyed spending time with them and speaking to them about school. Sam had managed to get them into his school which made sense, saved a lot of time on the school run and the boys had settled well. They would eventually go to Roger's school when they went on to senior school, there was an after-school club which the boys went to while waiting for Sam to finish his day at school, and occasionally if Roger finished early, he would come and pick them up, so it all worked very well.

They hadn't heard any more from their mother as their father had broken the phone in temper when Hari wouldn't tell him where it came from. The father had been prosecuted for child cruelty and assault and was awaiting sentencing. It had been suggested that he would probably get a suspended sentence, however, the boys didn't want to go and see him and hoped that their mother might contact Social Services to see where and how they were.

After some digging by Social Services, it would appear that the mother had gone back to her parents in India, so who knew whether she would come back for her sons at some point. Social Services sent a message to say that the boys were fine and happy but obviously missed their mother.

They enjoyed their life with their dads, Sam and Roger kept them entertained at weekend, long walks and playing in the park when the weather allowed and visits to the cinema, bowling and restaurants which they all enjoyed very much.

The boys shared quite a big room and were asked to keep it fairly tidy; the house rules were few but had to be observed. They had to look after their clothes, putting them in the laundry when necessary, and they were asked to clear the table after a meal. They appeared to be very happy and The Dads saw this developing into a long-term fostering, which didn't faze them at all. They were thoroughly enjoying the new challenge and had lots of fun. The neighbours had got to know them and said that it sounded a very happy household, and admired Sam and Roger for making a good life for these boys.

Chapter 54

In the New Year after the families had all enjoyed a great Christmas—Bobbie coped brilliantly and loved entertaining her and Jason's families—his parents had stayed over for a few days—so everything was very relaxed and a happy time was had by all—Sarah and Paul had their belated celebrations with Ma-donna and Derek. As usual, at this time of the year, talk was about holidays for the forthcoming year, and had anyone had any thoughts! Sarah said she would love to go somewhere hot again but appreciated that Ma-donna and Derek didn't need to go in August anymore and understood if they didn't want to join them. Ma-donna said to Sarah to dare to stop them going away together, it would be great as Sarah felt confident after her illness to go abroad again and all was left was for someone to decide where they should go.

After some thought, they decided on the Loire Valley, a very pretty part of France, not too hot and not too much driving. They felt they would prefer to sail and drive than to fly as they could take so much more with them. Joanne and Charlie's baby was due in June, so August would be perfect timing to go away.

Ma-donna and Derek were enjoying their retirement; however, Derek had been asked if he was available to work at different times and he did when they had no other plans, and did enjoy it. Elizabeth loved having them around but kept herself to herself to give them time to themselves. Errol visited them often, he was on his own now, missed his mum very much but got a lot of comfort from Elizabeth, who was always happy to speak about Ruth and their early lives, especially, and he was never tired to hear these stories.

Joanne's pregnancy was progressing well and she and Charlie were getting very excited. They had recently had their twenty-week scan where they were told the gender of the baby as they thought it would be nice to know, however, they were telling no one, not even their parents. They would enjoy that information for themselves, and give themselves a chance to think about names. That was quite hard as they couldn't totally agree initially, but then narrowed it down to about three names, and had settled on a middle name they both agreed on, saying that once their baby arrived, they would see which name would suit him or her best.

Ma-donna and Joanne's mum Yvonne went shopping with Joanne on a couple of occasions, the first time mainly to shop for maternity clothes and looking at prams and cots; baby clothes could come later. Elizabeth was knitting for the new baby, mainly little matinee jackets, bootees and bonnets, all in white and these little garments were lovingly and beautifully made. When Joanne saw them, her eyes filled with tears—obviously hormones making her very emotional, but amazed at this very elderly lady showing so much love for this, as yet, unborn great grandchild.

Although the ladies looked at prams and cots Joanne wanted to make the final decision with Charlie, he viewed prams as jig-saw puzzles and they terrified him; the thought of putting them together, complete with baby, then dismantling them to put them in the car at this stage, totally freaked him. Joanne wanted him to be with her when they finally made their choice to ensure that Charlie would be able to master the technicalities.

Their next shopping trip was just a bit of fun really, buying clothes for the baby, but keeping it very unisex as Joanne would not be drawn to reveal the baby's gender, despite hints being dropped by both mums to ensure that they could buy something suitable. Joanne said that when the baby was born, they would have plenty of time to pop out to buy something 'suitable.' The mums agreed good-naturedly as there was nothing else for it.

Apart from Joanne and Charlie's wedding and a few birthday and Christmas celebrations, the two mums had never really spent much time with each other, and they found that they really enjoyed each other's company. They took the opportunity to discuss the possibility of caring for the baby once Joanne went back to work and realised that they would both enjoy that so very much, while saving Charlie and Joanne expensive child care fees.

Ma-donna, Derek and Elizabeth were all so looking forward to the baby's arrival and she obliged at the end of May, arriving two weeks early! All went well, rather a shock for Charlie and Joanne, after a few twinges she felt she should go in to get checked only to find that she was well into labour—they all agreed that was the way to have babies!

Amelia Elizabeth entered the world weighing nearly 8lbs and was soon home with Mum and Dad, both so very proud of their little daughter. They had a few sleepless nights and Charlie managed to take some days off, not easy when self-employed but he picked and chose jobs for the first few weeks so that he could give Joanne plenty of support. She was a natural and was a great mum much to everyone's delight, her own mother had reservations as Joanne had been so reluctant to start a family, however, it just showed that all was fine when the time was right.

The next few weeks family and friends all wanted to meet Amelia but they were very considerate, choosing the right time and making sure it suited everyone. Amelia had settled down into a good routine, and when Sam and Roger took the boys to meet her, they were absolutely fascinated by her. They wanted to hold her so Joanne was happy to let them, she made them sit and made sure they supported her head and neck, and they absolutely loved her. Sam took photos of them with the baby and these would be shown to the social worker when she next visited them.

The social worker was very happy with how the boys were progressing—they were thriving both at home and at school and this was turning into a long-term placement; the social worker ensured that Sam and Roger were happy to carry on with this, and they were happy as long as the boys were happy.

They started to plan their summer holiday, they decided to have a traditional seaside holiday where the boys could play on the beach and enjoy amusements like Punch and Judy, donkey rides and all the fun of the fair. It was a great success as it had taken the older boy, especially, time to be a child again, after having to deal with his mother leaving, and deceiving his father over the phone situation; for a while he totally distrusted adults but now, he was a normal boy once again enjoying ball games and other activities, and this holiday was just perfect to fully recover the child in him. His younger brother followed whatever Hari did and really looked up to him. They were a lovely family and really enjoyed life.

Ma-donna, Derek, Sarah and Paul had a wonderful time in the Loire Valley, very reminiscent of their earlier holidays, however, this time they managed in one car, where previously they had the children and both cars were packed to the gills, this time, it seemed much more civilised.

They got to their gite which was on the outskirts of a small town, it was very well equipped with a lovely garden and a small pool, and the living area was lovely and cool. The bedrooms were quite luxurious with their own en-suite so the whole place was beautiful. Their host had left them a couple of bottles of wine and some fresh bread, which they would have with their evening meal.

They had brought food with them for the first evening in case they were a long way from the shops, but they needn't have worried as the town boasted two nice supermarkets, several bakers and patisseries and some lovely restaurants, so they certainly wouldn't starve during their holiday.

The first evening was really fun, they opened the wine and Ma-donna made a salad, Sarah had brought some cold meats and a quiche from home so it was a very simple supper but went down really well as they were all tired after the long drive, but realistically, they all agreed it was less stressful than flying. The last few years since going away without the children they had flown to various destinations, and some of the places they had flown to would have taken a long time to reach by road, but this made a really pleasant change, and was a good start to their holiday.

Elizabeth was at home on her own, she hadn't wanted to go with them, to be fair, if she had they would have gone in two cars, but she was quite happy knowing that the boys would pop in, Joanne would call in with Amelia who was a delight, and Hari and Suni were always pleased to see Elizabeth. They were in awe of her when they first met her, but when they could see how nice she was, they enjoyed their visits. She still baked so there was always something nice to eat in one of her tins and that was a great attraction to the two young boys.

The holiday was going well, it was a lovely area and they enjoyed visiting some of the beautiful chateaux and gardens in the Loire region, they had some lovely meals out but also went to the market for fresh produce and the food they cooked was delicious. Fresh fish on sale in the market, also some meats—they didn't go for the horse meat which was still popular in parts of France—and the fruit and vegetables were amazing—and not expensive. It was a great couple of weeks and they all had a wonderful time.

All too soon they were home, Elizabeth was really pleased to see them all and had prepared them a lovely meal. They constantly marvelled at her age and what she was still achieving, day on day. She told them that she had seen Amelia several times and they would see a change in her as she was putting on weight and had a real little chuckle! Sam and Roger had called in with the boys and she said it was lovely to see them all.

There was an official letter for Derek on their return and when he opened it, he had to sit down to absorb the contents. It was from a solicitor informing him that both his parents had passed away in recent weeks, first his father and then his mother. They were adamant that Derek shouldn't be told until after their funerals had been dealt with.

Apparently, his father had made rather a bad investment, he was usually very astute but on this occasion, he got it badly wrong and the result was they lost everything. They couldn't afford to pay the management fees so their accommodation reverted to the holiday village with the proviso that they could live there for the remainder of their lives. As they were both in their early nineties, the management didn't have long to wait and knew that they would eventually get their money back—Derek's parents had to sign ownership back to the village so this could happen, and in the end, they both died penniless.

Derek knew this would have totally destroyed both of them, they had always kept up appearances and when this had become general knowledge amongst their friends, they would have been devastated. Despite the way they had treated Derek and his family, he had written to them twice, once to tell them about Sam and Roger fostering two boys and how proud they were, and once to tell them about Amelia being born. Both times the letters were returned unopened and he knew it was his father's writing on the envelope saying to return to sender.

Despite everything, Derek felt for his parents, really wondering how lonely the end must have been for them, and what they had missed out in life; Derek and Ma-donna got so much out of their family, had so much fun with the boys and Amelia and had never understood his parents. However, he knew he couldn't have done anymore, so he told Ma-donna what had happened then tried to put the whole sorry saga out of his head.

A couple of weeks later Sarah was back at school with the autumn term starting far too soon, in her opinion and she really envied Ma-donna being retired. Paul had gone back to work straight after their holiday and Derek had gone in for a few days for holiday cover, and he was happy to do that, once in a while.

Ma-donna caught up with the grandchildren, as she now thought of Hari and Suni—she often thought that the day might come when they would need to go back to their mother, if she returned for them, or the social workers might find them a more suitable home, however, she hoped that this wouldn't happen as it would break all of their hearts. Sam and Roger were brilliant foster parents and they all had a lovely holiday in Norfolk, the boys had told her all about it and they were very happy.

They worried about Hari as he had taken a lot on his young shoulders when he was with his father, and had put up with a certain amount of abuse, and no one knew what the long-term effect of this might be. However, at the moment he had reverted to a normal ten-year-old and seemed happy with his lot, and was also very kind to his younger brother.

Once again it was Christmas and the plans were slightly different. Charlie and Joanne were going with Amelia to Ma-donna and Derek's with Joanne's mum as she would have been on her own this year. Sadly, Joanne's parents had divorced after thirty-five years of married life fairly recently. It was due to Joanne's dad having his head turned by a young woman he worked with— Yvonne had suspected for a while that something was wrong and when he told her he'd met someone else, she agreed to divorce him.

She was very hurt and angry but didn't want to make life difficult for the children, she'd had friends who had gone through a similar experience using the children as bargaining chips, and she was determined to be civilised about this and not make things awkward for Joanne and her sisters.

Sam and Roger were with his parents this year so they would visit Ma-donna and Derek on Boxing Day, thus making two very exciting days for the little boys.

Everything went really well and a great time was had by all. Bobbie and Jason were with Sarah and Paul on Christmas Day then were going up to Jason's parents for a few days after Christmas. Seb was home and had brought his girlfriend to spend Christmas with the family, Trudi was a sweet girl, they all knew her as she was one of Seb's regular waitresses and they had become really close. It worked well too as it meant that she went with him when he had a function and knew a lot about his work. She was very supportive and understood his passion for serving good food. Sarah and Paul were really happy that Seb had found a soul mate and someone who understood him and how he felt about his catering business.

Part 9

Chapter 55

New Year's Eve was upon them once again, and Ma-donna did a buffet for Sarah, Paul and any other family members who wanted to join them. Seb and Trudi popped in for a drink before going to a party, Sam and Charlie were there with the boys, but said they would go home before midnight, and Elizabeth joined them, but again, she said her bed would beckon before midnight, whether or not it was New Year's Eve.

At midnight, the champagne flowed for the four friends as everyone else had disappeared, and they once again reflected on the previous year, all the exciting things that had happened like the arrival of Amelia. Sarah said that they couldn't wait to be grandparents and Ma-donna told her it was wonderful, but they had plenty of time in front of them to think about this.

On New Year's Day they usually went for a walk where no driving was involved and Paul came to the door and said that Sarah was in bed with a migraine, she was feeling really poorly. Derek joked that she must be paying for the extra glass of champagne she'd had. It was a joke because Derek and Paul didn't really appreciate champagne, so they would have a small glass each and the girls would polish off the rest. However, Paul said that he would still come for the walk as Sarah was in bed resting and didn't really need anything and they wouldn't be out too long.

When he got home, she had got up and said she felt a bit better and had eaten a piece of dry toast, and she recovered. However, when term had started and she had gone back to work she came home one night with a really bad headache, said that she had never experienced anything like it. She took some painkillers and went straight to bed, but was determined to be at work the next day, as the children were doing a project that she had started with them, but really needed to be there. Again, her head cleared but Paul had begun to worry. When she spent the weekend feeling lethargic and doing very little, he said that she should contact their GP.

She did this on Monday afternoon after school to see if she could get an emergency appointment. This wasn't possible and the receptionist said that there was a bug going around that caused severe headache and nausea and Sarah had probably caught that. She should stay at home resting and wait for the symptoms to pass.

After a few days when she seemed to get worse, and by this time, was off work, Paul rang the GP and insisted that Sarah be seen. She felt too ill to walk to the car, so severe was the headache. However, once the GP saw her, he said he would refer her for a scan at the hospital, this sent alarm bells to both of them but the doctor said it was just a precaution, as it had gone on longer than a few days.

When Ma-donna and Derek heard the news, they were really concerned due to Sarah's previous health issues. She waited three weeks for the scan and during that time, managed to get to work and by the time her scan was due, she kept saying she felt much better, however, Paul insisted she had the scan anyway.

The result came via a phone call two days later. A consultant wanted to see Sarah and Derek to discuss the results—history told them this wouldn't be good news but neither of them were prepared for what he told them. Apparently, Sarah had a brain tumour and it was quite aggressive, so they needed to take immediate action to slow it down. The consultant suggested intensive chemo followed by radiation in order to shrink the tumour, and hopefully be able to operate to remove it once it was smaller.

Sarah and Paul were shattered, the consultant agreed there was a lot to process but suggested that Sarah stop work immediately as the treatment would be tough and she would be exhausted. Sarah then, stupidly, thought about her lovely hair that had come back after the breast cancer and that thought just finished her off. She broke down there and then emitting very loud sobs and all Paul could do was hold her until she had calmed down—he was close to tears himself but was trying to hold it together while still with the consultant.

He told them to take their time, obviously felt very sorry for the news he had delivered but they needed to know and there was no point in gilding the lily. He said he would be in touch with dates for starting chemo after which they left and made their way home. Paul phoned Ma-donna to tell her the dreadful news, rather than go round in person as he wasn't feeling very strong himself at this point.

Ma-donna, obviously was totally thrown by this news and really didn't know what to say apart from supporting them all they could in whatever way they could, and they would go and see them whenever they wanted, but understood they needed time to process this awful news.

Ma-donna was now herself in floods of tears and Derek wasn't far behind, they couldn't believe that this had happened to their dearest friend for the second time. When they told Elizabeth she said that she would gladly swap places with Sarah if she could, she would be ninety-six in the spring and apart from a few aches and pains, she was great.

A couple of days later, Ma-donna went to see Sarah, she had just had a phone call from the hospital with dates for her chemo and Sarah obviously was glad to get the call but she was dreading the treatment. Ma-donna just sat with her and hugged her, no words were needed, the pain was filtering through them both.

The children had been told and they were all devastated. Charlie and Joanne contacted Bobbie and Jason to offer their support, and Sam and Roger spoke to Seb. Trudi was being amazing and had taken over one of his functions, as he couldn't face it after hearing this news, and she calmly took the reins and did a brilliant job. Seb would never have let the clients down, but it was lovely just to be able to hand the job over and knowing that Trudi would do him proud.

The next five months were very busy with the treatment and the chemo took its toll, and was followed by a month of radiotherapy. Sarah lost her hair and felt very weak, however, a scan showed that the tumour had shrunk a little but not enough for the surgeon to be happy to operate. He suggested three more rounds of chemo which would take them through the summer.

During the spring bank holiday, while Sarah was going through all this chemo Bobbie invited them round for lunch on the Sunday. She cooked a lovely roast which Sarah wanted to enjoy, however, food wasn't tasting right but she did her best and Bobbie was pleased with what she had managed. She then got out the desserts and announced that she and Jason were expecting a baby due at the beginning of November.

Sarah was over the moon, as was Paul and for a moment she forgot her illness and focused on this wonderful turn of events. Unlike Joanne, Bobbie said that when they had the next scan, they would find out what gender the baby was so they could prepare the nursery with an appropriate theme, and deep down, Bobbie wanted to give Sarah something nice to think about.

When they got home, she went to see Ma-donna to tell her this wonderful news, and of course, everyone was thrilled. The gruelling treatment carried on but the surgeon kept putting off operating on Sarah, Paul thought he was probably quite worried about the risk element involved in such a procedure and when he asked him outright what the problem was, he said that the operation was very risky as the tumour hadn't shrunk as much as they had hoped, but after another round of radiotherapy they would do a scan and see what was happening.

Sarah had the scan one day in mid-September, she kept thinking of Bobbie and Jason and their baby son due in a few weeks, and the names that Bobbie had asked her to think about, and tried to think of everything bar the outcome of this scan. Again, the consultant called them both in the following week and the news was worse than ever. The cancer had spread through her body and, basically, there was nothing more to be done. They would, of course, go through the various options, whether Sarah could be nursed at home, or in a hospice where they would sort out painkillers and make her life as comfortable as they could.

Well, this was taking the agony to a whole new level, all Sarah kept saying was that she wanted to meet her grandson. The consultant said that should be fine, he really couldn't give her a time limit, only that no more treatment was available. He really hadn't envisaged the cancer taking hold of Sarah's body the way it had and he was also devastated. He said he would give them a list of phone numbers where they could ask for advice and help once they had decided on how to proceed and take things forward. He explained that Sarah would still experience some good days as well as some awful days and these phone numbers would have people at the other end who would be able to advise them and tell them what help was available.

The journey home was a complete blur, how Paul drove them home in one piece he really didn't know. For one mad moment he even thought that they could end it all together just the two of them, but that would definitely be a cowardly gesture, nevertheless, a tempting one just for a moment. However, they had their children, unborn grandson and friends to think about, and they knew in that moment that whatever life held for them, they would get through it together.

Everyone was devastated at the news; Bobbie was struggling trying to understand the new life growing inside her while her mum was hanging on for dear life to hers. None of it made sense, however, for the good of the baby she had to stay strong, and for the rest of them also. Paul had completely gone to pieces, just the fact there was nothing to be done made things so much worse, then he would snap out of it determined to make the most of the time they had left together as a family. Seb was distraught and Trudi was being very supportive, and had taken some of his jobs over so that he could spend more time at home with Sarah.

Ma-donna, Derek, Elizabeth and the rest of the family were totally shell-shocked also—Sarah had done so well and seemed so very hale and hearty, made them all realise how very precious life was. Elizabeth was reminded of the war years with the blitz when you could be speaking to someone one day, and they would be gone the next as they were in the wrong place at the wrong time. This was very different and totally heartbreaking. Elizabeth, once again, said she wished she could swap places with Sarah but that wasn't possible.

Some days Sarah was feeling reasonably well and wondered whether she should go to work but sadly that was not an option. She tired easily and due to the medication for the pain she could often fall asleep. She was determined to meet her grandson and was trying to support Bobbie through her pregnancy—Bobbie said all was going well but her hormones and emotions were all over the place she took maternity leave early so that she could spend time with Sarah. Her employers were very understanding and told her that they would keep her job open for her, however long she might be away.

Paul arranged to take Sarah to a spa hotel for a few days where she would have massages and treatments that would work with her medication and relax her so they could spend some time together. He got rather possessive about his time with her and Ma-donna visited Sarah or invited her round when Paul was at work. That way she got to spend time with her friend without eating into Paul's time with her.

Occasionally, Paul would go out for a drink with Derek which meant he could open up to him and said that he wasn't sure how he would manage without Sarah in his life. She was too young but he had the children to think about so he had to stay strong, like they all were.

At the end of September, Sarah took a turn for the worse, she was in much pain and the medication wasn't helping so she was advised to go into the hospice so they could monitor the pain relief and they assured her that she would go home again as soon as they had sorted this. After a week, she was home and feeling more comfortable and the MacMillan nurse was popping in regularly to see if there was anything she could do.

One day, they got a call from Jason, very agitated, to say that Bobbie had gone into labour but it was too soon for the baby to be born, she had another six weeks to go at least, but all Sarah could think about was that she would be meeting her new grandson very soon and felt very excited, despite worrying about Bobbie and how she was coping. In the event, Bobbie had to have a caesarean section as the baby appeared to be distressed and was quite small, so this was the safest option for mum and baby.

Edward Paul entered this world very quietly weighing at just under five pounds, initially everyone panicked but after a few seconds that seemed like hours, he let out a lusty yell and was quickly put into an incubator that had been prepared for him. Bobbie was understandably quite distressed and very disorientated but Jason held her hand and told her all was well and Edward Paul had made it safely into the world. Having reassured her, he then went to phone both sets of grandparents and they were all overjoyed at the news. Sarah wanted to go straight to the hospital but as it was late, Paul promised to take her the next day. She phoned Bobbie who sounded bemused but said she was fine and glad it was over.

She had been taken in a wheelchair to the neonatal baby unit to meet their little son and the proud parents just spent time gazing at the sleeping baby marvelling at how tiny he was but how very perfect. They were told that he would need to stay in until he could feed properly and started to put on weight—this could take as little as a week but might take longer—impossible to predict, they would have to wait and see.

The next day Sarah went to see Bobbie with Paul having first insisted on going shopping for clothes for Edward and by the time they got to Bobbie, Sarah was exhausted. However, she was taken to meet Edward Paul and she thought he was beautiful, of course, and so very perfect.

The tears came later when the realisation hit her that she would never see him grow up—however, she cried in private as she often did as self-pity didn't suit her, she felt. She went to see Bobbie every day for a week, then Bobbie told her that Edward had put on a couple of ounces and was feeding well, so they could take him home.

Jason spoke to Paul quietly and asked whether it might be an idea for Bobbie to stay with Sarah and him for a couple of weeks till Edward settled down, also to give Sarah the opportunity to spend time with Bobbie and the baby, if Paul thought it wouldn't be too much for them. Paul said Sarah would love it and it was a great idea and thanked him for thinking of it.

That worked well and Sarah even managed the odd feed so that Bobbie could rest, also Ma-donna popped in with meals she had prepared so that they could just spend time together and it all went really well.

However, by the beginning of November which is when Edward had originally been due, Sarah had really gone downhill and was admitted to the hospice, and this time everyone realised that she wouldn't be coming home. Paul was distraught and spent most of the time with her, he had taken a sabbatical a while ago for when this time came, and Bobbie stayed at her parents' house with Jason and took Edward to the hospice every day to see Sarah and when she wasn't too bad she would sit up in bed and hold him. It was a heartbreaking time for them all.

Chapter 56

Sarah passed away peacefully with all the family round her and it all felt very surreal. Even Edward was quiet in the last hour or so just sleepy in Bobbie's arms. Ma-donna and Derek had seen her earlier and said goodbye and tactfully retreated so that the family could say their goodbyes also.

They all came home later, Ma-donna realised that her friend must have gone and this hit her like a thunderbolt and she wept uncontrollably, not really believing that her lovely, funny and happy friend was gone for ever.

Jason phoned a little while later just to confirm the worse news and Derek told him that if there was anything they could do, like letting people know, or helping out in any way, he knew where to find them. Jason said that was fine, Paul would see them the next day but at the moment he was just inconsolable.

The next few days passed in a blur, lots of comings and goings, sorting meals out then Bobbie coming round with poems and readings trying to sort out the funeral, Paul seemed to have ducked out for a while, while realising they had to get this right but he really couldn't handle it. Derek spoke to him one day and said he couldn't imagine what he was going through, but after the funeral he would have lots of time to reflect but this was the next step, and Bobbie and Seb also needed support and this seemed to bring Paul up short, realising he needed to help Bobbie and Seb with the various arrangements.

Bobbie was grateful to Derek; he could always get through to Paul when things were tough and their bond just strengthened.

Sarah's funeral was a beautiful ceremony, extremely well attended, lovely readings and a wonderful eulogy written by all of them and read by Seb, with Trudi at his side when he struggled—it was all very moving and the wake in a nearby hotel was very nice. There were well over one hundred people and most of them came to the wake and Baby Edward stole the show, as babies often do, this was three weeks before Christmas and despite it being a wake, there were decorations in the foyer and the lights seemed to catch his eye, and he looked totally mesmerised and was extremely quiet while everybody talked and caught up with people, they hadn't seen for a long time, as is the thing with funerals. Jason's parents had come down and, of course, Sue was able to take Edward from Bobbie, which gave her a chance to talk to people, thanking them for their support.

On the whole it went very well, but was a very, very sad day, Paul struggled much of the time as did Bobbie and Seb but somehow, they got through it so grateful for the support of so many people. They were all glad to be home at the end of the day as they were all mentally exhausted.

Christmas was just round the corner and was a very difficult time, Ma-donna and Derek just couldn't get enthusiastic yet felt they had to make an effort, Amelia was walking and was very aware that this seemed to be a special time, so two days before Christmas they put up a tree with some lights and she loved this. Likewise, Bobbie felt she should put up a few things to get Edward's attention, this was his first Christmas, and Paul was going to spend it with Bobbie and Jason and Seb and Trudi would join them on Christmas Day. To be fair, none of them were looking forward to it but felt it would be good to be together.

Ma-donna and Derek missed Sarah dreadfully, and Paul too, as losing Sarah had really changed him. He had lost his sparkle and his happy carefree manner had gone, and they just didn't know how to approach him. Derek took him to the pub just before Christmas but they didn't stay long as it was full of people having pre-Christmas drinks and a very jolly atmosphere.

Derek realised as soon as they walked in that this wasn't a good idea, so ended up bringing him back to theirs and Ma-donna did them a meal. It would take a long time for all of them to get over their loss which affected them all. Elizabeth was inclined to avoid Paul and Ma-donna told her she was being silly, but she genuinely felt guilty for being there at nearly ninety-seven, when poor Sarah didn't even manage to enjoy retirement and see her little grandson grow up.

They all felt that they should take one day at a time, and while Paul was grateful for his friends' constant support, sometimes he knew he was awful company and preferred to be on his own. They did respect this but kept an eye on him, Ma-donna was in touch with Bobbie and Seb and knew that if Paul hadn't gone to work he was having a bad day, and she kept the children informed as best she could.

Christmas and New Year passed in a blur and Derek was working some of the time, a few people were off with winter illnesses and he had been asked to cover if he could. To be fair, he accepted gratefully as he felt he needed to get out of the house and do something normal. Things hadn't felt normal for several months since Sarah had her awful diagnosis and the thought of being in a different environment was very appealing. He also felt guilty for feeling this way but he was struggling to find a balance with Paul, didn't want to hassle him but equally, didn't want to ignore him.

Chapter 57

Spring came, Amelia was very cute and Ma-donna looked after her a couple of days a week, depending on how busy Joanne was, she certainly kept her on her toes as she was into everything but they all adored her and Elizabeth enjoyed playing with the little girl when Ma-donna was busy. This certainly brightened up their days. Bobbie would call in with Edward occasionally, he was a bonnie baby and had made up for being born prematurely, it was hard to believe he had started his first few days in an incubator. He was very alert and a friendly little chap so Elizabeth enjoyed rocking him. He would stare at her with big blue eyes and would give her big smiles, which she loved.

Bobbie was very worried about her father, he still didn't go to work every day, if he was having a down day he would just sit and watch daytime television and by the middle of the afternoon he would attack the whisky bottle. She asked Derek if he could pop in a couple of times a week if he didn't hear from him to see how he was getting on. Seb was spending more and more time at Trudi's.

She had her late grandmother's granny flat at her parents' house which she shared with Seb and this gave them a bit of independence, hence he was going home less and less, and when he did go home, he then stressed and worried about Paul. They all tried talking to him about his depression, as he was certainly heading towards deep depression with good reason, however, he needed to keep his job and needed his family on side.

Bobbie would pop round on her day off, as she was back at work now, thinking that Paul would be cheered up by seeing Edward. However, when she called in one day, Paul was watching the television without seeing what was on and showed no interest in his grandson whatsoever so she went to the kitchen to make a cup of tea. When she saw the state of the kitchen, she was speechless, the worktops were littered with dirty crockery, and a quantity of takeaway cartons and empty beer cans and wine bottles were piling up by the back door ready for the bin, as the kitchen bin was overflowing.

She went back in the sitting room, grabbed Edward and went to Ma-donna and asked if she would mind looking after the baby for a little while. Ma-donna realised something was wrong but she took Edward which was always a pleasure, and Bobbie told her she would be back shortly.

She then went back to see her dad and read him the riot act. She asked him, knowing how cruel she was being, what Sarah would say if she could see the state of the kitchen. Paul broke down and said he wasn't coping and didn't want to live without his beloved Sarah. Bobbie told him that was all very well, but did he not realise that Bobbie and Seb had lost their mum and they were also racked with grief, but had to keep going, keep working, and she and Jason had Edward to think about, so giving up wasn't an option.

Once she started, she really couldn't stop—she told her dad that he hadn't once asked her or Seb how they were, how they were dealing with their loss, and basically, it wasn't all about him and him alone.

She then went to the kitchen, filled the dishwasher, emptied the overflowing bin and got rid of the messy cartons and recycling, putting everything in the correct bins. She then cleaned the worktops, went through the fridge throwing out of date food out then cleaned the kitchen floor. She went through to Paul, told him she would ask Ma-donna to cook him a meal that evening, he would have a shower and tidy himself up and she would be back on the Saturday morning to clean the rest of the house and deal with his laundry.

He looked at her very sheepishly and kept saying he was sorry and he hadn't been thinking straight. She then hugged Paul and told him that it was six months nearly since Sarah had been gone, but he still had two children, a grandson and some great friends and family who all cared about him. She suggested he visited his doctor to explain how he was feeling as he was obviously depressed but he mustn't give up, as she said that they certainly needed him more than ever now that they had lost their mum.

She then returned to Ma-donna to pick Edward up and told her what had been happening, and she immediately said that of course Paul must join them for dinner and they would try and keep a closer eye on him. Bobbie said that she would return alone at the weekend, Jason loved having Edward to himself and she would go and tidy the house, and maybe suggest that it was time that they sorted out Sarah's things. Paul wouldn't move anything of Sarah's almost thinking that she would be back at some point, and this wasn't healthy, but Bobbie knew she had to tread carefully, however, she would broach the subject.

This was also upsetting for Seb, when he went in the coat cupboard and saw his mum's things hanging there, it felt wrong. He also would find things in the bathroom cabinet and that would feel strange too, and this is why he was going home less and less. Bobbie phoned Seb that evening and filled him in on her day and he thanked her for taking the bull by the horns, as it were.

Things did improve gradually after that, Paul would have dinner with Ma-donna and Derek once a week, and every now and then they would go out for a meal, usually Paul insisted on paying to make up for the friends' kindness. One night they went to their local Italian which they hadn't visited for about a year and, of course, the waiter greeted them, sat them down and asked where Sarah was.

Unfortunately, that evening was ruined and they ended up back at Ma-donna's and ordered a takeaway. Paul apologised for his reaction but it was obvious he was far from being able to deal with the situation. He was better at work now, everyone knew how fragile he was and would treat him with care but when the odd person turned up who didn't know, it affected him badly.

Ma-donna went back to the restaurant the next day and apologised for not thinking about warning them that they had lost Sarah but, of course, it was hard to think about everything. They were fine with it, just so very sorry to hear such sad news—they had known the two couples for years and felt bad for upsetting Paul. Ma-donna said that they would try again at some point.

One evening Paul brought up the subject of holidays, he felt he needed a break but didn't know where to go, he wanted to go somewhere that wouldn't be full of memories of Sarah. Ma-donna suggested that perhaps Derek and Paul could go away together for a few days for a 'lad's break'—Derek agreed although he didn't expect it to be a laugh a minute, but thought that Paul definitely needed a change of scene. They decided that Wales might be a nice place and they would camp if the weather was fine, and go to a hotel if it wasn't!

Chapter 58

A letter came for Derek looking very official and to his utter amazement it was from the government informing Derek that he had been awarded an M.B.E. for his services as a scientist/pharmacist. Over the years he had worked in the laboratory experimenting with different drugs to find remedies for different diseases, but never put his name to any of them as various people took part in the experiments and, basically, he thought nothing of this. It was just his job. Well, Ma-donna was very proud as were all the family and Paul was happy for his friend who had obviously been hiding his light under a bushel for years! He was told that he would be going to the Palace in September to collect his MBE and Ma-donna would accompany him, obviously. She thought that she would need to buy a new outfit, and immediately, thought about Sarah. She would have accompanied her as they often went shopping for special outfits together, and this was the first time that she had needed to get something special to wear since Sarah had passed away.

However, this was Derek's time and she would do her best to find something suitable, she may even ask Bobbie to go with her, or Joanne, of course. Charlie and Joanne were very busy and Amelia, now coming up to two years old, was as delightful as ever. Ma-donna and Derek were proud of this little family, they worked well together, and Sam and Roger were also frantic, between teaching and looking after their boys, they had very little free time but were very happy. At least they had the holidays where they could recharge their batteries.

Hari and Suni were growing up, they had lovely manners and were generally well-behaved, however, Ma-donna often worried about what it would do to them all if the parents came back on the scene and wanted the boys back. Social Services were happy for them to stay where they were, but if the courts got involved, they might have different ideas despite what Social Services might recommend. However, there were enough things to worry about without crossing bridges that they hadn't yet reached.

Paul and Derek had their break in Wales—the weather was glorious so the two of them had some lovely hill and coastal walks and in the end, they were away for over a week. This seemed to do Paul the world of good and apart from a few odd moments, he was in good spirits the whole of the holiday.

They came home looking happy and Paul returned to work the following week—his colleagues noticed a big improvement in his state of mind. Also, due to the good weather he had quite a suntan and he looked well.

Derek was still doing the odd day at work and tried to find out who had put him forward for the MBE but to no avail. He said he felt humble as the people he worked with were all dedicated and he wasn't sure why he had been singled out—however, he would look forward to the honour of receiving the award but felt it would be on behalf of all his colleagues.

The day came when Ma-donna and Derek set off for Buckingham Palace to receive his award from Prince Charles, it was a lovely day and they were both in awe of the opulence of the Palace and thoroughly enjoyed the occasion. They stayed in London overnight enjoying a morning of shopping the next day, with a show in the afternoon, returning home that evening.

Jason's parents Sue and Ted had invited Jason and Bobbie to spend a few days with them with Edward, Sue had a quiet spell at work after some busy weekends with lots of weddings, so she thought it would be nice to get cover for a few days so she could spend time with her family. Bobbie and Jason looked forward to the break as they hadn't been on holiday—quite difficult with a young baby but more so because Bobbie was worried about leaving Paul. However, Sue knew all this and suggested that Paul might like to go with them. He and Ted got on well and Paul agreed that it was kind of them to invite him so he accepted gratefully.

Sue loved seeing Edward, he was such a friendly little boy, just turned a year old so that brought back mixed memories as it was almost a year ago that Sarah had been lost to them—this is why Sue thought it would be a good time to get them all away in a different environment albeit a very homely and welcoming one. They had a lovely week; the weather was pleasant and they all enjoyed nice walks along the beach and a couple of lovely pub lunches. Paul was in good spirits which was a relief to everyone.

Soon after this, it was the first anniversary of Sarah's death and Paul invited Ma-donna and Derek for an Indian takeaway, which was Sarah's favourite and they had a pleasant evening reflecting and listening to music. Paul thanked his friends profusely for being there for him and apologised for behaving horrendously at times, however, they said no apology necessary, it was forgotten.

Then Christmas was upon them once again and Ma-donna hosted all the family as everyone was in a better frame of mind this year, she had Charlie, Joanne and Amelia and Sam, Roger and the boys and, of course, Errol. He joined them nearly every Christmas, but sometimes went to friends if he was invited.

Elizabeth loved having all the family round, Bobbie was hosting Seb, Trudi, Paul and Jason's parents so she had a houseful too, which she enjoyed. Edward was into everything as he was almost walking but there were enough people to keep an eye on him and as he was such a friendly little chap, he never minded who paid him attention.

At New Year, Ma-donna asked Paul and all the family round for a lunch on New Year's Day which worked better for the little ones and was totally different to what they had done in the past. This is when they often talked about holidays for the year, but this wasn't mentioned.

Sam said that he and Roger had some news, apparently, they had been told that they could now take steps to adopt Hari and Suni as there had been no contact with either parent for the last three years and Social Services could see how happy the boys were and felt that this would seal the family unit. Everyone was very excited for them at this news and the young boys spoke about this quite openly with Sam and Roger delighted that their future was going to be with them. The boys worried that they would be sent back to their father but were delighted that this wasn't going to happen. Sam and Roger were great parents and had done so much for, and with, these two little lads.

They had travelled with them, had some great holidays and ensured they were getting a good education and also helping them with homework. They did have an advantage but then they just wanted the best for them. When the boys showed an interest in something, they nurtured it and fanned their enthusiasm and they were doing very well at school and enjoyed lots of activities. Hari had changed schools in September so went to school with Sam now and loved it.

Once again, Derek was asked if he could work a few days in January, the usual winter bugs were working well and they were very short-staffed. Ma-donna recalled the cruise they went on immediately after their retirement and a selfish part of her wished that they could do the same again.

Paul seemed much more his old self, still had the occasional bad day and missed Sarah dreadfully. He found Christmas and New Year and general family get-togethers really difficult but knew he needed his family and friends round him so realised he just had to get on with it.

Just before Easter he was contacted by the Managing Director, Tony Loveday, who asked him out for lunch as he wanted to speak to him. Paul was puzzled by this and hoped that he wasn't in any trouble due to all the time off he had taken over the last year but felt that this would have happened before if this was the case. The lunch went well, then Tony asked him how he was coping at home and how the family were after losing Sarah. He said he struggled at times but was 'getting there' with the help of family, friends and colleagues.

What followed came as a complete curved ball—Tony said that they were going to have to lose a number of staff this year due to re-organisation and wondered how Paul would feel about taking early retirement! He was totally thrown but when Tony said that there would be quite a nice package, he would get a redundancy payment and his company pension even though he wasn't sixty yet. It was a wonderful deal but Paul wasn't sure what he might do instead, so he asked Tony if he could think about it. He said that was fine, he didn't expect an immediate answer, but the sooner he could let him know, the better.

Paul went home and phoned Derek asking him if they could go for a quiet drink. When he told Derek, he thought that was an amazing proposition, but he would have to think about what he would do with himself, being barely sixty and a fit and healthy man, he would need to keep himself occupied. Derek then suggested that he could do voluntary work as it wasn't essential for him to get another job, and Paul then started thinking about what he could do.

He thanked Derek for his input and told him he would think about what the possibilities might be, he said he had only ever had a desk job so wasn't sure what use he could be. A few days later, when Ma-donna asked Paul round for dinner she asked if he had thought about what he might do. He said he had been in touch with Tony and accepted the redundancy package, and had also been in touch with the hospice where Sarah had passed away.

Ma-donna and Derek looked at each other in surprise as Paul explained that he had never been back to the hospice, but felt he owed them a massive debt of gratitude as they had done so much to help them all when Sarah was dying, and he hadn't quite realised this at the time, as he was in a bad way.

When he contacted them, they said that they always had plenty for volunteers to do, from helping at fund-raising events to doing maintenance around the building, talking to patients who came into their Day Centre and helping them with activities so they felt that there were plenty of opportunities for him to get involved. He was due to finish at the end of May so would have the whole summer in front of him, he could also help Bobbie with Edward, Ma-donna occasionally looked after him when Bobbie was stuck and she loved having him, but it would be good for Bobbie to have another option, and it would be nice for Paul to spend more time with Edward.

Jason and Bobbie booked a holiday for the summer, thought they would rent a cottage for a week as it would be easier with the little fellow, he was nearly two and they could just do their own thing. They asked Paul if he would like to go with them and he was very happy to accept, he also said that he could stay in some evenings if Bobbie and Jason wanted to go out on their own. Bobbie quickly said that wasn't the reason they had invited him but wouldn't say no to a night out, now he came to mention it.

Ma-donna and Derek decided they would enjoy another cruise, in the Mediterranean this time, and they had two weeks in June, which they both absolutely loved. Ma-donna was anxious about leaving Elizabeth, but this dear lady at ninety-eight seemed to never change and also still had a fantastic mind. She really was amazing and said that she would be fine, and as usual, the boys and Joanne popped in to see her, also Paul was next door if anything went wrong and she needed help, so they were to go away and enjoy themselves.

Paul was enjoying volunteering, he was doing various tasks, from driving a van with donated goods to the warehouse to be sorted, to taking goods to the charity shops, and occasionally driving patients to and from the hospice if they had no transport to save them the taxi fare, and found that he thoroughly enjoyed what he was doing. He realised how valued he was and what a difference he could make and for the first time since losing Sarah, he found that he was enthusiastic looking forward to the day ahead when he got up in the morning.

Everyone noticed how different he was and when he thought back to the previous year and how depressed he had been, he felt rather ashamed. When he mentioned this to friends and family, they were all very sympathetic and relieved that he had turned a corner and found something useful to immerse himself in.

Soon it was autumn and a new school year dawned. Hari and Suni both loved school, Suni was in his last year of Junior school, the following September he would join Hari at the school Sam taught at! These lads were growing up fast, Hari was two years older than Suni but was a good head taller than him, everyone joked that he had fertiliser in his boots, he had shot up so much in a short time.

The adoption process was going through but progressing nicely and they hoped that it would be done by Christmas. Sam and Roger had actually booked to take the boys to New York on Boxing Day for five days but hadn't told them and if the adoption process was completed by then it would be a wonderful celebration for them all.

Ma-donna and Derek thought that was brilliant, however, when Christmas came, Joanne and Charlie also had some news of their own. Amelia was going to have a baby brother or sister the following June just after her fourth birthday and they were very excited about this; as they did with Amelia, they produced a picture of the twelve-week scan and Ma-donna, Derek and Elizabeth were so very happy for them. It turned out an eventful Christmas as the adoption process was complete and another grandchild was on the way. What a year 2020 would be! After the sadness of losing Sarah two years previously, everything was looking great.

Chapter 59

There was some slightly disturbing news over the Christmas period referring to a kind of influenza bug in China which caused breathing difficulties, and the media were getting concerned that this might spread to other parts of the world. However, scaremongering was all it was, Derek was the only one who showed concern as he had experienced in his work how things could sometimes spread, and felt that when he did go into work, he would try and find out a bit more about this peculiar illness.

In the New Year it became more of a reality as the numbers gradually grew and anyone who might be infected with this virus named Coronavirus was isolated but everyone just got on with their lives. As usual Derek was asked to go in for a few days early in the year and he was getting quite concerned about this virus, as it seemed to be gradually, but definitely spreading. There was news of a cruise ship where people were isolating in their cabins as there were report of the virus claiming casualties and at the end of February the first British person died as a result of Coronavirus, while on a cruise.

By early March the numbers were increasing and the politicians started to speak about 'a lockdown,' not something anyone had experienced—people, of their own free will, started avoiding going to busy places worried about picking up this virus which had now claimed quite a few lives. At this point, Derek was working every day, when not doing routine work, he was looking into this and thinking of ways to combat it.

Some people were blasé and continued to carry on with their normal lives, Cheltenham races went ahead in March, as did a big Champions League game in Liverpool against a Spanish team, despite Coronavirus being rife in Spain, France and Italy. It was a frightening situation, however, on Monday 23rd March the Prime Minister addressed the nation and announced that there would be a 'lockdown' for a period of time until they got this virus under control. This meant that schools would be closed, everyone where possible would work from home including teachers who would do lessons on line. Computers or tablets were provided to families who didn't possess any—so that the children would be taught remotely for a few hours a day and parents would help their children with their school work.

Essential shops would remain open but would only let so many people in at a time so everyone stocked up on household goods, soon providing a massive shortage of a variety of items until they were told that shops would remain well stocked and panic buying was unnecessary.

People were to remain indoors, apart from shopping and one walk a day to get exercise and no visiting other houses, no popping in to a neighbour for coffee or visiting relatives. Community nurses would still visit patients in their homes with the strictest hygiene rules in place. Gatherings like parties or weddings would have to be postponed and all hotels and restaurants would close for a period of time. Social distancing had to be observed.

This was such an unprecedented situation and made for a totally different way of life. Queuing to get into shops became normal, nurses were totally rushed off their feet, many of them abandoned their families where they could as they were caring for very sick people in hospital and chose not to go home to protect their loved ones. A massive sacrifice.

By now, the death toll was rising day on day. The virus affected people in many different ways, it could vary from a case of flu to a full-blown chest infection and the advice was to take paracetamol and stay indoors to calling an ambulance if the symptoms got really severe. The people who were the most affected were some elderly and those with health issues, and this virus would affect these people badly.

One day, in late March, Ma-donna got a phone call from the laboratory where Derek helped out, which he had been doing on a regular basis since the beginning of the year as they were so busy. He thought he may as well be at work as they couldn't go out and about with everywhere shut.

One of Derek's colleagues told Ma-donna that an ambulance had been called for Derek as he seemed very unwell. Ma-donna was horrified and asked what the problem was, apparently, he had felt unwell and was having trouble breathing, she asked which hospital he was in and immediately got in her car to drive over there. She left a note in the kitchen telling Elizabeth that she had to pop out as she didn't want to alarm her.

Derek had developed a cough over the last few days but seemed fine and had thought nothing of it. Ma-donna hadn't really noticed as he had been out of the house such a lot. When she got to the hospital, she initially wasn't allowed in—by this time she was very distressed but didn't want to ring the boys—she thought she would wait and see how Derek was.

After a couple of hours, she was shown into a room, given gloves and a mask to wear and told she could go and see her husband. He had Coronavirus or COVID-19 as it was now being called and he was having trouble breathing. He was given oxygen and hopefully this would help him. He looked pleased to see her and reached for her gloved hand and said he was sorry. He had obviously caught this at work, one of the people there had gone to Cheltenham races and was off with COVID-19 a week later, and this is where Derek had caught it from.

He told Ma-donna he would be fine but she was to stay away as he didn't want her picking anything up in the hospital, and the staff at this time were also discouraging visits, so she left him saying she would bring him some clothes and would be back soon.

When she returned, she told Elizabeth where Derek was and also phoned the children and Paul too. Everyone was very concerned about Derek and when Ma-donna went to the hospital with clothes and toiletries for him, the nurse took the case at the entrance and she wasn't allowed to see Derek on that occasion.

He phoned her that evening but he sounded strange and said he wasn't feeling too good. He said that he might need to be put on a ventilator if he didn't improve and he was frightened. He told Ma-donna that he loved her and the children very much and hoped that she would be allowed to see him soon. After the call Ma-donna shed some tears, this really was frightening but she didn't pass on her fears to the children. Paul then phoned to see how Derek was doing and she did confide in him that she was very worried but didn't want to say too much to the children, just that he was in the best place being well cared for.

Paul, sadly, could relate only too well with what Ma-donna was feeling but this was made worse as she wasn't allowed to visit whenever she wanted. The wards were very busy with patients and the nurses found it hard to deal with relatives with everything else they had to do.

However, the next day when Ma-donna phoned the ward she was told that Derek was on a ventilator to help him and she could go in the next day, if she wished, but would need to wear protective clothing and had to answer, truthfully, that she was well in herself. When she saw Derek, she was appalled, he was sleeping and opened his eyes when he heard her voice and she could tell by his eyes that he smiled, and reached for her hand. He asked if the children were coming to see him and she said she would speak to them, and to the nurses.

The nurse said that the children would be allowed in but would need to wear mask and gloves, and only if they were fit and well. She said that Derek was very poorly and still needed help to breathe, but hopefully the virus would be under control soon. When Ma-donna asked what would happen if the virus didn't go away, the nurse said that she didn't really know, but didn't look her in the eye when she said this.

Elizabeth was very concerned about them all, she didn't even go out for a daily walk, just walked round the garden and spoke to Paul over the fence with about three metres between them and kept him updated. He was terribly worried for them all but there was nothing he could do, couldn't even visit his dearest friend; he was still volunteering but on a much smaller scale, the charity shops were shut and all he was doing was driving patients for their care, and helping in the hospice itself with odd jobs and gardening. Anything to keep him occupied and stop him thinking too much.

That weekend Charlie and Joanne and Sam and Roger went to visit Derek, they decided not to take the children. They all had to wear protective clothing and when they saw Derek, they couldn't believe how ill he looked; he was wired up to machines and still on a ventilator, they had hoped that he might be able to breathe unaided but hadn't managed yet. He looked pleased to see them and they stayed for about thirty minutes. They were all very upset but managed to stay cheerful while they were there telling him to get his act together, get himself home and stop lazing around.

However, as soon as they left the room it was a different story, they were all visibly upset at how Derek was perfectly fine ten days ago and now was fighting for his life, as it dawned on them that this is what was happening.

Ma-donna got a call one evening a couple of days later from the ward saying that Derek had got worse and would she like to go to see him. She could bring someone with her if she wished. She told Elizabeth but thought it wasn't a good idea for her to go so Elizabeth suggested that Paul might take her. She wasn't fit to drive but Ma-donna said that would break the rules as they shouldn't socialise with friends—Elizabeth said that it would hardly be socialising and if she got a taxi to the hospital she would be sharing the space with a stranger, so what was the difference? As always, Elizabeth had sensible answers so she phoned Paul and he said he would see her in ten minutes.

When they got to the hospital and given the appropriate clothing, they were ushered into a side room, Derek had been moved from the ward which they felt wasn't good news. He was unconscious but they sat either side of him and talked to him quietly. Once or twice his eyelids flickered, the nurse assured them that he could probably hear them, so Ma-donna chatted about the new baby who would be due in a couple of months and Paul told him that he would buy him a pint as soon as he was home. However, there wasn't much response and Derek passed away a few hours later.

Ma-donna got the call early the next morning and many thoughts flashed through her mind, she asked the hospital what would happen and was told that Derek would be taken to the mortuary where the undertaker of her choice would take him to the Chapel of Rest where they would be able to say their final goodbyes.

After telling Elizabeth who was totally devastated for them all, as well as herself, she phoned Paul then told the children. They all sprang into action and said they would let other people know. They were not even allowed to go and see Ma-donna which was the worst part, children could be such a great comfort, but not at that moment.

After she had spoken to the undertakers, they said that they would let her know when Derek was with them and she asked about the funeral arrangements. She was told that they were extremely busy at the moment but someone could phone her or do a Zoom call and put her in the picture about arrangements. It would appear that only fifteen people could attend the funeral service and there would be no wake afterwards, however, the service would be transmitted on a Zoom link so anyone who wanted to see the service but was unable to attend could watch from wherever their computer or tablet happened to be.

Chapter 60

The funeral took place three weeks later, in the beginning of May amid the 'V' Day celebrations that would take place a few days later, again, rather low-key like everything else was at this time. In the end, fourteen people attended, all socially distanced apart from people from the same household. Ma-donna and Elizabeth sat together, as Charlie and Joanne did, Sam and Roger with Hari and Suni as they insisted, they wanted to say 'goodbye' to Grandpa Derek—Paul sat on his own with Bobbie and Jason sat as near to him as was allowed, and Sam and Trudi on his other side.

The service was taken by a humanist lady as neither Ma-donna or Derek were church goers and it was beautiful. Paul read the eulogy, first with Ma-donna's thoughts as she didn't feel she could do this, and neither did the boys, then he read his own tribute to his best friend which was, in turn, very moving and quite funny in places, he got that just right. Bobbie read a poem which she struggled with as she was suddenly reminded of having lost her mum not that long ago. Joanne was very pregnant at this point and she and Charlie were comforting each other so it was a sad little group of people who walked out of the chapel and after a brief chat, all made their way back to their cars and went to their respective homes.

When Ma-donna woke up the next morning and imagined that Derek was downstairs making the tea she put this down to the sleeping pill she had taken the night before. Not something she would be making a habit of but they had been prescribed as she hadn't been sleeping so she thought it might be worth taking one to ensure a decent sleep. However, her sleep had been troubled with various thoughts going through her head and this is why she had woken up totally disorientated.

She decided to stay there for a while and thought about her family, wondered how she would cope without Derek, how easy it would be to just stay there for ever, thinking about how Paul must have felt when he lost Sarah. Then she

263

thought about her dear mum who was now ninety-nine years old, she would certainly reach her centenary next year. Then she went back in her mind thinking about her Grandma Polly and her wonderful friend Dolly, they had all lost loved ones over time but they had all experienced what it was to be loved, and it dawned on her that they had all gone through what she was experiencing right now, and until this moment, hadn't actually realised how painful this was.

Suddenly there was a knock at the door, Ma-donna was shaken out of her reverie and, for a mad moment, thought Derek is here, however, he wouldn't have knocked so it couldn't be him. Then Elizabeth appeared in the doorway with a tray—something she had never done—her rooms were downstairs and she never went upstairs—as she carried the tray Ma-donna could see there was a cup of tea and some buttered toast and this took her back.

As a child, if she was ill or upset, Elizabeth always did tea and toast as everything would be fine after that, and that small act of kindness tipped Ma-donna over the edge. She took the tray from Elizabeth, reached out for her and sobbed and sobbed. Elizabeth held her daughter close until her sobs subsided and apologised for making her cry.

Ma-donna smiled at this and thought she should drink the tea before it went completely cold and said that she felt that everything would be fine. She had experienced the most amazing love with Derek, as Elizabeth had with Robert albeit challenging at times, and Polly with Thomas. Charlie and Joanne were very much in love, had lovely Amelia and a baby due very soon; Sam and Roger loved each other and their lovely boys—and this is when it dawned on her that love was an incredible emotion, came in various forms and would be excruciatingly painful at times, but Ma-donna decided then that the pain would be worth it for the love she had experienced and she would get through it with the love of her wonderful family and friends.

She then asked Elizabeth to get the kettle on; she would get up and they could have another cup of tea.

Printed in Great Britain
by Amazon

37602254R00150